Welcome to Paradise . . .

Aurelia came to Paradise Falls to find herself the object of veneration she could not understand—and the target of vicious attacks that left her bewildered and afraid.

What was the hidden truth about this place that her mother had been able to escape only in death? What was the truth about the strange powers that Aurelia felt stirring within herself?

The answer lay deep in the darkness of the cave where the nightmare children sang their song of welcome—and of horror . . .

CEREMONIES

JOSH WEBSTER

CEREMONIES

BERKLEY BOOKS, NEW YORK

CEREMONIES

A Berkley Book / published by arrangement with
the author

PRINTING HISTORY
Berkley edition / August 1982

ISBN: 0-425-05466-7

PRINTED IN THE UNITED STATES OF AMERICA

For Mary Lou Seno,
who taught me what was truly important

PROLOGUE

PLEASE LORD, the young woman thought, don't let it be me.

She looked at the woman marching in front of her—her friend and neighbor, the woman who had been her midwife, who had helped her through the time of great pain when she gave birth to her son. Choose her, she thought. Please choose her. Choose anyone but me.

As the hundred people marched two by two along the bottom of the high cliff to the cave, the same thought, the same fear was in all their minds. Tonight there was no friendship, no love, no humanity.

Only fear.

A gnawing, aching, blistering fear, that clawed at their hearts like some terrible, hungry beast.

The young woman, Sarah, glanced, with her eyes only, at her husband. In the darkness she reached out and touched his hand. His flesh was cold. He stared down at her, trying to look comforting, to reassure her that neither of them would be chosen, that the horror soon to come would be for someone else, but she knew him well, and even his forced half-smile told her of the terror he too felt.

1

Lightning cracked white and glaring above the cliff. The procession of people shuddered as one. Torches flickered in the night, throwing the marchers' dark, misshapen shadows upon the rock-gray wall to their left. The rain grew heavy, pelting them, driving them, bent-headed, towards the sacred cave.

And the chanting began again.

It started with the sound of the old woman's voice, then echoed through the procession until all voices were as one, low and sad.

A funeral dirge. The song of the doomed.

Please Lord, Sarah prayed, squeezing her husband's hand, take my neighbor, choose anyone but us.

The torch bearers assembled in a half-circle before the huge boulder inside the mouth of the cave. The wind cried outside.

From deep in the bowels of the cavern, a moaning echoed over the huddled mass of people.

"Can thee hear them?" the old woman cried. "The children? They call us from the grave."

Everyone in the procession wore black, old-fashioned clothes. The men had beards. Their faces were hard and weather-worn. This was their most sacred of rites.

The ritual of the Chosen One.

They stood silent and erect, and dared not look their neighbors in the eye.

The bent old woman climbed the boulder with the help of a huge man with a face like the gray-shadowed walls of the sacred cave. She stood above her people and they stared down at their feet. The old woman knew her power well and used it like a sword hanging over their heads.

Slowly, menacingly, her skinny, black-gloved hand rose and pointed, like the skeleton fingers of the plague itself.

The young woman felt all those around her shudder,

cowering as one massive, frightened creature.

"We have come to our sacred temple to choose the anointed one," the old woman said. She wore a black veil that covered her hair and face, yet the people could feel her eyes upon them, deciding.

And they kept their trembling heads bowed.

"The sins of our people are with us still. We must choose one to baptize us again upon this, our holy ground."

The crowd murmured in unison, "Amen."

"Without the baptism of the Chosen One, the holy of Holy Sacrifice, the act that touches our children's sacred blood, we would surely perish. The water, our life, would turn from us again. The river would become like the desert Moses was banished to." The old woman's voice grew loud and angry. Her words echoed in the cathedral-like spires of the cave. "Our crops would shrivel and die, as would the children, our immortal souls."

The crowd chanted, "Amen."

Sarah slowly inhaled, not to make a noise in the terrible silence that followed. Her legs felt weak. She did not know how much longer she could stand. Looking above her, at the roof of the cave, where shadows from the torch lights danced, she grew dizzy. The heavy rock ceiling seemed to sink down upon her, suffocating her like the closing of the lid upon her coffin.

The old woman screamed.

All heads jerked up to watch. Sarah felt her knees buckle. She grabbed her husband's arm for support. The crowd inched closer together. She could smell the thick, terrible, sweating stench of fear. Her eyes, too, were fixed upon the old woman.

The huge man clutched the old woman as she began to tremble. Her body shuddered in quick, violent spasms. Carefully, he laid her down upon the rock.

She screamed again.

White, foaming saliva dripped from below the bottom of her veil onto her black-clad chest. Her arms and legs flailed as if she were falling from some great height to her death.

The huge man tried to control her fit without hurting her. He was helpless. Her arms beat him about the face and shoulders.

The crowd, staring in awe, whispering, suddenly became silent.

The old woman lay still.

No one moved.

No one breathed.

A cloud of bats, squealing, darted down over the boulder, circled twice, then disappeared out into the night. Thunder boomed outside, rolling in toward them, then lightning exploded and the cave was momentarily alight.

Sarah screamed.

Her husband tried to muffle the sound, but was too late. All eyes turned toward the young woman. She gasped and shook her head.

"I am sorry," she whispered. "I did not mean . . ." She began to cry. Her husband held her close to stifle the noise.

"It is time," a voice called out. All heads snapped back to the boulder.

The old woman stood up with the aid of the huge man. Slowly, her black-gloved hand pointed out at the crowd. Its fingers curled and uncurled. Like a huge black spider, it dangled down in front of their faces. Slowly, it swept over the people.

As it approached, each person's breathing stopped for that moment. They stood stiffly poised in fear.

Sarah clung to her husband, shaking. She would not look up at the moving hand. Then she heard the others

4

begin to chant, and she felt her husband's body turn rigid.

They were chanting her name.

Terrified, she peered up at the boulder. The old woman's black hand was pointing at her.

"No!" she screamed. She twisted out of her husband's grip and pushed at the bodies surrounding her. "No! No! No!"

"She screamed because of the bats," her husband yelled. "She is not the Chosen One. We have a son." His voice grew hysterical. He threw out his arms helplessly. "He needs his mother."

The huge man helped the old woman down from the boulder. She walked to the entrance of the tunnel. On command, the huge man lumbered over to Sarah.

"Thee cannot take her," her husband cried. "Take me. I will go. Not her. Thee cannot. Please!"

The man swept him aside with one wave of his massive arm. Sarah glanced at her husband, her eyes pleading for salvation.

"Take me," her husband yelled. He jumped onto the back of the huge man. Bending forward, the man's arm engulfed Sarah's husband's head and flipped his body over onto the ground. Before he could push himself up, three men in the crowd pinned him down.

The huge man pulled Sarah towards the tunnel. She cried out for mercy. Turning, she reached out to her husband. He screamed to her, but could not break free.

Then Sarah saw the black, empty hole before her, beckoning. Her legs collapsed. The huge man held her by the arm and dragged her into the darkness.

The old woman commanded the people to follow. Once more in twos, they marched behind her, down the dark, dripping tunnel. Sarah wept silently, choking on her tears.

Again she called back to her husband.

But he was helpless, still held down by the three men at the mouth of the cave.

The chanting began once more. It echoed through the tunnel.

The procession edged ever downward through a maze of caverns, marching through one, then another, for what, to Sarah, seemed like an eternity in hell itself.

The old woman held up her hand, illuminated by the torch her huge companion carried above his head. The people halted. The chanting stopped.

Only the old woman, the huge man and Sarah went on. He yanked her by the arm. She kicked out at him, biting and scratching his hand.

Suddenly she was free.

Crawling backwards, she pleaded with her friends. "Please. Stop them. I do not want . . ."

The huge man dragged her back by the hair, tugging her quickly around the corner of the tunnel. He pulled her down a slow decline that ended in a small, blocked cavern no bigger than a closet.

"No. Please. Do not leave me here. I will die. Please." Sarah tugged at the old woman's long black skirt. "Please. I . . . I . . ."

The old woman stepped back in silence. The huge man ripped Sarah's hand from the skirt.

"For the sins of our fathers, the sins lurking within us still," the old woman chanted. "Blessed is the darkness. Blessed are thee who has been chosen to atone for our sins. Blessed are the children.

The huge man threw a candle down on the mud next to the woman, then two stick matches.

"Thee are in God's hands now. If thee are truly Chosen, thee will be saved. And the light of the Lord will be with thee always."

"No," the woman screamed. "Do not leave me!"

Slowly, the black-shadowed pair backed out of the

cavern. The light from their torch dimmed quickly. Blackness swept over Sarah like a massive tidal wave.

"Please!" she screamed. It echoed up through the tunnel, slowly diminishing in strength.

Trembling, Sarah crawled forward in the thick darkness toward the candle. With one hand, she felt the ground. Something twitched and scurried out from beneath her palm. She gasped and jumped back. Regaining her nerve, she bent forward and combed the ground again.

She found the candle first, then the matches. She lit the first match on the rock wall, and pocketed the second after igniting the small candle. It only dimly illuminated a two-foot radius in front of her, but at least it took away that cold, awful blackness.

Sarah stood up weakly. The candle flickered. She quickly cupped her hand around it.

Staring desperately at the flame, she began to pray to its light for her life.

The old woman met the procession and led them, in silence, back to the mouth of the cave. Hearing their footsteps echo closer to the tunnel's entrance, and knowing his captors had loosened their grips, Sarah's husband suddenly jerked one arm free and swung it. Kicking simultaneously, he broke free and somersaulted away.

Dashing into the tunnel, he ran straight into the procession. The huge man swept him up like a child and held him.

"I want to go after her," he yelled, seeing the old woman. The crowd murmured its disapproval. She silenced them with a brief sweep of her hand. "I demand my right. I am her husband. Her fate is my fate."

"To be the Chosen One is the greatest of honors. It is not to be challenged," the old woman said.

7

"I demand my right."

The veiled head nodded. "Hold thy arms above thy head."

He raised his arms. The huge man searched him carefully. He found no candles or matches.

"Thee are not chosen. Thee shall surely die."

"So be it. It is my right."

"Then let it be done."

The huge man gave Sarah's husband one candle and lit it. The people parted to either side as he passed through them, descending into the depths of the tunnel.

"Go then," the old woman called after him. "But know what thee does is a sacrilege. Thee shalt destroy thy wife and thyself with such a passion. It is written. Woe to the disobedient for they shall feed the mouths of the dead."

Sarah's husband kept blinking his eyes to focus them more sharply as he proceeded into the black catacombs below. He could not hurry for fear the candle would go out. Cupping it, he walked as quickly as the flickering flame allowed.

If it went out, he knew he was doomed.

For a long time—he did not know how long—time was lost in the shadowed world of the cave—he wandered, calling out to his wife at each new turn. There were many caverns. He could only pray, each time he chose one, that it would lead to his loved one.

"Sarah?" he yelled. The echo fluttered through the different tunnels, diminishing quickly.

The candle had burned halfway down before he heard it. A sound other than the constant dripping.

No . . . a voice. Distant and haunting in the swelling darkness before him.

"Sarah?"

The voice grew louder. But the words were incoherent, melding together in echoes.

Then, suddenly, the words became clear.

It was a song . . . like a Gregorian chant.

He held his breath. He could not believe what he heard. He shook his head hard, but the sound was still there, echoing around him.

Children, he thought.

Singing.

Sarah had climbed out of the cavern and passed through many tunnels when she finally turned the corner to face another dead end. She could no longer contain her terror. Defeated, she leaned against its cold, wet wall. Slowly she slid down onto her knees and wept.

A faint voice drifted behind her. Her head jerked around. She held her candle out towards the sound, squinting to see through the utter blackness beyond the feeble light.

"Who is it?" she whispered, almost too frightened to disturb the empty darkness with her voice. There was no answer. But she had heard it. She knew she had.

She stood and walked carefully back the way she had come. At a break in the tunnel, there appeared four passageways. She could not remember which she had come through.

"Is someone there?" She cocked her head to listen. A dim sound vibrated towards her.

"Help me," she whispered. "Please." She chose one of the passageways and entered. It wound steeply upward. The faint sound grew louder. The tunnel leveled off. She quickened her pace, stumbling over the rock-strewn ground.

"Sarah?"

She heard it. Her name.

Oh God, she thought, they've come back for me. She

dashed forward around a sharp corner.

"Help me," she cried. "I'm here."

She watched the candle closely as she tried to run and didn't see the rock jutting up from the tunnel floor. She cracked both shins into it. The candle flew out of her hands as she tumbled forward. Horrified, she watched its glow disappear down a dark ravine.

Blackness instantly enshrouded her.

She felt her way forward, to the edge of the hole. Fumbling in her pocket, her hand shaking so badly she could barely control her fingers, she found the remaining match and lit it on a dry stone. The tunnel ended where she lay. A deep, twenty-foot-wide ravine, too deep for her to see its bottom, stretched out before her. To her left, on the other side of the ravine, was another smaller tunnel.

"Sarah?"

She heard it again.

"I'm here," she yelled. "I'm here."

Pain suddenly shot through her fingers. She tossed the match down and stuck her burned fingers in the cool mud. As the darkness engulfed her again, she curled her knees up close to her chest. She tried to cry out, but her throat quivered and no sound emerged. She reached up to her collar and began to stroke the embroidery she had sewn herself, to make her drab clothing pretty for her husband.

Yellow, she forced herself to think. Yellow flowers. She ran her fingers over the stitching, tracing each small flower, trying to picture them, fresh and pretty below her neck.

I can see them, she thought, *my flowers. It is not dark. I can see them.*

Her body began to shiver. She could not stop it.

"Sarah?"

Her body stopped shaking and became rigid. She

tensed her shoulders and neck, trying to gain back control of her voice to answer.

"John? Is it thee, John?"

Only cold, black silence answered.

Then again, in the distance, she heard the faint cry; "Sarah."

"I am here," she screamed. "Oh God, I am here. Here!"

"Sarah?"

It was louder now, closer.

"Hurry, John. Hurry."

"I am coming, Sarah."

In the tunnel across the ravine, she saw a fluttering patch of yellow light.

"John. I can see thy light."

"Sarah? Do not move. I will come to thee."

She heard footsteps. She pushed herself up. She was able to stand, although her legs quivered badly.

"Hurry, John. Please."

The light grew brighter in the mouth of the tunnel, dimly lighting her small cavern. Looking down, she stopped at the edge of the ravine.

Suddenly she realized what would happen.

"John, wait!" she cried. She saw his shadow first. He followed it almost instantly as he leaped over the big rock at the mouth of the tunnel.

"Stop, John! Stop!"

"Sarah, I found you."

He dashed forward, and she screamed.

He saw it too late.

Sliding on the mud, he flipped over the jagged embankment and careened down into the dark, deep pit. The candlelight followed his fall, but went out long before he hit bottom. Sarah could hear his body snapping, dashing itself against the walls of the ravine, before it splattered onto the rocky bottom.

Cold silence gripped Sarah's throat.

"John? Are thee hurt? I cannot see. Are thee hurt badly?" Silence.

Dark, horrid silence.

Sarah fell to her knees by the ledge. For a long time she knelt there, petrified, unable to speak. Then she heard a faint voice-like sound.

"Is it thee, John?"

It echoed behind her. She gasped, twisting around to face it. It sounded like singing.

"Go away," she moaned. Huddling her knees against herself, she leaned back nearer the edge of the ravine.

"John? John? Please, John, answer."

The singing grew louder.

Sarah held her breath, terrified in that black abyss. She reached up and began to trace her embroidered flowers again.

Yellow, she thought.

The terrifying melody beat against her head. She could feel its horrible vibrations pounding inside her brain until she could no longer imagine her yellow embroidered flowers.

Her mind began to swim as wave after wave of the chant-like cacophony washed over her, suffocating her.

She gasped for a breath of air, but none came.

It was as if the something in the darkness, something dreadful, had swallowed all the oxygen.

Leaving her only that rotting, putrid stench of death.

CHAPTER I

AURELIA HILL slammed the front door to the town house and bounded towards the kitchen. She could smell the pork chops frying as soon as she passed the living room.

"Mom?"

She stopped to throw her jacket down on the dining room table.

"Mom?"

There was no answer.

Her quick exuberance faded suddenly. She did not continue into the kitchen.

In a whisper, she called out again, "Mom?"

Slowly, she slipped around the table and peered into the kitchen from the doorway. Her stomach fluttered. She hoped what she was thinking would be wrong.

It wasn't.

Becky Hill was hiding in the corner of the kitchen, peeking out of a crack in the curtain of the window.

Aurelia watched, breathless, frightened even to walk in. For over a month now her mother had been acting strangely, and it was getting worse. Becky Hill was scared of something that neither Aurelia nor her father,

Sam Hill, could fathom. It did not make sense. For the last three weeks, Becky had refused to leave their home. She would not take her turn with the car-pool or do the grocery shopping. For the first two weeks Aurelia had done the shopping for her, because Becky did not want Sam to know what was going on, but the secret did not last. In the past week Becky had become scared of being seen through the windows and kept all the shades drawn. It was then that Sam forced her to talk about it. What she said frightened both him and his daughter.

Aurelia took a deep breath and entered the kitchen. The pork chops were beginning to burn and the greasy smoke curled thick and gray up around the ceiling.

"Mom? What is it?"

Becky Hill gasped, yanked the curtain closed and spun around. Her eyes bulged as they focused on her daughter. Her hands were shaking badly.

"Mom? Are you all right?"

"They're out there."

"Who, Mom? Who's out there?" It was the same thing her mother always said, but she would never be more specific. Aurelia walked up to the window, pulled the curtains back and glanced outside. The small grocery shop across the street was closing. A few people were walking on the sidewalk, some carrying brown paper bags as if they'd just left the grocer's. Aurelia recognized two of them as neighbors.

"There's nothing unusual out there, Mom."

"Get away from there," Becky hissed, continuously rubbing her hands on her hips. Aurelia held the curtain open and smiled reassuringly at her mother, trying to act normal and not show her growing apprehension.

"Look for yourself. Just another closing at Bently's store. Look."

"Get away!" Her mother smacked Aurelia to the

side, then ripped the curtains closed again. "They're out there."

Aurelia backed away from her mother, hugging herself tightly. Until two weeks ago, Becky had never raised a hand to her in anger.

"Please, Mom. What's wrong?" Aurelia couldn't hold it back then. She began to cry. She couldn't stand seeing her mother like this any longer.

"Oh God, I'm sorry," Becky said.

She opened her arms to her daughter, and they embraced. All the weeks of fear and confusion bubbled up in Aurelia then, enclosed in the security of her mother's hug, and she wept fitfully. Becky stroked her daughter's long hair and whispered to her lovingly.

"I'm sorry. I didn't mean to hit you."

Aurelia sniffed, and Becky handed her a paper napkin from the counter. Aurelia blew her nose and wiped her eyes. They sat down together at the breakfast table. Then Aurelia looked back at the stove.

"Mom, the pork chops." Aurelia tried to smile, and sniffed again.

"Oh no! I didn't even notice."

Becky jumped up, pulled the frying pan off the stove, and flipped the chops over. They were charred.

"Your dad won't notice. I'll just scrape them with a knife like I do his burned toast in the morning." Becky grinned awkwardly, then winked.

Aurelia began to giggle. Relieved to see that, Becky giggled, too. Soon they were laughing uncontrollably, both happy to feel close again and normal. It had been a long time since they had felt this way.

The front door slammed, interrupting their laughter.

"Quick, get me a sharp knife," Becky snapped.

Aurelia burst out of her chair, grabbed one of the knives from the woodblock, and quickly handed it to her mother. Becky scooped the chops from the pan and, trying to scrape them too quickly, nicked a finger.

"Darn," she exclaimed, sucking the tiny cut.

Aurelia grabbed the knife from her mother's hand, and continued the scraping. Becky, her finger in her mouth, began laughing, trying, with her eyes, to tell her daughter to hurry.

"Now what do my two ladies find so darn funny?" Sam Hill asked from the living room. They heard his footsteps approaching. Becky pointed with her chin, still sucking her finger, to tell Aurelia to put the chops back on the stove. She made it just before Sam entered the kitchen.

"So what's the joke?" Sam had been tense driving home, wondering what strange things his wife would be doing today, but now he relaxed, seeing his wife laughing and having fun with Aurelia again, the way she always had before this last month.

Aurelia spun around, hiding the chops with her body. She glanced at her mother, trying to hold back her laughter.

"Trying to burn the place down, eh?" Sam waved his big hand in front of his ruggedly handsome face, where the smoke now curled. He was six feet tall, built thick and strong through the shoulders and back.

Aurelia burst out laughing.

"Burned the dinner again?" Sam shook his head, pretending to be upset.

"We got it in time," Aurelia injected quickly. Becky winked at her and grinned.

"That's good. You two are a hell of a team for a couple of ghosts."

"Bigot." Aurelia laughed.

Becky and Aurelia looked very much alike, as if they were two stages in the development of the same woman. They were small and thin and beautiful in a fragile way.

16

Both had white hair and pink eyes and snow-white skin. Sam liked to call them his ghosts.

Sam grinned and shook his head, his stomach finally settling down after the apprehensive ride home. He was hoping this was a sign that everything was getting back to normal again, that his wife's strange paranoia was finally at an end.

"All right. I'm sorry about the ghost joke. Those of Polish extract don't like Polack jokes, I guess albinos have the right to scorn ghost jokes."

"That's right," Becky said, trying to frown through her smile.

"Let's get rid of this smoke." Sam walked over to the window and threw back the curtains.

As he unlatched the window, Aurelia watched her mother. Becky was squeezing the edge of the counter until her knuckles turned white. Aurelia stepped next to her and held her arm. She could feel her mother's muscles flex, then begin to tremble.

Sam grabbed the bottom of the window and started to slide it open.

"No," Becky screamed. She darted towards the window and yanked at Sam's grip. "Please. Don't. Close the curtains. Please, Sam, please."

All the joy slipped away quickly. Sam felt a heaviness descend over him again. He glanced at his daughter.

There was nothing to say.

Becky was still . . . .

Sam sighed and closed the curtains.

Still?

He hated his thought, but he had to finish it.

Still going insane.

Becky served the dinner in silence, and they ate without talking. The silence grew more and more intense until Aurelia could not stand it any longer. She knew if someone did not speak soon she was going to cry.

"Can we still go to the baseball game, Daddy?"

Sam sat up straight, startled by the sudden interruption of the silence.

"Sure. I promised, didn't I?"

Aurelia tried to smile, as she glanced over at her mother.

"Do you want to go, Mom?"

Becky stared down at her food, but did not answer.

"It's their last game," Sam said. "Two of my students are on the team and they've been on my tail to watch a game. I think you should come with us, so I can show you off. Impress them with your good looks."

Becky slowly glanced up, then shook her head.

"Come on. You haven't left this place in a month. It'll be fun." Sam turned to Aurelia. "Won't it?"

"Sure. We'll have a great time. Just Daddy and his two ghosts."

"Thee should not joke of that," Becky barked sternly.

Sam threw his fork down on his plate angrily. "I thought you weren't going to use that thee and thou crap any more. You haven't used it in thirteen years."

"Thee should not . . ." Becky dropped her napkin on her plate and sighed. "I'm sorry. You shouldn't say that. I don't like that joke. You both know that."

"All right, I'm sorry too," Aurelia said. She reached out and touched her mother's hand. "But please, won't you go to the game with us? It's the last one."

"I can't. I've got too much work to do. I want to get that sweater I was knitting for Mrs. Baxter done tonight. We're going to need the extra money soon. You've only got a week left, Sam."

"Don't worry about that." Sam wiped his mouth with his napkin. "With this budget deficit, and Wilson High closing two months early too, it might be tough to get a teaching job, but I can always work construction.'' Sam flexed his big arms and winked at Aurelia. ''I'm still strong, you know.''

Motionless, Becky stared at her plate. Then she looked up and pretended to smile. Aurelia let go of her hand.

''I really want to finish the sweater. You two go. Have fun. I'll be fine.''

Aurelia glanced at her father sadly, then got up and cleared the table. Sam leaned on the back two legs of his chair and turned to Aurelia.

''Why don't you get ready? I'll be with you in a minute. Bring your raincoat too. There's a storm sweeping west over Tennessee towards Greenville. The game could get rained out. If it does, I'll take you to the mall. We'll check out that leather shop. See if they still have those boots you liked. If they do, I'll—''

''We can't start spending now, Sam,'' Becky interrupted.

''That's all right,'' Aurelia said, washing off her hands. ''I don't need 'em anyway.''

''We'll see,'' Sam said. He had never known his wife to refuse her daughter something she really wanted, and it bothered him.

The wind began to pick up outside, rustling the bushes under the kitchen window. A branch scratched against the corner of the back door.

Becky started to get up from her chair, but froze when she heard the scratching.

''It's only the wind,'' Sam said, asking Aurelia, with a glance, to leave the kitchen. Aurelia immediately went into the living room. Becky stood up, walked over to the sink and turned on the water to wash the dishes. Sam hugged her from behind. She leaned back in his strong arms.

''Becky, I want you to talk to Dr. Leonard. I really

think it would be good for both of us. I'll come with you. He said he'd enjoy meeting you.''

Becky pushed out of his grasp.

"I won't. Not a psychiatrist. I'm not crazy, Sam. They're out there. They want to take me.''

"Who? Who wants to take you where? Why won't you tell me what frightens you?''

Becky closed her eyes and shook her head. Sam reached out to her, but she backed away.

"I think you should see him. He's a good doctor.''

Becky shook her head again, then closed her eyes.

"Daddy," Aurelia called from the other room, "it's almost game time. We should get going.''

"All right. I'll be there in a second." Sam held Becky by the shoulders and waited until she opened her eyes. He smiled. "Think about it. Please? For me?''

Becky forced herself to smile, then nodded. "I'll think about it.''

They kissed quickly, and Sam hurried to the front door. Aurelia handed him his jacket.

"Do not forget thy hat," Becky called out from the kitchen.

Aurelia stared up at her father sadly as she closed the door.

The darkness came quickly. The wind was strong now. Becky listened intently as it whined, almost crying, through Greenville's streets. Then the rain began pelting the roof and the east window of the living room. It was warm in the house, but Becky pulled a shawl over her shoulders. She could not stop shivering.

As she knitted, she listened to every sound outside. She could not concentrate and kept losing count of her stitches. Finally, she gave up and threw the blue armless sweater back into the basket next to her chair. She stood up.

Tightening her shawl around her neck, she slowly edged towards the bay window. She started to peel back the bottom corner of the curtain, but stopped suddenly.

The lights, she thought. They can see me with the lights on.

Methodically, trying not to make a noise, she crept around the room, turning off all the lights. When the floor creaked, she jumped back, pressing herself into a corner.

When all the lights on the first floor were off, she went back to the window and peeked out the bottom corner. Rain was pouring down heavily, at a sharp angle because of the high wind. A man walked along the other side of the street, then passed under the street light. He stopped under an awning and glanced around the block as he shook the rain from his hat.

"I will not," Becky whispered to herself, backing away from the window. "Thee cannot make me."

Stepping backwards, she tripped over the footstool, but caught herself on the railing to the stairs.

The oppressive darkness tugged at her mind, as if forcing an unconscious door open, releasing spasms of a horror she had fled from years ago.

She had blanked it out for so long . . . so very long.

But now, in the last month, the fitful dreams came to her not only in her sleep. She would see those pitiful, anguished eyes staring at her once again. Red, glowing eyes looming at her in tortured, questioning horror.

Her sweat-cold face grimaced in agony. Her last hold on reality began slipping. She felt as if she were hanging by her fingers above that terrible abyss of insanity.

Vengeful, demonic eyes peered at her from every corner of the black-shadowed horror that now had swallowed her consciousness. Like a hideous, yellow-fanged monster, it devoured her mind, eating away the last vestiges of her sanity.

Then she knew.

"It is the only way," she told herself. She stood up and straightened out her dress. "I should have known all along. It's the only escape."

The wind blew hard, snapping the rain against the window. It seemed to be calling to her.

Becky gasped and held her breath.

"No. Go away. Please. Go away."

Voices.

In the wind.

Children's voices singing with the rain.

The eerie melody echoed inside her head.

She heard herself singing with them. She held her hands against her ears and shook her head violently.

"Go away," she cried, then turned and dashed, screaming, up the stairs.

At 9:30, Sam and Aurelia returned home. The wind was still strong, but the rain was only a drizzle now. Sam unlocked the door.

"Wonder why all the lights are out?" he asked.

"Maybe Mom went to bed."

"This early?"

"I don't know. Maybe."

"Becky?" Sam threw his wet coat on the antique brass tree in the hall. "The game was rained out. We went to the mall. Come see Aurelia's boots. They were on sale." Sam turned and smiled at his daughter. She reached under the shade and flipped on the lamp. "I'm going to get a beer. You want a soda?"

"No thanks. I have to go to the bathroom," Aurelia crossed her knees jokingly. "Quick!"

Sam laughed and walked through the dark into the kitchen. Aurelia bounded up the stairs two at a time then spun around the top of the railing.

"Mom? You gotta see my boots. They're beautiful.

Laura will be so jealous. Serves her right, too, for being so uppity lately.''

Aurelia pushed open the bathroom door, but stopped before going in. She was waiting for her mother's reply. There was only a dim, eerie silence and the sound of her father downstairs popping his beer can and walking into the living room.

''Mom?''

She didn't answer.

Aurelia shrugged, deciding she must be asleep after all. She leaned into the bathroom, turned on the light and sauntered in.

Suddenly she grabbed the sink with both hands, horrified.

Her mother was lying naked in the bathtub, her eyes bulging, reflecting the light, her body covered in blood, her face and torso slashed all over in long strips. Sunken down, she was half submerged in her own sea of watery blood.

Aurelia's eyes turned up into her head and she began to scream.

And scream.

And scream.

After a brief police investigation, Becky Hill's death was recorded as a suicide. They found a razor with bits of her flesh and blood encrusted on it still in her hand. There was no sign of a break-in or a struggle. The report said she had taken her clothes off and neatly folded them on the bed, then gone into the bathroom, sat down in the tub, turned on the water, and slashed herself to death.

Sam tried to keep the story out of the local paper, but that was impossible. Aurelia was in a deep state of shock. Sam took her to Dr. Leonard, who told him it was imperative that they leave Greenville for a few

Josh Webster

weeks; go somewhere together, somewhere far away from any reminder of what had happened.

Sam did not attempt to complete the last term of school. He and Aurelia moved into a hotel the day after Becky's suicide, and they left for Florida the day after the funeral. The doctor told him to try to keep Aurelia talking, keep her mind busy. It would be good, he added, for both of them.

The first week in Florida, Sam tried desperately to keep them both occupied; going to the beach, swimming, sailing, going out to eat. They tried, but neither could talk much. Their attempt to enjoy themselves was mostly mechanical.

The second week was a little better. They finally spoke at length about Becky's death and tried to understand what had happened. Neither could make any sense out of the suicide, but the talking brought the pain and confusion into the open and made them easier to live with. Sam let Aurelia drink screwdrivers the night they talked about it. They cried together often then, holding each other desperately, wishing it were all a dream, that they would wake up the next day and Becky would be making breakfast for them.

But it was not a dream.

After two weeks, Sam felt they were both strong enough to go home. If it hadn't been for his responsibility to Aurelia, he knew he would have gone off the deep end; Becky had been so much a part of his life. But Aurelia needed him, and because of that he willed himself not to give up. He knew how lucky he was to have her, and he let her know it. That knowledge made it easier for her to cope as well.

One aspect of his daughter's behavior still worried Sam, though: she was afraid to be alone. At no time during the two weeks in Florida had she gone for a walk by herself or spent any time alone in the hotel. She clung

24

to her father like a small child, never letting him out of her sight.

She had also brought her favorite doll from her collection of over thirty, most of which were antiques once owned by her mother. The one given to her on her tenth birthday was an especially old doll with a strange, pitiful sadness to its painted face. Sam had never found out where Becky had discovered it. Aurelia had been so delighted by it that she had named it after her mother. Now she would not sleep without it. The night before they were to fly back, Sam called Dr. Leonard to discuss the matter, and was quickly reassured that Aurelia's behavior was not abnormal, considering the circumstances. The doctor told him not to try to force her to be alone or to make her sleep without the doll. It would take time. When she was ready, she would put the doll away. It was probably a good emotional cushion, something tangible that kept part of her mother near her when she needed it.

It was ten o'clock at night by the time they returned to their town house from the airport. Sam put down their bags and felt in his pocket for the key to the door.

"We can go to a hotel if you want," he reminded her before he pulled out the key.

"I'm all right."

They looked into each other's eyes for a long time before Aurelia finally smiled. Sam nodded and took a deep breath. He was trying hard to be strong too as he unlocked the door.

"Welcome home, Aurelia."

"You too, Daddy."

They held hands and entered the darkness. Both felt the warm, sweating apprehension in the other's grip.

"I'll put the groceries in the refrigerator," Aurelia said.

"All right. I'll take the suitcases upstairs."

"No," Aurelia snapped.

Sam stopped and stared at her nervously.

"Don't go upstairs, Daddy. Sit down. I'll get you a beer. There should still be some in the refrigerator."

Sam smiled, understanding, and went into the living room. Aurelia flipped on every light as she passed through on her way toward the kitchen.

"I'll make us a sandwich, all right?"

"That'd be fine."

Sam got up from his chair and turned on the television. Soon Aurelia came back with two ham sandwiches, a soda and a beer. They had just settled down to eat when someone knocked loudly at the front door. Aurelia jumped up from the sofa, spilling her can of soda.

"I'm sorry." She was shaking badly as she peered up at her father through her long, white lashes.

"Don't worry about it. Scared me too." Sam hugged her close, then went to answer the door. He opened it to find Bob Higgins, the neighbor he had asked to get his mail.

"How's Aurelia?" He handed Sam the pile of envelopes.

"Better."

"Good. Glad to hear it. That letter on top, the one with no stamp—" He tapped his finger on the large blue envelope. "The day you left, my wife saw this man with a beard, dressed like the Amish, deliver it. He caught her attention because he was so big and he kept banging on your door for a long time. She went out and asked if she could help him. Told him you were gone. He just grunted, handed her the letter and left. Strange, huh?"

"Sounds like it." Sam peered down at the envelope. "Listen, thanks for getting our mail and watching the place. I gotta go back in. Aurelia . . ."

"I understand." Bob patted Sam on the back. "We'll talk later."

Sam closed the door and flipped the top letter over. It wasn't even sealed. He put the other envelopes on the table in the hall and sat back down with Aurelia. Then he opened the blue envelope and read the letter.

It was an offer for a teaching job in a town called Paradise Valley. The school, the letter explained, was in an orphanage. Sam was to reply within two weeks—and those two weeks were up tomorrow. He showed the letter to Aurelia, who read it quickly.

"Isn't that where Mom was from?"

"That's the place. An immediate opening for a tutor. They need an answer by tomorrow. What do you think?"

Sam watched Aurelia as her thoughts seemed to drift somewhere else. It was the look she had worn so often the first week in Florida, before they had had their long talk.

Sam took her hand gently. "It's your decision as much as mine. Either way, I'm going to have to find a job pretty quick. Money's getting low."

Aurelia jerked her head up and looked him in the eye.

"If you don't want to go, that's fine," he added, startled by her penetrating glance.

She turned her gaze toward the window for a moment. Sam watched her and waited, wondering what the problem was.

She looked back at him. "It *is* a teaching job."

"Yeah." He sat up straighter, waiting for her to continue.

"And you're a good teacher." Then she grinned. "One of the best, I've heard."

Sam laughed and hugged his daughter. She was not just his little girl anymore. He saw that clearly now. She was old enough to understand what his profession meant to him and strong enough to be able to tease him playfully in a time of great sadness and loss for her. Sam was glad for her support, but somehow the loss of her childhood bothered him.

"But do you want to go? That's what I'm really asking. Don't agree just because you think I want to."

"It'd be fun." She peered at him seriously. "In a way—I don't know—it's like we'd be closer to Mom. You know what I mean?"

Sam nodded. "Remember what your mother told you about the Holy Children? There'll be no electricity. No movies. No TV. It will be like entering a world a hundred years behind us."

Aurelia grinned. "An adventure."

"And an inconvenience."

She shrugged. "Maybe. Maybe not. I'd like to see where Mom grew up. It's hard to put into words, but I know I'd like it there. It's almost as if I've already been there. I can just picture the whole valley. And I know they'd like me. We'd have fun. There'd be horses and candlelight and farms and cows and . . ." Aurelia's bright, happy expression slowly faded. She stared down at the floor, bleakly.

Sam knew what she was thinking about. He sighed, trying to kill that same slow, stabbing pain he felt in his own chest when he thought about his wife, how she lay in bed in the morning with the new dawn caressing her wonderfully fragile curves, how she'd roll over, smiling that smile that was only for him, that told him to come back to bed, that everything would be good and warm and close in a matter of seconds, as soon as he returned to her.

Aurelia was crying.

Sam took his daughter in his arms and held her tightly, stroking her neck. The tears did not last long this time. He was glad to see that. She was getting stronger every day.

Aurelia pushed away from her father's chest. "I . . . I can't stand being here, Daddy. I mean it. I'd rather live somewhere else for a while."

Sam sighed and nodded. "So would I, honey. What do you say we drive to Paradise Valley tomorrow? Check it out?"

"Can we really?" Her face lit up.

"Why not? A deal?" Sam stuck out his hand and they shook on it. "It'll be a long day. It's across the state in the mountains. I think we'd both better get some sleep."

Aurelia picked up the empty plates, took them into the kitchen, then returned and kissed her father's cheek. They both said good night, then she walked towards the stairs. But as she neared them, she slowed down. Sam peeked out of the corner of his eye, pretending to watch television.

At the foot of the stairs, Aurelia stopped and peered upward. She tried to lift one foot up on the first step. Her body began to tremble. She lowered the foot back down and grabbed the railing.

"Aurelia?"

"Daddy, Daddy, help me."

Sam leaped off the sofa and embraced her. Her body was already soaked with sweat. He squeezed her close to stop her trembling.

Sam held her and petted her, telling her that everything would be all right. Then he picked her up, carried her back to the sofa and laid her down. He took a blanket from the closet and gently covered her. She pulled herself closer to him and rested her head on his lap. He caressed her hair.

"Daddy, where's Becky?"

For a terrifying moment, Sam felt his insides tightening, then he realized she meant her doll. He went into the hall, opened her suitcase, and brought back the strange, hauntingly sad-faced doll. He had hoped she would not need it tonight.

Aurelia tucked the doll in next to her and hugged it close. In a while she was breathing evenly. Sam lifted her head and put a pillow under it. The movement didn't awaken her.

Looking down at his daughter, her sleeping face calm now and serene, his mind began to drift away. Closing his eyes, he could picture his wife upstairs, lying in bed, her arms open, waiting for him.

He could not control it any longer, not now, at home again, in the dark, alone, with all the pain, the confusion, the disbelief, and that sharp grief that clawed at his throat, making his guts feel like he had just swallowed a mouthful of razor blades.

Leaning over, he dropped his head in his palms and wept quietly.

Why? he asked himself.

Oh God, Becky, why?

CHAPTER II

THEY HAD driven for over three hours when they reached the pinnacle of the winding mountain road.

During that time, the same horrible question had kept haunting Sam.

Why had she done it?

It was the same question Sam had been asking himself day and night since her death. The question he kept seeing in his daughter's eyes. Perhaps the answer will be found here, he thought, in her childhood home. Maybe it was a disease, some hereditary mental disorder. He hoped the answer would be that simple. Sam knew he would find no release from the constant, nagging, sometimes overwhelming guilt that question created until he found the answer.

He tried not to, but he kept blaming himself for his wife's suicide. He did not want to tell Aurelia, but that was a major reason he had decided to come here. Without an answer, he did not know how much longer he could keep up his facade of strength for his daughter. Justified or not, his guilt was gnawing at him like a spreading cancer.

Sam stopped the car. They both got out to survey the valley below them.

"No wonder they named it Paradise Valley," he said.

Aurelia walked next to him. He put his arm around her shoulder.

"It's beautiful," she cooed.

A river, blue and sparkling, wiggled its way through the middle of the valley. Clean, well-kept farms divided the land into different geometric patterns. There were cows grazing in some sections, wandering up the gentle slopes of the green foothills. Mountains, thick with pines, with patches of oaks, maples and white birch, enclosed and protected the land. After yesterday's heavy rain, the land seemed new again, clean and bright in the sun's caress. On the mud-brown road that ran alongside the river, Aurelia spotted a small black buggy pulled by a thin gray horse.

"It's like entering the Twilight Zone," Sam laughed. "Going back in time a hundred years." For the moment the amazing beauty of the valley let him forget that haunting guilt.

"Look," Aurelia pointed. "That big red barn over there. There's some kind of painting in a circle above the doors. It's really pretty."

"It's an old superstition. That symbol is supposed to protect the barn, the animals, and the land. I don't remember what they call it." Sam turned and started back to the car. Aurelia still stood, staring in awe. "Come on," he called. "Let's drive on down."

Aurelia hurried to the car. As they began the slow, winding descent, she leaned over the seat and sat her doll, Becky, on the pile of suitcases, as if she wanted Becky to see the valley too. That bothered Sam, but he said nothing. Near the bottom of the mountain, the paved road ended. They turned onto a dirt road, muddy from the rain. Sam glanced at Aurelia. Her wide eyes constantly darted from one view to the next. She could not sit still.

"You like it, don't you?"

"It's wonderful," she sighed. "So green and open and lovely."

Sam grinned. He hadn't seen his daughter happy, really happy, since before Becky's death. "Can't argue with that. But remember, I haven't gotten the job yet. Besides, I may not even want it. The job description in the letter was nebulous to say the least."

Aurelia folded one leg and sat on her foot, leaning towards her father. She decided not to ask him what "nebulous" meant. She understood his general meaning.

"I know you'll take the job. I just know it."

They passed a big farm with six horses grazing in a pasture. A black and white colt leaped, twisting in the air, its long, stiff, delicate legs bucking. Aurelia stared until it was out of sight.

"Think I could learn to ride, Daddy?"

"Why not? If they let you."

A brown leather buggy, pulled by a brown and white horse, appeared around a clump of white birch and bounced towards them. Inside rode a man and woman dressed in black: the man wore a round-brimmed black hat and had a full beard. They were somber looking and did not smile as they passed, even though Aurelia waved at them frantically.

But then the buggy stopped.

Sam glanced out his rearview mirror. The man and woman were straining to peek back at the car through the small rectangular window in the rear of the buggy.

"Did you see the way they were looking at us?" Aurelia asked.

Sam nodded. "Maybe they've never seen a car before."

"Do you think so? That's weird."

Sam shrugged. "With these mountains, who knows how much of the outside world has filtered in here? All the highways go around the valley. It's like entering a foreign land with different customs and attitudes. I'm sure we look as strange to them because of our clothes as they do to us."

"Wow." Aurelia shook her head slowly, letting that sink in. The dirt road rose in a gradual incline. At the summit, they saw the town. "Is that all of it?"

"Guess so. They don't need bars or grocery stores or restaurants or shopping malls. They're self-sufficient."

The town consisted of five buildings: an old church, a hardware store, a blacksmith shop, a livery stable or barn, and one building that was boarded up.

Strange, Sam thought, looking back at the church. It looked run-down and in need of paint. Some of the windows were broken and boarded up. For a strongly religious community, that seemed especially odd to him.

There were two buggies parked in front of the hardware store and three in front of the blacksmith shop. Sam stopped the car by the hardware store.

"I'll ask inside where the orphanage is. Be back in a second."

As Sam stepped up on the wooden sidewalk and sauntered into the store, he did not notice the three men in the blacksmith shop peeking out the half-closed doors, pointing at Aurelia.

The store reminded Sam of an antique shop in an East Coast tourist town. There were heavy wooden butter churners, many old-fashioned farm implements, assorted lanterns and elaborate candle holders. Rows of nails and other handmade tools leaned against the walls.

"Hello," Sam said at the front counter. The short, heavy-set man behind it scratched his beard but did not look up. Sam raised his eyebrows and waited for some acknowledgement of his presence. The short man gave him none. He rose out of his chair and walked over to the other three men, all in black, grouped in a circle at the far end of the store.

Sam sighed and walked towards them.

"Could any of you give me directions to the orphanage? I've been offered a teaching job there. My name's Sam Hill."

The four men stared at him and said nothing. One of them, by far the oldest, bent-shouldered, with a bald head and long gray beard, walked out of the circle and up to Sam. He stopped two feet away and carefully scrutinized the intruder. Then he coughed, hobbled over to the window by the front counter and stared out at Sam's car.

The other men whispered amongst themselves, constantly glancing at the stranger.

"I just need directions. Come on now, gentlemen. I was invited."

The leg Aurelia was sitting on had begun to ache after the long drive from Greenville. As the old man stood watching the car, Aurelia opened the door, got out and stretched. The bright sun hurt her eyes. She spun around to escape its glare.

The old man at the window gasped and, stepping back, knocked a lantern off the counter with his elbow. The metal frame clanged in the heavy silence. Sam's head snapped towards the noise.

"It's a '68 Chevy," Sam announced, taken off guard. "But it's in good shape." He grinned, but no one smiled back.

The old man slowly gazed up at Sam. His hands were trembling. One eye twitched. He stared for a long time, then quickly turned back to the window again, as if to make sure what he had seen was real.

Aurelia peered through the dark window. Seeing the

cute old man with the fuzzy beard watching her, she smiled. Again he jumped away from the window. Aurelia shrugged and got back into the car.

The three other men hurried to join their friend. He was leaning, breathless, against the wall, holding the shelves with the candles for support.

"What affects thee so, Jacob?" the short, stubby one asked, clutching the old man by the elbow. Jacob shook his head and pointed towards the window.

"Is he all right?" Sam asked. He wanted to help, but decided it was best to let them handle it. It was obvious strangers were not exactly welcomed here.

One of the men helped Jacob into a high-backed rocking chair, then the threesome gathered at the window. Sam watched, confused.

"It's just an old Chevy. No big thing," he said.

The three men stared, open-mouthed, as Aurelia rolled down her window and waved. Sam walked up behind them.

"That's my daughter, Aurelia."

In slow motion, the three men turned as one to face Sam.

"I am Ezekiel," the one in the middle announced. "How can I help thee?" The other two whispered to each other nervously, watching Sam out of the corners of their eyes. One of them quickly grabbed a chair and offered it to him. Sam waved it away and grinned.

"All this for a Chevy?" he laughed.

The men stared at him solemnly. From then on, they interrupted each other to answer any question he had.

They followed the same road through the small town, splashing the car in the mud puddles, then up over a long, easy-rising hill. At its flat crest, they saw the orphanage. It was a massive Victorian house, painted a drab brown, with steep roofs and cone-shaped spires above the rounded turret-like corners. The house over-powered its own miniature valley. It was strangely ornate compared to the simple architecture of the other houses. A tall, jagged rock cliff, like a gigantic, gray curtain, separated the orphanage from the rising mountains. Across from it, on the grounds, was a small red barn and next to that, a pasture, with cows chewing grass within its wire fence. Connected to the barn was a gray, dilapidated woodshed. Pigs wallowed in the fresh mud outside it. At the other end of the shed a white chicken coop glistened in the sun. Aurelia could hear their squawking when Sam turned off the motor.

"Ominous looking," he said as he got out. Aurelia climbed out of the car and walked around to stand next to him as he perused the area. A half-mile along the cliffs, an attractive one-story white house with a woodshed behind it sat like an island surrounded by a green and yellow sea of long, waving grass.

"It's like a story-book picture," Aurelia sighed. "Like I used to read when I was a kid."

"Kinda eerie, though." Sam straightened his tie and shook the wrinkles from his jacket. "I'm still waiting for Rod Serling to come out of those huge doors."

"Maybe that's where we'll live." Aurelia pointed at the white house in the distance. Sam glanced at it, then inspected the cliffs.

"Look at the size of the entrance to that cave." Sam whistled to emphasize his awe. Between the white house and the orphanage, a huge dark hole, over thirty feet high and at least as wide, stared back at him like the angry black eye of a Cyclops.

"Well, I suppose it's time to face my interview. Shall we?"

Sam Hill graciously offered his arm. Aurelia, chin high, trying to appear lady-like without giggling, looped her arm in his and walked toward the front doors. As they approached, Aurelia saw many children's faces pressed to the glass on the second- and third-story windows. When she smiled, they only continued to stare half hidden in the darkness of their rooms.

On the small fourth story, a curtain that hung at one of the long windows was cautiously drawn back. A shadowed face peered down at them, too blurred to be distinguishable.

Before Sam could knock on the door, it creaked open. Aurelia's up-turned head snapped down, startled. When she saw the size of the bearded man in black, she backed around behind her father.

"Hello," Sam said. He stuck out his hand. "I'm Sam Hill. I've come about the teaching job. Perhaps you were the one who delivered the letter?"

The huge man did not utter a sound. His stern, unfriendly face and six-foot-eight-inch frame frightened Aurelia. She inched closer to her father. Sam looked awkwardly at his outstretched hand, then let it fall back to his side. Glancing down, he saw Aurelia staring in awe. He rolled his eyes to reassure her, and she swallowed to keep from laughing.

She was not scared then. No one in the world could hurt her when she was with her father. She knew that for a fact.

The huge man stepped back silently to let them enter, then beckoned with his hand. Sam shrugged, smiling at his daughter, and followed. They ascended four flights of stairs. Aurelia checked out each floor as they went. The woodwork in the house was beautifully ornate, but there was a strange emptiness, a lack of warmth to the halls that made her uneasy. In the open rooms at the end of each hall, the shades were drawn. Each floor was dark and cold looking. The place reminded her of a haunted house she had seen once, maybe in a movie or on TV. Thinking back, she could not remember what the movie was, or even if she had really seen a similar house, yet the place seemed oddly familiar to her.

The huge man stopped in front of two large sliding doors. He glanced back at Sam and Aurelia, as if to reassure himself that they really should be allowed here, then knocked on the doors. A woman's voice answered. The man slid one door back into the wall and waited at attention outside.

A tall, pretty, dark-haired girl put her feather duster down and scowled at Aurelia. She stomped out, purposely shoving Aurelia aside as she passed. Sam and Aurelia looked at each other for a moment in surprise, then entered. The room was small and cluttered with antique dolls. Thick red and black drapes hung down to the floor. Each was pulled tightly closed. Not even a crack of sunlight filtered in. Long cream-colored candles were scattered everywhere, and the room twinkled in their flickering light.

The door behind them slammed closed. The noise startled Aurelia. She jumped forward towards her father. Sam spun around, annoyed at the strange reception they had been granted so far.

"Thee must forgive Matthew. He is a mute. He knows only his own people. And the girl, Ruth, she is upset. She is always pouting. It is her way. Nothing seems to make her happy," the old woman said. She walked towards them out of the shadows across the room. She was short and thin and bent, clad in a long black dress that covered her feet and buttoned up to her neck. She wore a black hat with a black lace veil that draped down past her neck, and black gloves. No part of her body could be seen. Yet, behind the veil, Sam could detect the blurred outline of a face. He could feel her scrutinizing them both closely.

"Is he the one who brought the letter?" Sam asked.

"He is. Matthew helps me run the orphanage. He is a

39

good disciplinarian. The children respect him."

Sam smiled wryly. "I wouldn't want to show him any disrespect." He stepped closer to the woman. "I'm Sam Hill, as I'm sure you've deduced. And this is my daughter . . ."

"Aurelia," the old woman interrupted. She waved him aside and hobbled up to the girl. "Please sit." She took Aurelia's hand and led her in front of a high-backed chair covered in red velvet. Aurelia smiled politely and sat down. The old woman lifted Aurelia's chin with her black gloved hand. "Thee are truly lovely. Just like thy mother."

Sam stood awkwardly watching. "How did you know Aurelia's—"

"I am called the Blessed Mother." The old woman let go of Aurelia and gestured for Sam to sit on the sofa. He obeyed. "I am the founder of the orphanage. There is nothing sadder in this world than a child who has lost its parents—unless it is a mother who has lost her child. Does thee not agree?"

Sam squinted slightly, disturbed at her interruption and at the turn the conversation had taken. His daughter did not need to be reminded by a stranger of her mother's death. He said nothing.

Aurelia looked around the room. Dolls sat everywhere, on the chairs, the shelves, the windowsills. They were all clad in old-fashioned dresses, their wide, blank-eyed faces staring in every direction. Aurelia was overwhelmed. They were even more gorgeous and delicate than her mother's collection, which Becky had given to her.

"I love your dolls," she cooed. "They're so different. They're beautiful."

Sam was still watching with a frown. He wasn't going to be sidetracked.

"How did you know my daughter's name?" he asked loudly.

"I am the spiritual leader of the Holy Children. I know all my people well. Becky always said that if she had a girlchild, she would name her Aurelia."

Sam nodded suspiciously. He did not feel comfortable here. He decided it was time to get down to business.

"Your letter didn't inform me as to what exactly my function here—"

"Would thee like some tea? Thee has traveled a long way."

Sam sat up straighter and sighed with annoyance. He was getting tired of this. The Blessed Mother pulled a long felt cord hanging from the ceiling by the chair next to Aurelia.

"We are all in mourning for thy mother," she said, patting Aurelia's hand. Sam leaned towards her. Aurelia tried to smile politely.

"We appreciate your concern, but I don't think we have to discuss that," Sam said finally.

The door slid open and a girl of about thirteen, clad in a long black dress, her blond hair arranged in looping braids, entered, carrying a silver teapot and china cups on a silver tray.

"Cream and sugar?" the Blessed Mother asked as the girl placed the tray on the table next to Aurelia.

Sam sat back in resignation. "That would be fine."

The Blessed Mother poured the tea. Aurelia got up to give her father a cup. Then the old woman pulled a chair closer to Aurelia's.

"She has been raised well," she remarked as she sat down.

Sam took a sip, then set his cup down and peered at the woman until she finally stopped staring at his daughter and faced him. If this is the spiritual leader of the Holy Children, he thought, I can see why Becky left.

"I'm sorry," the Blessed Mother said. "I know thee must have many questions. It's just that . . ." She glanced at Aurelia. "She looks so much like her mother. I sorely missed Becky when she left. It hurt me so." She gazed back at Sam. "Thee must put up with my silly tangents. I am an old woman. Now what is it thee wishes to know?"

Sam forced a smile and took another sip of tea. Maybe she's just a little senile, he thought.

"First, how did you know where we lived? Becky had told me once that she had had no communication with the Holy Children since she had left here. I've been curious about that."

The Blessed Mother smoothed the veil covering her face. "We try to follow our people, even if they stray. We are always ready to greet them with open arms when they discover that this is their home, that the outside world is not for them."

Sam cleared his throat for his next question, but before he could ask it, the Blessed Mother leaned towards Aurelia again.

"Does this talk of thy mother hurt thee, child? I was not thinking."

"No. That's all right." Aurelia smiled and shifted her weight. "It's nice to know people cared about her so much here."

The old woman nodded her approval, then turned her attention back to Sam and waited for him to continue.

"You implied in your letter that you thought I would have an easier time teaching here because I was married to one of the Holy Children. I have to confess, Becky never really spoke about her religion or this valley. No offense. She just didn't."

"Thee must be a good teacher. Thee are a good father." She looked back at Aurelia. "Is that not true?"

Aurelia nodded quickly. "The best."

"What other qualifications could I ask for?"

Sam sighed and leaned back. "There's a lot more to teaching than that."

"So there is. We contacted thy high school and they had only good reports to give us."

Sam thought he would have been told by the principal if that were true. He and Ralph played poker together. But then, he hadn't seen Ralph in the last two weeks.

"What exactly is the job here? You said tutoring, but—"

"It is a state requirement that our children be able to pass the high school equivalency tests. I forget what they are called."

"G.E.D.'s," Sam said.

"Yes, those. I would like thee to tutor the children between fourteen and seventeen. They are well educated and disciplined, but I'm sure there are areas that need development in order for them to pass the tests. I would like thee to teach them enough to pass it. Sometimes we must deal with the outside world in order to secure our privacy. It is a strange irony. Personally, I feel education is overrated. Schooling is good, but after a point, it can be dangerous."

Sam leaned forward. "I'm not sure I agree. There are—"

The old woman raised her hand. Sam was startled at how easily she wielded authority. He had actually shut up in midsentence. He would never have done that in Greenville, not even before the school board.

"As a teacher, I am sure thee does not agree, but we are an agricultural people. God's land is our life's blood. To know the land, how things grow, when it will

43

rain, these things are more important to us than knowing that in 1066 the Normans invaded England. Our true learning comes from the Bible and the land. It is the way of our forefathers and . . .'' She put her hand on Aurelia's arm, and Aurelia could see her strange eyes peering through her black veil. ''. . . the way of our grandchildren as well.''

Sam stood up and walked to the window, then turned. ''To a point, yes, but—''

''If you have more specific questions, Mr. Hill, I suggest you ask them of Grace Fromm, our own teacher.''

The sliding doors opened again and a heavyset woman with a round childlike face entered.

''Grace, this is Mr. Hill.''

Sam put out his hand. The woman bowed her head, watching his hand, then glanced at the Blessed Mother awkwardly.

''It is not our way to shake hands,'' she told Sam. ''Or for a man and woman to touch in public.''

Sam let his hand fall back to his side. At least now he understood why his hand had been refused so often today. He nodded slightly. ''Nice to meet you, Grace.''

The old woman stood up and adjusted her long dress. It was then Sam noticed that her clothes were much fancier than the simple black wool and cotton garb worn by the others he had met so far. Must go with the job, he thought.

''Grace, would thee show Mr. Hill our school and explain whatever he wishes to know?''

Grace nodded and walked to the door. Sam looked at his daughter.

''Would thee like to see the grounds, Aurelia? I will show thee thy new home.''

''The little white house?'' Aurelia asked. Her eyes lit up with hope.

44

"That is the one." She patted Aurelia's hand, then glanced back at Sam. "If, of course, thy father agrees to teach our children."

Seeing the joy in Aurelia's face, a joy that had not been there for weeks until she had looked down at the valley from the mountain, Sam knew he had to take the job. Actually, he had known he would last night; that was why they had packed most of their clothes for the trip. But the way Aurelia's eyes had lit up here reassured him it was the right choice.

"Seems I have no choice," he said. It only aggravated him slightly then that the old woman, who for some reason veiled herself from the world, had tried to force his decision. Aurelia was much more important than his minor dislike of her blatant authority complex.

The Blessed Mother nodded. Sam wondered if he detected a smirk behind her black veil as she offered her arm to his daughter and led her to the door.

Grace Fromm moved aside as the pair departed, then stood waiting for Sam.

"The school rooms are on the first floor. Shall I take thee to them?"

Sam was thinking about his daughter and only half heard her.

"Oh. Sure." He walked into the hall, then abruptly stopped. "Just a minute." He listened for Aurelia's voice and the sound of her footsteps. She's at least two floors down now, he estimated.

Grace watched him, confused. He turned and faced her.

"Did you know Becky?"

She raised her eyebrows, surprised by his question. "Yes, I did."

"And her parents?"

"She was raised with me at the orphanage. I never knew her parents."

"How about a brother or sister?"

"She had none." Grace nervously rocked back and forth on her heels, glancing constantly at the stairs.

Sam could see his questions made her uncomfortable, but he had to ask. "What happened to her parents? Do you know?"

"I do not. Please Mr. Hill, let us speak only of the school." Again, she glanced down the stairs.

Sam shrugged. He would have to ask someone older about it, he decided. But not the Blessed Mother. He already distrusted her. It was very hard for him to believe she had contacted Ralph, his principal, without his being notified.

As Sam and Grace's footsteps faded, the door of a closet at the end of the hall eased open. Ruth stepped out and edged quietly to the top of the stairs to be certain of their descent.

She had been hovering outside the door of the Blessed Mother's room, trying to listen to the conversation within, but had fled into the closet when she heard the approach of the girl with the tea tray. Now she stood, her face twisted angrily, listening to the stranger's voice drift away. Her hand curled into a fist by her hip. Unconsciously she began to bang it against the wall. Her eyes squinted narrowly.

"Bitch," she mumbled. "Pink-eyed little bitch."

A girl a little younger than Aurelia quickly grabbed the handle of the big front doors and opened them for the Blessed Mother. The darkness of the orphanage's foyer burst into light. Aurelia shaded her eyes with one hand.

"I have to get my hat." She trotted to the car, reached in the open back window and put on the yellow, wide-brimmed straw hat she had bought especially for the trip.

The old woman watched and waited patiently.

"I have to wear it. Daddy gets mad if I don't. It's either sunglasses or a hat. Sunlight hurts my eyes. It's because I'm—"

"I know." The Blessed Mother patted Aurelia's shoulder. Aurelia smiled, glad not to have to explain the limitations of her albinism.

They walked slowly along the foot of the cliffs. The sun glared off the jagged gray rocks, its warmth soaking in through Aurelia's longsleeved blue blouse and jeans.

"I used to hate it when all my friends wanted to do was lie in the sun and get tan. Everyone thinks being tan is so pretty. The boys would come over to the lake in the park and they'd all swim and play in the sun. I used to try to play with them, but . . ." Aurelia stared at the ground as she walked. Somehow she just knew the Blessed Mother understood her loneliness. She glanced up at her black-veiled face. She could almost see the sad smile behind it.

"Thee are very beautiful already. Matthew wrote after the resurrection in Chapter 17: 'And after six days Jesus taketh Peter, James, and John his brother, and bringeth them up into an high mountain apart, and was transfigured before them; and his face did shine as the sun, and his raiment was as white as the light.' Thee does not need others' false security. Thy skin is like the light of God, like the snow, pure and clear and unblemished. It is a rare and wonderful gift."

Aurelia had never thought of albinism as a gift before. She had looked on it more as a curse. She liked thinking about it as being special instead of odd. As they walked in silence, the old woman's warm, blackgloved hand on her shoulder, she thought about her "gift." It made her feel unique, but in a good way.

"Do the other children take care of the animals at the

orphanage?'' Aurelia asked.

''That is how they learn the ways of nature, which are the ways of our Lord.''

''Are the cows dangerous?''

The old woman shook her head. Aurelia could detect a muffled laugh.

''Cows are scared of their own shadows. The chickens are more dangerous than the cows.''

''Wow.'' Aurelia glanced back over her shoulder at the barn.

''Do the pigs always—''

''Becky loved the animals too.''

Aurelia felt a quick, biting sadness. Yet the pain was not overwhelming now, not the way it had been before. She wanted to hear more.

''Did my mother take care of the animals?''

''No. She was not allowed.''

''Why?''

''It was not her place to work. Work was for the others. Thy mother was special. I loved her very much. Everyone did. I am so terribly sorry she died. Seeing thee brings a flood of grief to my old heart. Thee looks just like thy mother when she was thy age.''

''Do you really think I do?''

''Exactly alike. Exactly. Both as beautiful as a winter sunrise.''

Aurelia felt better then than she had since her mother's death. She felt a strong kinship between herself and the old woman. She had felt it as soon as they had met.

They walked in silence until they reached the huge mouth of the cave. Its shadowed throat looked dark and ominous compared to the sun-glaring rock cliff that surrounded it.

''Come.'' The Blessed Mother waved her hand as she entered the cave. ''This was thy mother's favorite place, where she always played as a child. It felt safe to her. The sun could not hurt her here. Nothing could harm her here.''

''It's so big.''

Aurelia walked into the mammoth cavern. The ceiling was over sixty feet high. Spiraling, colorful rocks twisted down from it like pointing fingers. Huge boulders lay against the walls like monstrous broken marbles. A breeze, dark and wet, washed over her. She shivered. It was as if the cave itself were breathing on her, trying to cleanse her of the outside world and make her a part of its dark, hidden secrets.

''Let us rest.'' The Blessed Mother led Aurelia to a couple of flat, smooth rocks. They sat on them, facing a round, ten-foot-high entrance to a tunnel. It was pitch black a few feet into its mouth.

''Thy mother was happiest when she was here.''

''It's overwhelming. It's so huge and . . .'' Aurelia perused the vastness of rock, shadow and space, then shrugged and glanced at the Blessed Mother. ''I don't know, spooky, I guess.''

The Blessed Mother looked down at the dust. ''Thee will get used to it. Thy mother did.''

''Really?''

''Yes.''

''If she liked it, I guess I do too.'' Aurelia looked into the blackness of the tunnel before her.

Suddenly she gasped and jumped off the rock. ''I saw something.'' She pointed at the tunnel. ''Over there. In the tunnel.''

Calmly the Blessed Mother looked over her shoulder. ''Tell me what thee saw.''

Aurelia stared, standing stiffly, her arms, straight and rigid, pressed to her sides.

''I don't know really. Something stared at me from the darkness.''

49

The Blessed Mother arose and lifted Aurelia's face to hers.

"Thee are truly chosen, child."

Before Aurelia could ask what she meant a cold breeze swept over her from the tunnel. With it, a distant, eerie sound flooded the cavern.

Then it stopped.

Aurelia felt her body heave, as if it had just swallowed something heavy and foreign deep inside it. Beads of sweat rolled down her forehead and ribs.

"What was that? The wind?" She wiped her forehead and shifted her weight from one foot to the other, trying to get rid of the numb, prickling feeling in her limbs. She rubbed her hands. "It was weird. Did you hear it?"

The Blessed Mother quickly walked out of the cave. Aurelia followed her, nervously waiting for an answer. She felt as if she were being watched by something in the cave as she left it.

"It was only the wind," the old woman said as they entered the bright, green sunlit world again. It felt wonderful to Aurelia to be back in the warmth and beauty of the valley.

"Weird," Aurelia repeated, looking back at the cave.

She did not see the strange knowing smile that wrinkled the old woman's face.

They are pleased, the Blessed Mother thought.

Already they sing to her.

As they sang to her mother.

Soon, my children, soon.

CHAPTER III

BEFORE DINNER, after the sun had set, Sam and Aurelia discussed their immediate future. The job was good for at least two months, until the middle of June. That was his trial period, Grace had said. They were to live in the little white house for free. It was a charming place with lots of big windows and dark wood floors. The furniture was sturdy and comfortable, and there was a sense of home that had swept over both of them as soon as they had unpacked. Sam's neighbor, Bob, had a friend who would rent the town house in Greenville. That took care of his only real financial worry. Everything they needed—cooking utensils, sheets, blankets, pillows, everything—was already here in the house.

It was part of the contract, Grace said. Sam's salary would be minimal, but all the food they wanted would be delivered to them whenever they asked, free of charge. In fact, the house was already stocked with food.

They cooked dinner over the wood-burning iron stove, experimenting with how many logs were necessary. They did not talk much during dinner, both being tired from the long day, but they did discuss the Blessed

Mother for a while. Sam was relieved to hear how kind and understanding Aurelia thought she was. It lessened his anxiety about the old woman. She was the only problem he thought he might have in Paradise Valley.

The next morning Sam had breakfast ready by the time Aurelia had bathed and dressed, which took quite a while. She had tried on six different outfits before she finally gave up and put on the first dress again. It was light blue with pale yellow flowers. Wearing it made her feel fresh and new, like spring.

The breakfast was delicious. Both of them had a good appetite for the first time in over two weeks. Sausages, eggs, fresh bread, jelly, tea and peaches—now that's the way to eat breakfast, Sam thought.

He sat back from the kitchen table and looked out the east window. The sun was bright in the blue, cloudless sky. It shimmered on the wet morning grass, glowing warmly across the outstretched land.

"It's like being on vacation," he sighed, stretching.

Aurelia smiled shyly as she turned slowly in a circle, modeling her dress.

Sam grinned. "You look radiant. It's a perfect first day attire. Especially with the beginning of spring and everything budding." Then he laughed teasingly. "Including my daughter."

Aurelia grinned proudly and put on her hat. "Do you really think so?"

"If I were one of the boys at this school, I'd be dying to meet you. But I'd probably have been too shy to talk to you. Pretty girls always made me stutter."

Aurelia laughed, a little embarrassed, but pleased. She was nervous about her first day in a new school.

Sam rose and started to stack the dishes.

"I suppose we should get going. It's almost 7:30. School starts at eight."

"Daddy, why do you think the Blessed Mother wears all black, with a veil and gloves and everything?" Aurelia asked as she helped with the dishes. "Do you think she's deformed or something?"

"I don't know. Probably for the same reason nuns used to wear their black habits. They all wear black here. It's part of their religion. It's not our place to question it, honey. It's just their way."

They walked out onto the porch together. Aurelia stopped.

"How many kids go to school at the orphanage? Is it just, well . . . orphans?"

"All the kids in the valley go to school there. About a hundred of them, Grace said. There will be about thirty in our class, sort of a combination of tenth through twelfth grades. I have no idea how advanced they are. We'll find out today."

"Do you think they'll think I'm weird? You know, coming from a different way of life, dressing different, not in black. I saw some of the kids, the orphan kids at least, staring at me from the windows yesterday. And that girl—Ruth? She certainly wasn't very friendly."

Sam put his hand on his daughter's shoulder. "Don't worry. It might take a little time for them to get used to you, but it'll be fine, just fine. Grace assured me they're a nice group of kids. Just take your time, be polite and I'm sure you'll make lots of new friends."

Aurelia stared down the long dirt road towards the orphanage. Sam opened the screen door.

"Shall we?"

Aurelia nodded. They started across the lawn to the road. There were still a few puddles, but most of the mud had dried already. All around them, the farms were being tended. Sturdy men in wide black hats and beards were feeding their livestock or hitching teams of horses to their plows.

"Now that's hard work," Sam said, pointing to a man, bent-shouldered, leaning in against his plow, the leather strap strung tight across his back as the two thick-legged, big-chested horses dragged the plow through the black earth.

"Why don't they use tractors? And electricity? They could get a lot more done in a fraction of the time."

Behind them Aurelia heard the approach of a horse's hooves and the soft rattling and squealing of a buggy.

"It's their religion. Like wearing black all the time. They believe in being close to the land. Working it the way their fathers and fathers' fathers worked it. They don't need to over-produce and sell their crops for a profit. They till just enough land to feed themselves and let the other fields lie fallow so the nutrients return to the soil and keep it strong." Then Sam chuckled. "Listen to me. The city kid. Already they've begun to convert me."

Sam stopped walking. Aurelia looked up at him. He held her gently by the shoulder.

"You certainly are full of questions. You sure you're ready for this?"

The concern in his face made her feel warm inside. She smiled and touched his big hand on her shoulder.

"I'm sure. It's wonderful here, so . . . so different. Another world. I don't need to make friends right away. Just being here with you and knowing this is where Mom was raised . . . well, I don't know, it's just nice, that's all. Peaceful and nice."

"Good." Sam winked at her and they began to walk again.

The clippity-clop of the horse grew louder. They both turned around at the same time.

"Good morning," Sam called out.

"Thee are surely right," the man called back. He pulled the reins back. The horse snorted, tugged at her reins, then halted next to Aurelia. She could smell its dank, sweating body. She thought it was a wonderful smell, like the way the rodeo had smelled when her parents had taken her to Nashville as a child to see it.

"My name's Sam Hill. This is my daughter Aurelia."

"Aurelia," the man repeated with a grin, as if the name were something very special. He was a short man, probably in his seventies, with a big belly that stretched at the buttons on his black jacket. Sam was startled by his pudgy, happy, cherubic face. He realized this was the first person he had met in the valley who had smiled freely and openly.

"I am called Thomas Borg." The horse whinnied and tried to pull the buggy forward. Thomas yanked the reins tight against his big belly. "Whoa. Hold on there, Gretchen."

Aurelia cautiously walked up to the gray mare. "Can I pet it?"

"Sure. She is friendly. Scratch her under the ear. She loves that. Not too much though. Should not spoil her."

Aurelia carefully stretched out her arm. She could see the horse watching her, its big, brown eye turning as her hand moved. It jerked its head. Aurelia yanked her hand back.

"Do not be afraid. She is just not used to strangers."

Aurelia stepped closer and petted the animal's soft neck, always stroking downward with the lay of the hair. "She's beautiful."

"Getting old. Cannot plow anymore. But she pulls the buggy all right." Thomas shifted to one corner of the seat, then patted the other side. "Come. I will give thee both a ride. Going to the orphanage, I suspect. Everyone in the valley has heard about thee. I came especially to give Aurelia a ride." He slapped his leg. "But they didn't tell me she was so pleasing to the eye."

Aurelia walked around the horse to the buggy. Thomas eased his large body down to the ground, took her hand and helped her up. Then he got back up and waited for Sam to climb in.

"Do not tell anyone I said so, but that is a mighty fine dress thee are wearing." Quickly he glanced behind the buggy. "Get awful tired of black sometimes." Then he roared with laughter. Sam smiled politely and glanced at his daughter. He could swear he smelled liquor on the old man's breath. He knew that was a ridiculous assumption, but he didn't think he was mistaken.

As they trotted down the dusty road, Aurelia felt a great elation, watching the gray speckled horse, feeling the morning breeze, listening to jolly Thomas Borg.

"Going to be a good year. Planting is done for some already. Peas are in. Beans. Corn is still to be planted. It is a good warm spring. Lots of rain."

"Glad to hear it," Sam said. "We're city people. Never lived near a farm. Just grocery stores."

"Too bad." Thomas rubbed his big belly. "The land, growing things, that is important."

Sam smiled. "So's teaching."

Thomas laughed heartily. "No doubt. Growing ideas. Just like farming. Plant an idea in a child's head. Nurture it. Let it grow. Same thing. Just a different way. No doubt about it."

Sam decided he liked this old man. He held the joy Sam had expected to find in Paradise Valley. A joy he hadn't seen in the other faces he had met so far. Perhaps he had been too busy scrutinizing every look, every gesture, yesterday, and hadn't given the others a real chance. Certainly the men at the hardware store had been friendly enough, after an initial period of awkwardness. Sam leaned back in the buggy and watched as they rode onto the orphanage grounds.

Be a little more open-minded, he told himself. We're the strangers here, the odd ones, not the other way around. Patience is still a virtue. Give them a chance to get used to us . . . like you told your daughter.

He laughed at himself. He should listen to his own advice more often.

Thomas Borg pulled the reins and the buggy jerked to a halt. The horse snorted, then bent its head and began to munch the short grass.

Aurelia hopped off the buggy. Sam started down, but stopped, one foot on the metal step.

"Mr. Borg, would you do us the honor of coming over to visit? I would like to talk to you, if that's all right? We're strangers here and I would appreciate your advice."

"My pleasure, Mr. Hill."

Sam jumped off. "Good. Soon, I hope."

Thomas nodded, cocked his black hat down over his eyes, pulled back on one rein to turn the horse and trotted away. Sam watched the buggy bounce and sway. It reminded him of a rowboat in choppy water. He decided that Thomas Borg was the one he could ask about Becky and her family. He was old enough to know more than Grace and he didn't seem to be nervous the way Grace or the men at the hardware store had been.

Even though they had only just met, he knew he could count on the truth, good or bad, from Borg.

The school was on the first floor of the orphanage. It consisted of three classrooms, one for the first through fifth grades, one for sixth through eighth, and Sam's, which was also the smallest, for ninth through twelfth. There was a large kitchen, a dining room, and a parlor room. White lockers narrowed the width of the long hallway so that no more than three people could walk shoulder to shoulder. Sam Hill went directly into his classroom to prepare for the onslaught at 8 o'clock. It was now 7:50.

Aurelia wandered in the hall, looking about apprehensively, waiting to meet her classmates.

They appeared all at once, coming from the dining room. She watched them from the safety of the shadows at the other end of the long hallway near the front door. They all wore black. The girls had long, thick, flowing dresses that buttoned to their chins. The boys wore black slacks, white shirts and black jackets. They all carried hats or bonnets in their hands.

Aurelia watched, without seeming to stare, at the military-like procession. No one spoke until the huge mute closed the dining-room doors behind them. Then, like a distant, erupting gusher, they all began to whisper at once.

Aurelia could see different cliques form as the kids broke up into small groups. She wondered what they would be like, these children of another century. She began to tap her hip unconsciously as she became aware of the glances that darted her way.

A short, heavy-set girl, about fourteen—it was hard for Aurelia to guess their ages with their bulky clothes and wide, clean faces—approached. They all looked strangely childish to her. Yet when she caught them staring, they could suddenly look very old and alien.

Aurelia took a quick gulp of air and began to walk down the hall. She felt out of place in her brightly flowered dress. She tried not to think about it as the girl came closer. The others were watching.

"Hello," the short girl said, smiling. She had thick brown hair pulled back tight under her bonnet. A quick survey showed Aurelia that most of the older girls wore their hair in braids looped and pinned to the back of their heads. "My name is Mary."

"I'm Aurelia."

"We all know that."

Aurelia smiled shyly. She was not sure if that was good or bad.

"It is my first year in the third class," Mary beamed proudly. "I am going to finish all the studies in two years. I am a fast reader."

"That's a nice talent." Aurelia shuffled her feet and kept smiling. She saw, out of the corner of her eye, that the other kids were slowly moving closer. She wondered if Mary was a misfit, someone who didn't fit in with her peers and was quick to befriend a stranger because no one else wanted to hang around with her. Aurelia scolded herself for being so catty and suspicious. At least Mary had made the effort to come and talk.

"To tell you the truth, I'm a little nervous." Aurelia glanced down the hall. A tall, big-shouldered, curly-headed boy stepped out of the crowd. He looked much older than the others and, even from a distance, she could see he needed a shave.

"The others are pretty shy," Mary said. "They have never seen an outsider, a nonbeliever before. Thee must forgive their staring. They are rather childish."

The tall boy stopped a few feet away and pretended to be looking in a locker. It was obvious he was eaves-dropping.

"Do you live . . ." Aurelia felt a little awkward finishing her question, "*here*?"

Mary smiled to show that did not offend her. "I am one of the orphans. There are over fifty of us. The rest have families and just come in the morning for school. Everyone has breakfast and lunch here, though."

The tall boy stuck out his tongue and blew hard to make an obnoxiously loud spitting noise.

Mary spun around. He glared at her, taunting her. She looked back sheepishly and whispered behind one hand.

"That is Richard. He is an orphan too. Everyone is scared of him. Personally I think he is retarded." Richard blew out again, even louder. Mary inched closer to Aurelia. "No one knows exactly how old he is. I think he is at least . . . well, twenty anyway."

Aurelia smiled and glanced at the boy. He was staring at her and would not look away. She turned back to Mary.

"He scared the other teacher, Miss Fromm. He even made her cry once. But he was punished."

Again Richard made the noise with his tongue. He walked up behind Mary and pinched her arm.

"Quit talking." He spoke so fast the words blended together.

Aurelia could tell Mary really was scared of him. She gave Richard a dirty look, but he sneered at her until she averted her eyes. Mary adjusted the books she was holding against her large chest.

"Sometimes he—"

"Quit talking," he repeated.

Mary glanced over her shoulder.

"Quit talking." Richard frowned mockingly at Mary, then machine-gunned the next phrases. "Time for school. Do not talk."

Mary smiled uncomfortably at Aurelia and, without a word, walked away down the hall.

Aurelia glared at Richard. He grinned proudly. Then she heard the muffled giggling. Looking down the hall, she could see the other kids watching intently, covering their mouths as they tried to control their snickering. Aurelia's stomach churned. Her throat went dry. She wished that she were anywhere else but there.

She quickly realized she was being oversensitive. Not

a good start, she told herself, regaining her poise. There's always a show-off, in any school. It's no big deal. Pick on the new kid till she knows her way around. It's the same anywhere.

She took a deep breath and walked towards the others, pretending that nothing was wrong. Their laughter echoed down the hall.

Suddenly they were silent.

The hush startled Aurelia. She stopped and stood on her tiptoes to look over their heads. The dining-room door was partially open. The huge, gray-bearded mute was standing behind it, peering out sternly.

Without a word, all the children shuffled, bent-headed, not even glancing at each other, into their respective classrooms. Aurelia quickened her pace and followed the older ones into a door on her right.

The classroom had twenty-five desks. It was easy to count, five rows of five. One wall was all windows, overlooking the yard. The red barn and gray shed filled the view.

Aurelia glanced at her father. He winked at her. She sighed, relieved and comforted by his presence. The kids quickly chose their seats. There seemed to be more desks than students. Richard sat in the back with two other boys. Aurelia sat between Mary and a blond boy. The boy kept watching her, but always averted his glance when she met his eyes.

Once Aurelia took her seat, Richard instantly got up and sat directly behind her. She pretended not to notice, but she felt him staring at the back of her head.

Miss Fromm entered the room. No one spoke. The silence made Aurelia feel even more awkward. She looked over at the blond boy. He was staring straight ahead, but Aurelia could tell he knew she was looking at him. He was thin but muscular; his biceps pushed out against the jacket that was two sizes too small for him.

There was a gentleness to his face that appealed to her. As she stared, she decided he was really cute. She liked his big green eyes. When he looked over this time, he finally grinned sheepishly, then quickly stared back at the front of the room.

"Class, this is your new teacher, Mr. Hill. The Blessed Mother has brought him here from the outside. And this is Aurelia, his daughter. Now show them thy manners."

All the students stood up and introduced themselves from left to right, front row to rear. Aurelia waited for the blond boy to speak.

"My name is Joey," he said softly, then glanced at Aurelia. She smiled. He grinned. She thought he was very handsome when he smiled. After that she lost her feeling of awkwardness and forgot about Richard's moving behind her.

Miss Fromm adjusted her long skirt, nodded to Sam and left abruptly.

"Now that we all know each other, I'd like to ask a few questions. I'm here to help you pass your G.E.D.'s. That's equivalent to a high school diploma."

Sam walked around his big oak desk and sat on its front edge. Aurelia watched him proudly. It felt strange to be his student.

"I don't know what skills you have already acquired and what you need to learn. I have you for four hours each morning. You seem like a nice group and I'm sure we'll get along just fine. If you have a question or want to answer one of mine, of which I'm going to ask many, just raise your hand and I'll get to you."

Aurelia glanced around the room as her father spoke. All the pupils sat stiffly in their chairs, watching his every move. Something about them bothered her. Then she realized what it was. There were no sneaking glances or playful smiles—no quick whispers. They all sat like stone statues, staring forward, their hands on their laps, listening and waiting. Aurelia glanced out the corner of her eye at Mary. She too sat stiffly, staring.

Behind her, Aurelia noticed the girl, Ruth, who had been cleaning the Blessed Mother's room yesterday. She wasn't sitting like the others. She was leaning back on her seat, her legs crossed, her skirt hitched up past her knees, flirting with Richard. She was the only girl who wore her hair down, not in braids wound on top of her head. Ruth caught Aurelia watching and frowned.

Aurelia quickly turned around.

None of the students spoke unless Sam asked them a direct question. When he did, they stood at attention to answer. He told them standing was not necessary, but they did it anyway, always ending their answers with "sir."

"I'm putting these mathematical problems on the blackboard. I want you to copy them, then solve the ones you can. It will help me decide what areas you need help in and what areas you are strong in."

Sam Hill turned his back on the class and began to chalk the problems on the board. He was an English teacher, really, with a minor in history, but he was proficient enough in math to determine their levels of competence, and he would brush up later.

Suddenly Aurelia heard whispering behind her, then a few quiet giggles. She did not want to turn around. She knew they were laughing at her.

Richard, after making sure he had Ruth's attention, removed a three-inch square wooden box from his jacket. Leaning forward across his desk, he opened it. A large, furry brown spider crawled out onto the lid. He inched the lid close to Aurelia's back.

The spider's long, woolly legs twitched as it crept onto Aurelia's dress. Slowly it began to inch up towards her shoulder. Richard put the box back in his jacket and gazed around the room proudly. Everyone behind Aurelia was watching intently, trying to keep from laughing.

Sam began to write his third problem on the board. The chalk screeched. Aurelia felt her skin crawl. She shivered, but the feeling did not go away. She heard the kids behind her whispering again. She wondered if they were really making fun of her, or if her imagination was playing up because Richard's move to the seat behind her had made her paranoid.

She decided to at least glance over at Joey. Somehow she knew his shyness and his big smile would take away her foolish suspicions.

When she turned her head to her right, she saw it on her shoulder—big and hairy, creeping up towards her chin. For a moment she just stared in horror, face to face with the spider.

Then she leaped up, flailing wildly at it. It jumped on her hair and held on, crawling up the side of her neck.

The class burst out laughing.

Sam spun around to see his daughter slapping at her neck hysterically. He dashed around the desk.

Joey bounded out of his seat, yanked the spider from her hair, threw it on the ground and squashed it with his heel.

The class quieted. Only Richard's deep-rumbling guffaws continued.

"What happened?" Sam pulled his daughter to him and glanced angrily at the students. As each saw his eyes, they stared down at their desks.

"A spider, Mr. Hill," Joey said, pointing down at the splattered remains.

Sam let go of his daughter and looked at Joey. Joey sat back down.

"What was your name again?"

"Joey, sir."

"Well, thank you for your quick assistance. As for the rest of you, laughing at someone else's fears is sick and very cruel. You should think about what you would feel like if you were the one everyone was laughing at."

Sam did not want to alienate his daughter from the other students on the first day, but he realized it was too late already. He walked back to his desk and let his accusing glare rest heavily on Richard.

Richard leaned back in his chair defiantly and smirked.

Suddenly, standing there alone, Aurelia felt horribly foolish. Everyone was watching her. Their laughter echoed in her head. She quickly sat down.

She would not look at anyone, not even Joey. She knew if she did, she would cry.

Sam thought about accusing Richard and chastizing him in front of the class. His heart was beating rapidly. His hands were sweating. It was all he could do to control his anger. But he knew if he made a big case out of it, it would only embarrass Aurelia still more, make her feel even more segregated than she did already. He felt terribly sorry for her, but couldn't show it now, not in class. It would only make matters worse.

Teacher's daughter . . . teacher's pet.

Sam probed the class for the next two hours with different types of mathematical problems and oral reading assignments. He was a little gruff with them, but he thought they deserved it. He discovered that the students were very capable and quite advanced in their basic skills.

The incident was slowly forgotten as he did his job, the job he loved—teaching.

But Aurelia did not forget.

For two hours she sat in her seat, staring straight ahead, never looking at anyone, feeling her heart break every time she relived the incident.

She had so wanted the day to go well. She had really been ready to make friends, to learn from these strange children about their way of life, the farming, the animals. She had planned it so wonderfully in her head last night in bed, but now . . .

Now, she thought, it's ruined. No one likes me. They laughed at me, made fun of me. They . . . they . . .

As she fought back the tears for the tenth or eleventh time, she felt her hip being nudged. She didn't move.

She just wished it would go away.

She could hear her father's voice lecturing, but she didn't hear the words. She hadn't heard anything since the incident.

She felt it again.

Gathering up her strength, she turned her head slightly. It was Joey. He half-smiled and nudged her again. In his hand was a note.

She looked at him defiantly. He nodded at her reassuringly, then nudged her with the note again.

She took it and glanced up at her father. She could tell he had seen the note but was pretending he hadn't. That made her feel better. It gave her the courage to open it.

"Don't let it bother thee so much," the note read. "I came to the orphanage two weeks ago. They put a snake in my bed. Everyone laughed. Richard does that to all the new kids. He is crazy. Do not worry about him. The others are nice once thee gets to know them. I will help thee. Thy friend, Joey."

Aurelia glanced at him. She could see he was embarrassed. She waited a long time for him to return her look.

She smiled and mouthed the words "Thank you."

Joey quickly stared back at the blackboard. He didn't want her to see him blushing.

At noon, Sam dismissed the class. They marched out in silence. As soon as they hit the hall, Sam heard that familiar teen-age buzz. He liked its sound. It made him feel at home in his new job.

Aurelia remained in the classroom.

"Rough first day, huh?" Sam said, packing his books on the desk.

"I feel better now."

"I didn't want to talk about it too much. I thought it would embarrass you even more. The sooner it was forgotten the better."

"Thanks, Daddy. I'm glad you didn't."

Sam shook his head and smiled, then patted her on the back.

"That one boy, Richard—the big kid. He's a nasty one. I'm sure he was responsible for the incident. I could make him sit somewhere else. I saw him move behind you after you sat down."

"I'll move if I want to. Please don't treat me any differently than the others. They won't like me if you do."

Sam was startled at his daughter's growing wisdom. He wished she'd be a little more childish sometimes—at least for a few more years. He wasn't used to her becoming a woman.

It made him realize she'd be leaving him in only a few years for someone else—someone she'd give her love to. He walked back to his desk. He did not like thinking about that.

God, she's only fifteen, he reminded himself. Then he thought about what he had been like at fifteen. That only made him worry more.

"I saw Joey pass you a note." Suddenly even that gentle-faced blond boy was a threat to him. He forced himself to laugh at his foolish jealousy.

"He told me he just came to the orphanage. Richard put a snake in his bed. It made me feel better knowing I'm not the only one."

Sam gazed at his daughter. It was as if he were seeing her for the first time. Her face seemed different. Each feature stood out by itself. He stared at her until he again saw the child he knew so well.

"Wonder what happened to Joey's parents?" Sam asked finally.

"I don't know." Aurelia looked at him through her long white lashes, slightly embarrassed. "I think he's kinda cute."

Sam sighed. "I guess he is." He shuffled the books on his desk. "Anyway, I'm going home for lunch. Are you ready?"

"I'm going to eat here if that's all right. I want to try to make friends. It'll be easier if I do what they do. All the kids in the valley eat lunch here. I don't want to be different. Besides, if I go home for lunch with you today, they may think I did it because I'm scared of Richard. I'm not going to let them think that."

"Getting awful smart in your old age," Sam laughed. "And brave."

"Well, I gotta go. They're already in the dining room. See ya at home later, Daddy." Aurelia walked to the door, then stopped and turned. "Or should I call you Mr. Hill?"

"Daddy is fine with me. As long as class is over." Sam Hill watched his daughter leave, then sat at his desk. He was wishing he could turn the clock backwards and start all over again.

He never used to think about time much.

Now he did.

Since Becky's death, it seemed to rush past him. He used to feel he had some control over it, but not anymore.

It was the same feeling he had about his class.

Sure, they were well-disciplined. Except, maybe, Richard. But they acted so strange, so unnaturally stiff and polite, especially for kids that age.

They had no imagination, no fresh ideas. They acted as though they were always being watched and were frightened to stand out as individuals. Even Joey seemed apologetic about helping Aurelia, as if he thought he shouldn't have.

It felt all wrong to Sam.

It was as if they all lived in a constant state of . . .

Fear.

But why? Sam wondered.

What possibly could scare them here?

CHAPTER IV

LUNCH CONSISTED of chicken, pork chops, green beans, corn, applesauce, bread and milk. No one spoke aloud, except during grace. Across the table, Aurelia kept watching Ruth whisper to Richard and glance over at her. She had never seen eyes as vicious as Ruth's before. Their malevolence would have taken away her appetite, had it not been for Joey. He had saved her a seat next to him. When he noticed Ruth's quick, purposeful sneers, he rolled his eyes in mock disdain. Then he and Aurelia giggled silently. After that, Aurelia did not feel nearly as intimidated. But for the rest of the meal an uneasy tension still permeated the silence. This time Aurelia knew the tension wasn't·hers alone. It was everywhere in the room.

After another prayer led by the Blessed Mother, the children herded into the hall. Aurelia stepped next to Mary, and the girl smiled shyly.

"Do you always eat like that for lunch? That was a full-course dinner." Aurelia wanted to, but decided not to ask about the children's obvious tension.

"Twice a . . ." Mary was shoved forward before she could finish. Her head spun around. Seeing Ruth, she immediately sidestepped away from Aurelia.

All the kids passed by next, chattering to each other but ignoring Aurelia. She began to tap her side again, unconsciously. Once more she felt alone and conspicuous.

But she was also getting mad this time. It didn't hurt so much when she was mad. She took a long, deep breath. If they don't want to like me, the hell with them, she told herself. I don't need them anyway. She took another deep breath to calm down.

And I won't be beaten that easily.

She forced a smile on her face and began to walk, alone, down the hall towards the others. She could tell they were waiting to see what she'd do. As she continued down the hall, she suddenly realized she had no idea where she was going. She slowed her pace.

"I'll show thee to thy locker," a voice announced behind her. She almost jumped to the side, it had startled her so much. Then she saw Joey's warm smiling eyes, his shy grin, and her anger melted. "Thee must forgive Ruth," he whispered. They walked together towards the others. "She is jealous."

"Why?" Aurelia stopped and stared, puzzled. Joey averted his eyes and shuffled his feet.

He shrugged and spoke with his head bowed. "She was the Blessed Mother's favorite. Now thee are. Everyone knows it. They tease her about it. So she takes it out on thee with Richard's help."

"But I don't see why they think that. I haven't done anything. Heck, it's only my first day."

Joey got up his nerve to look at her. "She was also the prettiest girl in the orphanage until . . ." He glanced back down at the foot he kept circling on the floor. "Until thee came."

No one except her parents had ever told Aurelia that she was pretty. She pushed her long white hair back off her shoulders. Neither spoke; they just looked about nervously. She had never felt like this before. She wasn't even sure she liked it. She didn't know what to say. Her stomach felt funny.

"Come," Joey said. "I will take thee to thy locker. It is at the end of the hall. Then thee can get thy books."

Aurelia was glad he had broken the silence. It seemed, for a moment, to have overcome both of them.

As they walked, the other kids moved aside. It reminded Aurelia of the time she had sat on the bow of her girlfriend's speedboat and watched it slice through the waves. She forced herself to smile again. A few kids smiled back as she passed, but not many. She could feel their eyes following her as they broke through the last group and halted at the end of the row of lockers.

Joey felt them watching too. Suddenly he wasn't so sure he should show her to her locker. He looked over his shoulder. Ruth and Richard pushed their way to the edge of the crowd. Ruth was staring intently.

"Which one is it?"

"Maybe we should—"

"This end one?"

Joey glanced back at Ruth as he nodded.

"Maybe thee should get thy books first," he said. He could tell something was up. If Aurelia went to get her books, he could check her locker before she came back.

But he was too late. Aurelia was already raising the metal latch.

"Wait," Joey whispered, grabbing her hand.

She swung open the door. A terrible stench attacked her. Her stomach wretched. She gasped, covering her mouth with both hands, swallowing to keep from being sick.

A skinny white rat, tied by its pink tail to the top of the locker, dangled inside. Its eyes bulged grotesquely. Its yellow-toothed mouth gaped open. Its neck was slit wide open. Blood dripped down into a sticky puddle at the bottom of the locker.

Aurelia felt her knees buckle when she stepped back. She caught Joey's arm and squeezed, gulping air. Her throat clenched in a spasm.

Regaining her balance, she turned. All the children were watching. Some were laughing. She wanted to scream at them, but she couldn't. Her throat locked. She inhaled slowly, then squinted back at them defiantly.

She wasn't going to let them see how terribly hurt she was. A tear pushed out of one eye. She didn't wipe it away. She didn't want them to know it was there.

Suddenly there was complete silence. No one was laughing. The children quickly dispersed into small groups. Joey saw the mute's head above the others, shoving his way through. Leaning back, he inched his hand to the locker door and closed it.

"Do not say anything," Joey whispered out the side of his mouth. "Act as if nothing happened."

Aurelia sensed the urgency in his voice. She wiped her eye and looked down the hall.

The children were obviously terrified. Ruth and Richard had hidden in the crowd. That pleased her.

The mute stopped in front of Aurelia. As nonchalantly as she could under the circumstances, she looked up at him and smiled. The huge man stared at her. Slowly he turned and perused the hall. No one dared look at him. Even Joey kept his eyes to the floor.

The mute gazed back at Aurelia. His big, bearded face, those dark, deep-set eyes, no longer frightened her the way they had when she had first seen him. She was too angry now. She met his stare straight on. His face changed. She saw a strange, almost sad yearning in his eyes.

He reached for her locker. Aurelia stepped over,

blocking his arm, and leaned back against the locker.

The mute grunted.

Aurelia's smile broadened. She never lost eye contact with the man. The silence in the hall was overwhelming. Joey peeked out the corner of his eyes at the other children.

They were all watching in awe.

The mute mumbled and walked back down the hall. The children quickly bowed their heads again. He stomped past them and closed the dining-room doors.

Aurelia felt a power grow inside herself that she had never felt before. It took away the horror of a few moments ago. When she stared down the hall the children still averted their eyes, even Ruth and Richard. Mentally she taunted them until all the hurt inside vanished.

"I . . . I have never seen that before," Joey stammered. "Never." He exhaled loudly, realizing he had been holding his breath the whole time the mute had been there. "Thee stopped him from opening thy locker. No one stops the mute, except . . ." Joey's eyes widened. He glanced down the hall, then back at Aurelia. ". . . except the Blessed Mother."

All the orphans had chores to do after lunch. The other children went home to help with the work on their families' farms. Joey told Aurelia that he had to clean the barn and feed the sheep and pigs.

When he had left, she was alone in the hallway.

She walked back to her classroom and from the windows watched the orphans begin to work outside. The horrible laughter and the sight of the dead rat still clung to her.

She tried to think about something else.

Maybe I should help with the chores here at the orphanage too, she thought. Do like everyone else. Then I won't seem so different. They'll accept me quicker, not tease me. But if what Joey said about the mute was true, I sure shocked them. I could see it in their faces.

She turned away from the window. Who cares, anyway? The heck with them, she thought. She saw Joey take a pitchfork into the barn. She smiled unconsciously. I care. That's who.

Besides it's just like any other place. There are good kids and bad.

Joey sure is nice. She watched him disappear into the shadows past the big barn doors. More than nice. A strange tingling began inside her. She felt like giggling to let it out, but didn't know why.

She looked over the grounds thoroughly. She did not see Richard or Ruth anywhere. A few bad ones aren't going to hold me back, she told herself. She pulled her shoulders back and marched out of the classroom.

Joey was pitchforking fresh hay into the stalls when Aurelia entered the barn.

"Can I help?"

Joey hadn't heard her enter and spun around. He quickly regained his composure.

"Hello," he said, obviously glad to see her.

Aurelia smiled. She liked the way he looked at her. It made her feel special. The last of her anger melted then. "Well, can I?"

"I'm not sure thee should. The Blessed Mother would not—"

Aurelia strutted next to him, rolling up the sleeves of her dress. "I'm going to and that's that. Now what should I do?"

Joey grinned. He walked around her, peeked out the barn doors, then pulled them nearly closed.

"Grab a pitchfork. I am almost done. Fresh hay is over there. We only have six more stalls to go. Then I will show thee something special.''

The forkfuls of hay were much heavier then Aurelia had expected. She tried not to show the strain, but Joey did most of the work. Aurelia was amazed at the amount of hay he could lift with each forkful.

''You're pretty strong,'' she said.

Joey stuck out his chest and grinned. ''I guess.'' He glanced at the barn doors and his grin faded. He stepped closer to Aurelia. He seemed very serious then. ''Do not tell thy father.''

''About the rat?''

He nodded slowly. ''If thee told him and the Blessed Mother found out—'' Again, he checked the doorway. ''Someone would be punished. Probably Richard. Maybe more, I do not know. But the others would not like thee, especially the orphans. Punishments here are harsh. Very harsh. Most of the children are nice, really. They will accept thee soon. But not if thee tells on them. Does thee understand?''

''Sure. It's just like my old school. Kids don't fink on other kids. I won't tell, I promise.''

Joey sighed. ''Good.''

Finished with their work, they stabbed the pitchforks into the huge pile of hay.

''Now, what's so special?'' Aurelia asked. She just wanted to forget about the locker incident then.

''Come. I will show thee.''

They walked to the far corner of the barn. Aurelia liked the strong animal smells combined with the scent of fresh hay. She had never smelled anything so thick and pungent before—it was almost as if she could taste it. But it was pleasant to her and she inhaled deeply. Joey glanced at her and smiled, as if he could guess her thoughts.

In the far corner there was a three-foot-high, half-sized door with a wooden latch. Joey bent over and opened it. A dozen or so sheep milled around in the pen outside.

"Wait here." He bent over and went through the door. She heard the bleating of the sheep as he chased them. He came back with a small lamb cradled in his arms. Aurelia watched the muscles in Joey's forearms flex and tighten, the veins bulging hard against his skin, as his calloused hands comforted the kicking lamb. She felt her body shudder slightly, wondering what it would be like to have those strong, gentle hands holding her like that.

The lamb baaed. He put it down in front of her, holding it under the neck. She knelt down next to it.

"It's so cute," she murmured.

The lamb looked up at her and baaed again. She reached out slowly, letting it watch her, then petted its head and back. It was soft and warm.

"I just love it."

"It is just a baby. Its mother died. I take care of it, feed it with a bottle. It thinks I am its mother. Watch."

He knelt down and put his fist in front of its face, his thumb sticking out towards it. The lamb nuzzled his hand, then took his thumb in its mouth and began to make sucking noises. Aurelia was captivated.

"It is an albino," he said.

"How can you tell? All sheep are white."

"That's what they say about Caucasians too." Joey looked up at her and grinned. "But look at the others. They are more gray or brown than this one. Look at its eyes. They are pink."

Aurelia lifted the lamb's face close to hers and kissed it. "Can I hold it?"

Joey pushed it into her lap. "Sure. It likes to be held. I can tell it likes thee already."

Aurelia swept the lamb up into her arms. It kicked for a moment.

"I'm not going to hurt you. You're so pretty," she whispered. "Just relax."

The lamb lay down in her lap and didn't move. It watched her constantly, its head tilted sideways.

"It takes to thee. It was never that calm with me."

Aurelia stroked slowly and evenly down its back, then scratched it under the chin.

"I already fed it."

"Is it a she or a he?"

"A girl."

"Have you named it?"

Joey shrugged. "No. Perhaps people who have one or two animals as pets name them. On my parents' farm we had many animals. We could not name them all."

The lamb kicked and Aurelia let go. It hobbled, long-legged and awkward, to the door. Joey leaned back on one arm and pushed the door further open. They watched the lamb wobble out into the pen.

They both lay back on the fresh hay and laughed. The closeness suddenly made Aurelia nervous in a way she had never been before. "Joey?" He looked into her eyes. She felt that nervousness tighten her throat. She swallowed. "You said you came here about two weeks ago. Where are your parents?"

Joey fidgeted and looked at the small door. He stretched to close it. "Those sheep were ours. All our animals are here now."

"You don't want to talk about it?"

Joey still had not looked at her. He began to chew unconsciously on his lower lip. Then he stood up and walked towards the other end of the barn. Aurelia quickly caught up with him. She wished then that she hadn't asked about his parents.

"There was a ceremony," he began. "My parents—"

The big barn doors rattled. Light flooded into the barn as the doors swung open. Outlined in the blaring light, the Blessed Mother stood like the black shadow of death.

Joey grabbed the pitchfork next to him. Aurelia glanced from the door to Joey and back again. He was shuffling the hay he had already piled in one stall. She could see the pitchfork trembling with each awkward stab.

"Joey?" she whispered.

He ignored her and kept turning over the hay.

On the horizon, above the highest pine-thick mountain to the east, two hawks circled together, gliding slowly and easily in the bright blue sky. Aurelia rolled her sleeves down and buttoned them as she walked along the bottom of the cliffs away from the orphanage.

As quickly as the Blessed Mother had appeared, she had gone. Yet Joey would not speak to her after that. Aurelia wasn't really angry with him for ignoring her; she felt sorry for him. She would hate to be as scared of anyone as Joey had seemed to be of the Blessed Mother. She pictured all those young innocent-eyed children bowing their heads, terrified, when the mute had entered the hall. Then she remembered what Joey had said about punishments at the orphanage. Nothing was quite as simple here as it had first seemed.

Aurelia decided simply to walk, and look at the valley and not think about any of it for now. She stopped for a time to watch the soaring hawks, squinting her eyes until they circled down over the other side of the mountain out of view.

She looked back at the orphanage. The sun was high above it. Its dark-windowed carcass seemed to stare back at her.

That was when she saw him.

Richard ducked behind the bushes in a clump of white birch about fifty yards away. Aurelia started to walk again but she quickly glanced back. She could see him at the far edge of the birches, watching her.

She walked faster. She tried not to look back again, but couldn't help herself. This time she didn't see him. Her house was still a long way off, but she had almost reached the mouth of the cave. She tried not to break into a run as she quickened her pace towards it.

Its cool darkness immediately engulfed her. Knowing he couldn't see her, she ran to the far end by the entrance to the big tunnel. Slipping into the tunnel's blackness, she stopped, held her breath and waited.

She didn't see Richard enter.

A warm breeze swirled up from the tunnel. It seemed almost to whisper to her as it tingled against the nape of her neck. She held her breath again. She wasn't sure, but she thought she saw a shadow brush quickly behind a rock near the mouth of the cave.

She spun around and squinted to see farther into the tunnel. Her eyes adjusted to the dark, but she couldn't see far into its depth. She decided to hide farther down in the tunnel even if it was a little scary. The darkness would protect her if Richard tried to follow.

She inched her way down the black, damp tunnel. That eerie whispering sound that came with the breeze floated around her. It became clearer as she descended. She cocked her head.

. . . *Aurelia* . . .

Someone was calling her.

No, it can't be, she told herself. It's just the wind.

Suddenly the tunnel became very hot, almost steamy. Aurelia instantly began to sweat through her dress. She started to hurry back up the tunnel, but it was getting harder to breathe. The air seemed almost too heavy to suck into her lungs. She felt her body tottering, and had to stop and lean back, reaching for the rock wall. Its coldness startled her. The heat and lack of air grew worse. She glanced up at the entrance to the tunnel. Its bright opening began to flash like a strobe light. She was getting dizzy. She gasped desperately for some air.

. . . *Aurelia* . . .

She could breathe again.

. . . *Aurelia* . . .

She began to follow the voice. She didn't know why, but she had to. Something inside her made her. Twice, when the voice beckoned, she turned into another tunnel. It was as if someone else were inhabiting her body, using her limbs to move.

After climbing a small embankment, she bent down and crawled through a short, dusty cavern. There did not seem to be any way that light from the outside could filter in here. She should not have been able to see and yet . . .

It was like watching a movie unfold in her head or closing her eyes and walking through a room she knew well. She could see the cave, the tunnel ahead, see it as if from memory. Not with her eyes, but with her mind.

. . . *Aurelia* . . .

She followed.

After turning a sharp right-angled corner, she found herself at the edge of a huge lake. The ceiling of its massive cavern was at least forty feet high. Water lapped at the rocky embankment she was standing on. The sound of moving, rippling water echoed across the shore.

She wondered if this lake fed the valley's long winding river. She knew the river did start somewhere in the mountain that housed the cave. She could remember that.

But not other things.

The memories of her life before she had come to Paradise Valley seemed so vague and foggy now, just dim, flickering shadows that kept disappearing in the recesses of her consciousness.

Then the voice stopped calling her. A chill rushed across her body.

The cavern quickly darkened. It was becoming black.

Terror engulfed her. Whatever had brought her here and had given her the power to see in the darkness, had fled. She turned, horrified, and felt her way back into the short-ceilinged tunnel. Looking over her shoulder once at the horrible abyss behind her, she thought she saw slight wisps of gray shadows.

What was she doing here? How had she gotten here?

Her head began to explode with each quick surge of her heartbeat.

She couldn't remember.

She was lost.

And blind.

Her body trembled viciously. She fell over a jagged rock and blackness, utter blackness, consumed her. She felt as if she were drowning in it.

A girl's voice, faint, distant, almost laughing, whispered ahead of her. The words were unintelligible.

With all her strength, Aurelia forced herself to stand, to bend over in the tiny cavern, and step forward.

One foot at a time.

She concentrated, forcing each muscle to move.

The voice grew louder, repeating itself. It seemed to force her body forward.

. . . Aurelia . . .

She could see again, in her mind.

Other voices joined in.

They were coming closer . . . closer . . . closer . . .

Aurelia opened her eyes and inhaled deeply. The afternoon sunlight edged far into the mouth of the cave. Her head pounded as the light angled up over the rock and reached her face.

She was lying on a thin flat rock, as smooth as a fallen gravestone, at the edge of a tunnel on the right side of the cave's entrance. She sat up, feeling weak and dizzy. She shook her head. That only made it hurt more. She rubbed her eyes, then glanced around the cave.

No one was there.

She pushed herself up and walked out, shielding her eyes from the sun.

What had happened? She tried to focus her mind, to think back in a logical progression.

Richard had been following her. She had gone into the cave. Run to the tunnel. Then . . .

Waited to see if he followed. And he hadn't. She looked down at her dress. It was muddy and slightly torn at the hem.

He must not have been following her after all, she thought. She had hidden in the cave and wrecked her dress for nothing.

What a day!

She tried to laugh the experience off, but something stopped her. She kept thinking there was more to remember, but couldn't figure out what.

As she stared towards her new home, a warm breeze washed over her from behind. It felt as if the cave had just exhaled. She spun around, wide-eyed.

The cave, like the black mouth of a gigantic demon, loomed above her.

Aurelia hugged herself and backed away, trembling.

She knew it was childish, but she had the most frightening feeling that something in the cave was watching her, and waiting.

Just waiting.

CHAPTER V

AURELIA OPENED her eyes before the alarm went off. The sun's brightness illuminated her room. She remembered, in her groggy, half-conscious state, that she had screamed herself awake during a terrible dream sometime last night. She tried to focus her mind back to it, but couldn't. All she could remember were strange gray, shadowed faces surrounding her.

And she couldn't move.

And the eyes . . . horrible reddish eyes, glowing, staring at her like night creatures frozen in the headlights of a car.

She stretched her arms and yawned. A real beaut', she told herself, trying to laugh away the last vestiges of the nightmare.

The new day smelled good. She slipped quickly out of bed and strolled over to the window facing the cave where she had sat Becky down last night.

The doll was gone.

Aurelia glanced anxiously around the room. She knew she had placed it on the corner of the windowsill. The screen was partially ajar.

But it had been shut last night. She was positive of that.

Aurelia swatted the screen open and leaned out to survey the ground below. The doll wasn't outside the window.

She dashed out of her room, through the big living room and onto the porch. She ran barefoot to the back of the house, parted the bushes, and checked below the windows of her room, shading her eyes against the strong angle of the sun.

Her doll was nowhere in sight.

She circled slowly away from the house, looking for tracks, a sign, something. She found nothing.

Across the valley, farmers were working their fields and feeding their livestock. Aurelia stared out at them. Each had suddenly been transformed from an idyllic and intriguing curiosity to a potential thief. Once more she felt like an intruder, a distrusted foreigner. She hated that feeling.

She hurried back to her room, checked her desk, under the bed, in the drawers of her dresser. She was hoping, somehow, she had just misplaced the doll. She sat on the corner of her bed and tried to think. She was *sure* she had put it by the window. She clearly remembered doing that last night.

She walked slowly over to the window, took a long breath to stop that terrible sinking in her stomach and stared out at the valley.

The new day suddenly became painful to look at. For a moment, she thought of going back to bed. When she awakened again, the doll would be where it belonged and everything would feel right again.

It was the same hope she had had every day in Florida after her mother's death. She knew it would do no good.

She heard her father in the kitchen starting the fire in the iron stove. She sat at her dresser, pulled her long T-shirt up over her head, and stared numbly at herself. She felt horribly ugly and different from everyone else. She turned away from her reflection and brushed her hair slowly, then got dressed.

"Daddy?" she said, sliding around the door to the kitchen.

"Putting the eggs on right now, sweetheart."

She halted in the doorway, leaning her shoulder against the wall. He glanced over and, seeing her forlorn look, quickly put the eggs down.

"What's wrong?"

"Becky's gone."

Sam felt a lump in his throat. He suddenly realized why he had been watching his daughter so closely lately. He was scared, waiting for a sign that his daughter would . . . would go insane. Just like his wife. Cold sweat dribbled over his ribs.

"I know," he said quietly. His heart skipped another beat.

"I put her on the windowsill last night and she's gone. The screen was opened somehow."

He almost laughed, realizing she meant her doll. It was the second time that had happened. He was too paranoid. He would have to do something about that. He couldn't live the next few years always watching, waiting, constantly misinterpreting his daughter. It wasn't fair to her . . . or to him.

"Let's have a look." Sam put his arm around her shoulder and led her back to her bedroom.

"I already checked my room," she said. "I know I put it on the sill."

He pushed the screen open and scrutinized the bushes and the grass below.

"I'll check outside."

He climbed out the window and leaped over the bushes. Aurelia leaned out.

"Maybe a raccoon took it," he said. "They're very clever. Can open anything a human hand can. I don't see any prints, though. But it's dry here. Probably wouldn't find prints anyway."

"Do you really think so?" Somehow the idea of a raccoon stealing her doll made her feel better.

"Could be." Sam looked at his daughter. He did not believe a word he was saying, but he tried not to show that when he met her questioning stare.

As he walked around to the porch, out of Aurelia's sight, he swore under his breath and kicked a rock hard into the side of the porch. He stomped into the house, but caught himself in the living room and took a deep breath before entering the kitchen. He did not want to make Aurelia feel worse by letting her see how upset he was.

She doesn't need this, he thought. She just doesn't need this.

"I don't know," he said, taking out the eggs and cracking them quickly into the hot iron pan. "Must have been a Mama raccoon. Needed it for her kids, you know?"

"Daddy?" Aurelia grabbed his arm. He could see his attempt at a joke had failed. "Shouldn't you put the butter in first?"

He tried to smile. "Forgot."

She handed him the butter, then sliced some bread and began to toast it with a wire-mesh holder in the iron stove's fire.

Neither spoke during the meal. Aurelia made herself eat, but she wasn't hungry. She was pushing the eggs around on her plate when someone banged on the screen door to the porch. "Hello? Are you up?"

Sam pushed his chair away from the table and leaned back until he could see who was at the door. But Aurelia had already jumped up.

"I'll get it," she said and dashed through the living room. Sam still couldn't see who the visitor was but he could hear two voices talking rapidly. And then he saw Aurelia returning, pushing a shy-looking Joey ahead of her.

Sam waved him into the kitchen. "Want some eggs?"

"No thank you, Mr. Hill. I have already eaten. We get up at five in the spring and summer to do chores. I help milk the cows. Then we eat. We don't have to eat breakfast in the dining room with the other kids."

Aurelia hurried into her bedroom and returned with her purse and hat.

"I'm going to walk to school with Joey," she called as she headed out the door. Joey promptly followed.

"You haven't finished breakfast," Sam said.

"I'm not hungry."

Sam shook his head and went to the kitchen window. He watched the two kids half walk, half run across the meadow to the road. He smiled to himself at how easily kids could change their moods. She had been angry and hurt moments before, and now she was happy. Just because Joey had come over, the doll was almost forgotten.

If only if could be that easy all her life, he thought.

Suddenly he missed Becky terribly.

"I cleaned thy locker," Joey said, slowing the pace, now that they had reached the road.

"That was sweet of you."

They walked together in silence. Joey felt himself becoming nervous again, as he had when he was nearing Aurelia's house a few minutes earlier. He was trying to think of something to say, but his mind kept going blank. He fidgeted awkwardly with his hands.

"Does thee always wear that hat?"

"Don't you like it?"

He felt his stomach quiver. He could have kicked himself for saying the wrong thing.

"Sure I like it. I was just . . ." He didn't know how to finish. At that moment he wished he hadn't gotten his nerve up to go to her house. He knew he should never have thought she could like him the way he liked her.

Aurelia noticed his self-critical frown and smiled. "I have to wear it. Keeps the sun off my face and out of my eyes. I'm allergic to the sun because of my skin."

Now Joey knew he should never have come. Unconsciously he increased their pace. Aurelia tried to keep up and had to break into a trot. All of a sudden she stopped.

"Joey," she called. He froze and turned his head. "It doesn't bother me that I have to wear the hat. I like it."

Joey waited for her to catch up.

"I like it, too." He grinned. When she grinned back, he felt better about coming. They walked in silence then, but it was not so oppressive to him anymore.

Aurelia touched his arm. "Why did you ignore me when the Blessed Mother came into the barn yesterday?"

"I do not know. I mean, well, thee was not supposed to be helping me and . . ." He shrugged. "All the orphans warned me never to disobey the Blessed Mother."

"I think she's nice. She has a wonderful doll collection, just like I do. Collecting dolls is kinda like why I have to wear this hat." Joey peered at her, concerned, the way someone looks at a sick friend. She stopped walking and looked in his eyes. "I'm not feeling sorry for myself. I just meant, she understands how it is for me. I played with dolls a lot when I was a kid because it wasn't so easy for me to go outside and play with friends. That's all. And I don't play with dolls now, I just collect them. It's a hobby." She decided, then, not to tell him about the missing doll. She could see he didn't understand.

Joey stood a few feet away. He knew he had upset her. But he felt an obligation to make her understand about the Blessed Mother.

"She's not so nice," he said. Even if it made Aurelia mad, he had to warn her. "She hates the orphans. They know it. She likes to punish them. Even if thee does not believe me, it is so. That is why I told thee not to say anything yesterday. I was trying to warn thee to protect the others."

Aurelia frowned, and Joey felt his heart sink.

"Did she punish you for being with me in the barn? You said you disobeyed her."

Joey looked down at the ground. "No."

"There, see? She's not so bad then. You're new at the orphanage. Don't believe everything the others tell you. Maybe they're just trying to scare you again."

"Maybe." Joey raised his eyebrows. "But it is not just the orphans. It is all the people in the valley. They are all scared of her." As he began to walk again, they brushed shoulders. He glanced at her shyly. They were nearing the orphanage, and Joey slowed the pace. He did not want the walk to end.

"Joey?" Aurelia put her arm in his.

He knew boys and girls were not allowed to touch in public, but he didn't care. It was worth any punishment they could give him. It felt wonderful.

"You didn't finish telling me about your parents yesterday. What happened to them? Do you mind talking about it?"

Joey stopped. "I do not mind. Two and a half weeks ago. On Wednesday night. There was a special ceremony. A holy day. Everyone in the Valley acts different for weeks before it."

"How do you mean, different?"

"Nervous, I guess."

He looked up at the sky, blinking his eyes. Aurelia sensed he was drifting back to that night and squeezed his arm reassuringly. She wished he did not feel he had to hide his emotions in order to make her respect him, but she knew enough about boys to keep her thought to herself. She thought it was silly that they had to pretend to be so strong when she knew they weren't.

"My mother died that same Wednesday." Her words came out so suddenly that she herself was surprised she had spoken them.

Joey turned his head sharply and looked at her. "Really?"

She nodded.

Seeing the pain in her eyes made Joey feel a little better. It was easier to cope with that terrible sense of loss when he could share it with someone who understood, who was going through similar feelings. Joey half-smiled, trying to give her back the support she had just given him. It helped him gain the self-control he had been battling for.

"So what happened at the ceremony?" Aurelia thought the date was an eerie coincidence but she did not want to talk about her mother anymore. The details of her mother's suicide were a secret. No one would ever make her reveal how she had died . . . ever.

Joey shrugged. "After the ceremony they just never came back. No one would talk about it. The next day, the mute came and took me to the orphanage. None of the kids would speak to me. They still do not. If I tried to ask someone in the valley, a friend of my parents, about it, they would tell me to leave, to go back to the orphanage and not ask questions. That is all I know. Except that they are dead."

Aurelia couldn't believe what he had just told her. It

was so sad, so horrible . . . and so final. How could people refuse to tell him what had happened to his parents? And why? It seemed so cruel. It made no sense at all. Yet he was standing there, explaining it to her as if he had almost expected something like that to happen.

Aurelia's big eyes stared at him. "Maybe they just had to go somewhere quickly. Somewhere in secret."

"No," he said. "They are dead. I prayed they were not. God, how I prayed. But I could see it in the faces of the people I questioned." Joey's lower lip trembled. He knew he could not go on without crying. "They are dead. That is all."

He looked away and began to walk again. His shoulders hunched suddenly and he bowed his head. Aurelia could tell he was crying. She ran up next to him. He turned his head away. She felt like crying then too. She reached out to touch him, but he tucked his head further into his shoulder. Slowly she pulled her hand back.

"I'm so sorry, Joey. It's awful what happened."

He nodded, then ran towards the stairs to the front doors of the orphanage. In the last two weeks he had learned it was better not to talk about his parents. It hurt too much. But that wasn't the only reason. There was something dangerous about it too, something that terrified the people he had questioned. He had seen that in their eyes as well. It would only make things worse for him and Aurelia if they talked about it any further.

Aurelia shuffled up the stairs, not knowing what to do or what to say. Joey wiped his nose with the sleeve of his coat.

He had to act like a man, he thought. It would not be good for her to see him crying.

He clenched his jaw, took a deep breath, and turned to face her. Seeing the pity in her beautiful face made him feel like a child again. He wanted to throw his arms around her, and weep and be comforted.

But he was going to be strong now. A man, he told himself. Like his father.

"I will come over to thy house after chores this afternoon," he said. "I have a surprise for thee."

"What is it?" Aurelia was glad for the change of subject. It was hard to be comfortable with Joey's grief when he couldn't be.

Joey shook his head. "It is only a surprise if I do not tell thee." He forced a grin and opened the big doors for her. He was relieved she did not see the tear edge out the corner of his eye as she walked in.

The class was seated when Sam entered. Aurelia was examining her desk. She really hadn't noticed yesterday, but all the desks were wooden, with iron legs. The tops opened up like suitcases. She had never seen anything like them before. They must be a hundred years old, she thought.

She noticed all the kids were standing. She quickly closed the lid and stood up too.

"That's not necessary," Sam said, waving his hand as he walked to his desk. "Sit down, class."

They sat in unison.

"I realize you're used to a very formal classroom. However, I'm not." He sat on the edge of his desk, one leg swinging above the floor. "It will not be necessary to stand when you answer a question. Or when I enter. Also, you don't have to call me sir. If you want my attention, just raise your hand. If I don't see you . . ." He looked around the room, then smiled. "Wait. I'll get to you soon enough."

Sam began to discuss the events that had led up to the Civil War. He asked simple questions as he lectured, but only Aurelia could provide any answers. After responding to two questions in a row, she quit raising her hand.

She did not want to embarrass the others, or act as if she knew more than they did. She already stood out too much from the rest of the group.

Sam was startled at their ignorance of American history. He knew the kids' basic skills were excellent, better than those of his senior classes in Greenville High. At the end of an hour he decided to give the class a break by arranging a seating chart. He did not want them to feel defensive because they couldn't answer his history questions, so, with seeming casualness, he tossed out a Biblical question.

All hands rose in unison. He picked a boy in the back corner. The student's answer was perfect, and he even quoted the full Biblical passage pertaining to the question. Sam listened intently, then put down the seating charts.

"I can see by your names that most of you are of Scandinavian descent." He walked around behind his desk and leaned both hands on the back of his old leather chair. "Have you ever heard of the Vikings? The Norsemen?" They looked at him blankly. "They were your ancestors." He walked back around the desk, tapping it loudly with one finger. "Did you ever study any history? I mean besides Biblical history."

Mary raised her hand, and Sam pointed to her.

"Helman Strode was our founder. He established the Holy Children in 1796," she quoted. "Our people came across the Atlantic in 1847, from Denmark. They landed in North Carolina. They moved westward and settled here in Paradise Valley in 1848. We have been here ever since."

Sam rubbed his chin, then turned and looked above the blackboard. There were no maps. He wondered why he had not noticed that before.

"The Vikings . . ." He walked to the closet in the corner by the blackboard and checked inside. No maps.

Not even old books of history or literature. He tried not to look shocked when he faced the class again. "The Vikings were among the best seamen in the world. In what we would now consider very small boats, they crossed the ocean years before Columbus. You know who Columbus was?" Many in the class glanced at each other, then looked back at Sam as if he were speaking another language. "Christopher Columbus discovered America. That's the country we live in." Now don't get sarcastic, he told himself. Their ignorance is not their fault.

Aurelia looked over at Joey. She knew he had been watching her. When she caught his eye, he glanced away shyly. Aurelia opened her desk slightly and took out a piece of paper. She quickly wrote, asking him what his surprise was, saying she couldn't stand the suspense.

"But Mr. Hill," Ruth said, standing up.

"You don't have to stand," Sam said, a little too abruptly. Ruth looked at her peers, embarrassed, and sat down.

"Now, what is the problem?"

"Our ancestors were not . . ." She thought the word out. ". . . Vikings. Our first ancestor was Helman Strode. He is the father of us all."

"Religiously, in a symbolic way perhaps, Ruth, but . . ."

As Sam tried to explain, Aurelia passed Joey her note. He smirked after reading it. Aurelia playfully frowned and nodded at his desk for him to write her back. After checking to see if Mr. Hill was watching, he opened his desk slightly and reached in.

Suddenly he jammed the desktop upright. All heads snapped towards the noise.

Aurelia leaned over to look.

She gasped and, pushing out of her desk, began backing away towards the window, covering her mouth.

Sam darted through the aisle. Aurelia's horrified eyes

were glued to the inside of Joey's desk. Sam looked inside.

The doll, Becky, its face painted white, its eyes dabbed pink, its hair dyed an awful grayish-white was nailed through the chest into Joey's desk. Where the nail stuck out, red paint, like blood, oozed from the wound.

The Blessed Mother was sitting in a chair by the fireplace when she heard the commotion. She knew what had caused it. Quickly, she arose, drew the shades back from the window and watched as Sam and Aurelia, entwined together, slowly made their way home. She could see Aurelia's shoulders heaving as she cried.

She felt Aurelia's pain then, too; like a dull, wooden knife, it pushed in below her ribs. She knew that pain well. It was not so sharp anymore, the years had taken the edge off, but she could still feel it.

And remember.

Aurelia must learn, the Blessed Mother thought, staring at the girl. She truly must. It is the only way. It is her destiny. Her soul must burn first, as mine did. Then, and only then, will she be cleansed for what is to follow.

CHAPTER VI

SAM HELD his daughter tightly as he walked her home. Her small body convulsed against his side. She could not stop crying. By the time they got to their house, she was finally breathing regularly, and her body no longer quaked in short spasms.

Sam helped tuck her into bed after she had undressed. He went to the kitchen and brought back a glass of cold water. She reached for it, but was still trembling badly, so that he had to sit on the bed, lift her up and hold the glass for her as she sipped. Tears edged down her pale cheeks.

"Daddy, how could they be so cruel? How?"

He laid her head gently back on the pillow. "I don't think the class knew about it. They looked as shocked as Joey." He stroked her hair. "No one laughed. They were concerned about you. They really were."

Aurelia glanced through her red, swollen eyes. "Do you really think so?"

"Yes, I do."

Aurelia turned her head away. The horrible image of her doll poured into her mind again. She bolted upright and swallowed. She had almost vomited.

"I don't feel good."

"Just relax. Lie back." He put his big hands on her shoulders. She was sitting stiffly, every muscle of her torso tensed. "Come on, now. Lie back." He pushed her down slowly. "Try to sleep."

Aurelia felt her father's warm touch on her cheek. She reached up and held his hand against her face. In a while she was asleep. Sam gently slipped his hand from hers, then raised the blankets up over her shoulders, tucking them under her neck.

He sat for a moment, watching her sleep. She looked so beautiful, so innocent.

How the hell could someone want to hurt such a lovely child? he wondered. Never in her entire life had she consciously hurt anyone.

Staring at her tear-swollen face, his anger intensified. He stood up, shifting his weight from one foot to the other as he watched his daughter's fitful sleep.

Richard did it, he thought.

He couldn't prove it, but he knew. Richard was the only one who had not looked shocked.

Except Ruth, he remembered suddenly.

She had actually been smiling.

Sam sat on the front steps to the porch, one hand clenched into a fist, unconsciously pounding the outside of the stairs. He did not know what to do. His temper kept clouding his ability to think logically.

Maybe we should just leave, he thought.

Slowly, he gazed out across the land. The morning sun lit the peaceful valley. The small farm houses, clean and white and shining, dotted the rolling land. Farmers in black clothes cleared and tilled the soil. The big-shouldered horses, glistening with sweat, pulled hard at the plows and the old planting machines. Beyond the slow, easy-sloping horizons, the mountains stood green and protective.

It's beautiful here, he thought. Why should the acts of one or two spiteful kids ruin all that? He wouldn't let them. Aurelia loved this place too much for them to give up so quickly.

And he hadn't lied to her. The other children really were concerned. That one girl, Mary, had actually been crying for Aurelia's sake.

Sam heard the sound of a horse trotting and the squeaking of badly oiled wheels. Thomas Borg's buggy turned off the road from behind Sam's house and bounced its way up the path around to the porch.

Sam stood up and waved. He was glad to have company then, especially Thomas Borg's. The chubby little man waved back, then pulled the reins and bounded down out of his buggy with surprising agility.

"Hello, Mr. Hill," Thomas called as he ambled up to him.

"Call me Sam. All my friends do."

Thomas grinned. "And thee should call me Thomas."

"I'd invite you in, Thomas, but, well . . ."

Thomas's face saddened. "I know. I heard what happened."

"News travels fast here," Sam said dryly.

"Thee dismissed thy class early. All the children went home. The whole valley knows. The people are ashamed. It was no way to treat our guests. When one of the Holy Children does a harmful, mean thing, we are all responsible. Therefore, I offer my apologies first. Others will come. Thee shall see."

"I appreciate that. I wish you'd tell Aurelia."

"Let her rest. It is good."

Sam put his hand on Thomas's shoulder. "Let's

walk. I need to do something besides sit here.''

They strolled eastward together, past the woodshed and across the long meadow to a newly furrowed field. Sam thought he smelled whiskey on the old man's breath again. He did not want to comment, but he was intrigued. The Holy Children were definitely teetotalers.

"Guttard has planted peas here already. They are an early crop,'' Thomas said as he knelt to feel the black, moist soil. He arose and looked at Sam, the dirt still cupped in his hand. "It is good land. The Valley is fertile. The people here are like the land. They are basically good and . . ." He laughed loudly. "Fertile. Many children.''

Sam laughed too, patting the old man's back. He was glad to find humor again today. He sat down on a big, white boulder that pushed out of the edge of the field.

Thomas sat with him. He watched Sam stare across the field, clenching and unclenching one hand.

"Thee has a right to thy anger,'' Thomas said, staring across the field. "We do not take sinful ways with a smile either. Sin must be punished. We are not a people to turn the other cheek.''

"It was that older boy, Richard. I know he did it. That girl, Ruth, too. But I can't prove it.''

"They have been orphans for a long time.'' Thomas let the dirt fall through his fingers. "It is a hard life for them.''

"I guess so, but it doesn't excuse—''

"No it does not. I cannot argue with that. What will thee do? The Blessed Mother is the only one with the right to punish. It is our law. Our way.''

"So I should tell her, huh?''

Thomas sat up stiffly, blinking his eyes as he pondered. "I cannot advise thee. The Blessed Mother's punishments are severe. She does not treat sin lightly.''

"What would she do? I mean if she knew Richard did it."

"I cannot advise thee."

Sam detected a growing nervousness in Thomas's voice. He wondered if he should pursue the matter further. He could tell Thomas did not want to.

"I wanted to ask you something, Thomas." Sam stood up. Thomas arose too. They began to stroll back to Sam's house. "About Becky, I mean. My wife. It's important to me."

Sam watched Thomas begin to play with the buttons on his long, black coat as they walked. The old man would not look at him.

"Did you know her?"

Thomas nodded. "The Valley is small. Everyone knows everyone else."

"Did you know her parents?"

"She was raised in the orphanage. She was abandoned as a baby and left on the steps of the orphanage."

"In a group as closely knit as yourself, how could a pregnant woman keep that fact hidden? It would be impossible, I would think."

Thomas stopped, took off his black hat and scratched his head. "I do not know. But that is the way it happened."

They began to walk again, but now Sam moved with eyes downcast in dejection. His hopes of finding an answer to his wife's suicide were nearly destroyed now, and that realization sank heavily into his belly.

They turned the corner of the house and walked to Thomas's buggy. Sam offered him a hand, but the old man pulled himself up without assistance.

"Would anyone else know more about Becky's family?" Sam asked.

Thomas Borg looked down, frowning, then shook his head, no. Sam clutched the brass handle on the side of the buggy, and an uncomfortable silence followed as Thomas watched him think.

"I'm going to tell the Blessed Mother about the doll," Sam said finally, backing away from the buggy. "Aurelia doesn't need any more pain. She's had enough already."

"That will probably not be necessary, Mr. Hill."

"Sam," he corrected.

"I am sure the Blessed Mother already knows . . . Sam." Thomas smiled, but Sam thought there was something very sad about the expression.

"Thank you for stopping by, Thomas. Come again soon."

Thomas lifted the reins to go, but put them back on his lap and looked at Sam. "Beware of the Blessed Mother. Do not ask her what thee has asked me, about thy wife. I like thee, Sam, that is why I offer thee this advice. I was hoping it would not come to this. Beware of her. If I were thee I would leave well enough alone. For thy daughter's sake. Thee did not come here merely by chance."

Thomas Borg flipped the reins and the horse leaped forward across the grass. Sam stared at the buggy until it disappeared over the ridge to the south.

After Thomas Borg left, Sam went back inside to Aurelia's room. She was sleeping quietly. He sat and watched her for over an hour. He kept thinking about Thomas' warning. It seemed awfully melodramatic. Maybe the man was drunker than he had thought. He seemed nice enough, but . . .

Sam shook his head in resignation. The people here were a little strange, that's all. One thing he was sure of, though. They were a non-violent people. That was part of their religion. He couldn't imagine what Thomas could have meant.

Of course he hadn't come here by chance. He was invited.

Sam rose and tiptoed out of Aurelia's room. As he stepped out onto the porch, it came to him that he could not give up, he could not leave the valley until he knew who Becky's parents were and why they had abandoned her. He knew he couldn't live his life always waiting for signs of paranoia in Aurelia, waiting for her to begin to go insane too.

And he still wondered if he could have prevented his wife's death. Maybe he should have forced her to see a psychiatrist. Was it possible he had somehow pushed her into committing suicide?

Sam rubbed his hands together and walked outside. He couldn't live with any of those questions.

If Becky's instability was hereditary, he would finally be able to dismiss his guilt, but then what about Aurelia? And if it wasn't, how would he ever know for sure her death was not at least partially his fault?

Either way, he suddenly realized, he was a loser.

The screen door banged closed behind him. He spun around.

Aurelia smiled. She had washed her face with cold water to take the puffiness from her eyes. Her hair was brushed back neatly. She looked wonderfully young and naive again. Under her arm she held her backgammon set.

"How are you feeling?"

"All right." She looked around the valley from the steps. "Beautiful day, huh?"

Sam grinned. She was stronger inside than he gave her credit for. Sometimes a little touch of sarcasm could be an awfully healthy sign, he thought.

"Sure is. I see you're ready to try to beat me again."

He pointed at the wooden set. He was relieved not to be alone with his thoughts anymore. They had been getting more oppressive by the moment.

"For a buck?" She hopped down the last two steps and hurried to the big oak in the front lawn. She sat down in its shade, opened the board and began setting up the pieces.

"A buck a game it is." Sam sat across from her.

They played four games, and during the second Aurelia began to giggle, as she usually did during their mock-ferocious contests. She won the last three.

Afterwards Sam leaned back against the thick, black trunk, yanked out a blade of grass and began to chew it. Aurelia could tell he had been waiting to say something during the whole last game. She closed the board, latched it, then looked into his eyes and waited.

"Do you want to leave here?" he asked. "I know you liked it here, at first but . . . if, after today, well . . ."

Aurelia carried the backgammon set to the porch steps and put it down. Sam watched her closely as she walked back and knelt before him. She picked a thick blade of grass, placed it tightly between her two thumbs, raised it to her mouth and blew. A high-pitched screech pierced the air. She laughed and threw the grass away.

"Is that your answer?" Sam grinned.

Aurelia looked at him seriously. "They're not going to scare me away so easily. I like it here. Joey's nice. So's Mr. Borg. And the Blessed Mother and Mary. The others are a little harder to win over. Same as any place. I'll be accepted soon. You should have seen what Peter Stone did to the new girl in our class in Greenville this fall. I felt more sorry for her then, than I do for myself now."

Sam threw up his hands and laughed. "Just a question."

Aurelia smiled. "I'm going to have fun here, I know

it." She looked to her left. A buggy with a brown mare trotted up towards their house.

"Good afternoon," Sam called. A heavy, broad-shouldered woman stepped out of the vehicle. She had the kind of unexpressive face that Sam couldn't begin to guess the age of.

"To thee too," she said. She pulled a basket off the seat and approached the big oak. "I have brought thee cold chicken, potato salad, lemonade and a big apple pie." She shoved the basket into Sam's chest.

"Thank you," he managed to say.

"I am Gertrude Throm, Ezekiel's wife. Thee met him at the hardware store."

Sam nodded. "I remember. How are you?"

She walked up to Aurelia. "How does thee fare, child?" She clasped Aurelia's shoulders with her big, calloused hands.

"Fine, thank-you." Aurelia smiled shyly.

"Good. Do not let one troublesome incident cloud thy day. We are all concerned. The people asked me to come and apologize for them and to welcome thee." She almost lifted Aurelia off her feet as she kissed her on the forehead. She turned to face Sam. "And thee too."

Sam bowed slightly and grinned.

Gertrude took the basket back from Sam. "Mr. Borg came by earlier?" she asked.

Surprised, Aurelia looked at her father. "He did?" she said.

"He came to see how you were, but you were sleeping," Sam explained.

Gertrude flapped a checkered cloth out into the air and draped it on the grass, then spread the food over it.

"Come," she called. "Eat. Thee are too skinny, child. We must put some meat on thy bones."

As they ate and talked, Thomas' words of warning

soon seemed ridiculously out of place to Sam. But the guilt and the gnawing curiosity about Becky's parents still clung to him.

He couldn't get it out of his mind.

Sam was behind the house chopping wood when he heard a male voice at the front of the house, where Aurelia sat alone, reading. He walked along the side of the house and stopped at the corner.

Aurelia was on her knees, her face beaming with joy, her eyes sparkling. Joey bent over next to her. A small lamb wobbled unsurely between them, licking Aurelia's hand.

"It's for thee," Joey was saying.

"But the Blessed—"

"It was my family's. I own it. Not her. If I want to give it to thee, it is mine to give."

Aurelia stood up, hardly able to contain her excitement.

"Thank you, Joey. It's the most wonderful gift I've ever gotten."

She threw her arms around his neck and kissed him. Sam laughed inside, seeing the shock on Joey's face. The obvious innocence that flowed between them was fun to watch. He leaned closer against the corner of the house so they wouldn't see him.

Aurelia began to leap and run, playing tag with the stiff-legged, energetic lamb. Joey jumped away as the lamb turned to chase him.

Sam was glad to see the warm understanding Joey showed in both his timing and in the present that he had brought. He could tell how much the boy loved the lamb; it must not have been easy for him to give it away.

Sam realized he felt quite impressed with the Holy Children. One bad kid hurts Aurelia and the whole valley comes to comfort her, he thought. It was a good place after all. Good for Aurelia. Even after that doll incident, she still seemed happier here in the last two days, than she had been since her mother's death.

"Daddy, I'm going for a walk with Joey, all right?" she called.

Sam stuck his head around the corner of the porch. "Fine. Have a good time."

With the lamb between them, they walked through the open meadow behind the house then down near the river and over the hill to Thomas Borg's farm.

Thomas watched Aurelia and Joey's approach from his toolshed, where he was sharpening his axes. He called out through the open window, and they stopped.

"I see thee has a new addition to thy family, Aurelia," he said, strolling out to meet them. Joey did not trust anyone in the valley since his parents had disappeared, but he knew Thomas better than most. The old, smiling-eyed man was not like the others. The boy was glad to see him again.

"How old is it?" Thomas leaned over, groaning slightly and rubbing his stiff back, to pet the lamb.

"Three weeks," Joey answered.

Thomas straightened up stiffly. "Does thee still wish to learn to ride a horse?"

Aurelia glanced at Joey, wide-eyed. Joey smiled and nodded at her to answer.

"Sure do," she said.

"Good. Follow me."

They all walked together, the lamb bounding in a circle by their feet, and entered the barn.

"I have no saddles, but old Hilda there and Amos, they would not buck off a fly. Used to pull the plow, then the wagon, but they are too old for either now. I do not have the heart to get rid of them. I feed them and let them roam the pasture. They more than deserve their retirement. Worked hard all their lives."

He slipped the reins over each one's head as Joey helped.

"Thee has ridden them before. Thee can teach Aurelia." Thomas grinned and winked at Joey. "I have work to do."

Joey proudly led both horses out into the field behind Thomas's house. A path wound around its perimeter, hard and worn from years of use by Thomas's crop wagon. It was a good trail for the horses.

Joey helped Aurelia up on Hilda, the white-nosed mare. She was slightly swaybacked and very round-bellied. In fact they were both short, thick horses, even tempered—docile really. Joey remembered trying to get Amos to break into a gallop last fall. Perhaps lazy, he thought, was the best description for the animals. Or maybe just old.

Aurelia petted Hilda's thick brown neck. Joey jumped up, holding the horse's mane to swing over onto its back. He demonstrated how to use the reins to turn and to stop.

"The hard part," he laughed, "is to get them to start. Thee must kick them so." He jammed his heels in behind Amos's ribs. The horse began to walk. He turned back to see how Aurelia was doing. "Do not be so gentle. Thee cannot hurt her with those soft shoes. Kick. That is it. Kick."

Slowly, Hilda began to move. Aurelia held the reins tight in her small fists. The horse's wide back began to sway and bounce. Aurelia squeezed her legs tighter around her.

They circled the big field slowly. Aurelia loved the feeling more each second she was on the horse. Her imagination soared. She pretended she was a beautiful princess riding with her suitor in the fields of England. Then, grasping her hat and squashing it tight on her head when she finally got old Hilda to actually trot, she imagined herself a Southern beile, riding across her big plantation. Joey was her fiancé who was soon to go to war against the North. In his black hat, jacket and pants, he almost looked as if he were wearing a uniform. Aurelia laughed out loud, no longer able to contain her swelling joy.

After an hour, they walked the horses back to the barn, watered them, and fed them the sugar Thomas gave them on their way in. After Aurelia had run out of sugar, Hilda nudged her big, hard head against the girl's cheek, almost knocking her over.

Joey laughed and grabbed her around the waist to keep her from tripping over the hay bale. Aurelia spun around in Joey's arms and looked up into his eyes. Suddenly they both felt terribly self-conscious. Joey quickly let go.

As they walked home, the lamb, tired after chasing after the horses for over an hour, had a hard time keeping up with them. Aurelia edged closer to Joey and slipped her hand in his. She stopped and pulled him towards her, then stood on her tiptoes and kissed him. It was soft and wonderful. Joey put his arms around her tentatively, and she felt her body molded against his.

"Thank you so much," she whispered, resting her head against his chest. "You made an awful beginning turn out to be the best day of my life."

When they were within a hundred yards of her house, Aurelia stopped again. She sat on a big rock, still warm from the sun. The lamb lay down, exhausted, on her feet.

Joey glanced up at the cliffs. While they were riding he had thought he had seen Richard spying on them from the woods. Now he glimpsed a dark apparition jump behind a tree above them near the point in the cliffs that jutted out like the hull of a small ship.

He decided not to tell Aurelia. She was so happy now.

"I should get back soon. The Blessed Mother does not know I came here. Or that I gave thee the lamb."

"She won't mind. You were just being nice."

"I could get into trouble. They have been watching me more lately." Joey kept kicking his heel into the dust, digging a small hole. "I think it's because I . . ." He kicked harder and would not look at Aurelia. "I like thee. The Blessed Mother does not approve."

"Why? I'll tell her how kind you were. That you brought me—"

"No." Joey's eyes darted at hers. "Don't tell her anything. Please?"

Aurelia smiled to reassure him she wouldn't. "She's really not so terrible."

Joey quickly glanced back at his heel and squashed it into the hole he had dug. Aurelia could tell he was upset.

"Thee does not understand," he sighed.

Aurelia didn't want to pursue the subject. She already knew they would not agree. Pushing it would only cause an argument. Besides, she had something else she wanted to ask him before she got home. She held Joey's arm and looked up into his eyes.

"Is Richard always mean to everyone?"

"Yes. But with thee . . ." Joey straightened up. "Not if I can help it." He did not want to worry her anymore by telling her that he thought Richard and Ruth really seemed to have it in for her.

Aurelia smiled and started to walk again. "I thought I saw him watching me yesterday after I left you in the barn."

"Are thee sure?"

She shrugged. "I don't know if he was following me but I saw him. He jumped behind a tree." She halted again and grinned proudly. "I tricked him though. I hid

in the cave. If he was following me he . . ." She stopped
when she saw the look of horror spread over Joey's
face. "What'd I say? What's the matter?"

"Thee went into the cave?"

"Sure." Aurelia smiled again. "It was . . ." Her
smile faded.

Joey backed away from her, his mouth hanging open.
He slumped down on the rock next to the road. She immediately sat next to him.

"No one is allowed to go there. It is a sacred place,"
he said.

"But the Blessed Mother—"

"Only once a year, during the special ceremony, are
the people allowed to enter the cave. Even then, only
some can go. It is the ceremony my parents went to
when . . ." Joey rubbed his forehead. His expression
changed. He suddenly looked cold and distant. Aurelia
squeezed her hands tight between her thighs. "The
Blessed Mother took them there, and whatever happened to them was her fault. I know it."

"Why do you say that?"

"I just know. Everyone does. But no one will admit
it. That is why no one in the Valley will speak to me
about it. She frightens them too much." Joey looked
down at the grass, trying to figure out how to verbalize
what was only a terrible, haunting suspicion. "If thee
stays here long enough, thee will see. She holds this
valley in fear. It has always been so."

"I just can't believe that she . . ."

Joey shook his head hard. "The children have a
legend about the cave. My mother had never told me
about it. I heard it from one of the orphans two years
ago. When I asked my mother if it were true, she turned
sort of pale and nodded, but she never said a word."

Aurelia inched closer to Joey. Ever since they sat
down she had been feeling as though they were

strangers. It was a feeling she knew well, especially in Paradise Valley, but Joey had been able to take it away. Now alienation edged between them like a thick, gray mist. She hated it. She had upset him. She had only been trying to draw him closer to her with her secret, and instead she had driven him away.

Silently, she stared through that terrible mist and waited.

"The children say that the cave is the Devil's hole. That it is cursed. But that our life comes from it as well. They say if anyone goes in it, except during the Holy Ceremony, they will never be seen again." Joey sighed and, leaning forward, brought his knees up against his chest. "They say there are creatures in it. Strange horrible spirits. Spirits that feed upon our people." He let his legs drop and stared with a terrible urgency at Aurelia. "Stay away from there. The spirits, the cave—they are a part of the Blessed Mother's power over the valley. They are the reason everyone is scared of her. They will destroy thee." Joey jumped off the rock and pointed at her. "For thy own good, Aurelia. I warn thee."

"But I like her. She's—"

Joey backed away. Aurelia felt that cold mist close around her.

She stood up and reached towards him. He shook his head, turned and ran down the road.

"Joey?" she yelled frantically.

He stopped and looked back. "Stay away from there. It is a place of evil. It is *her* place." Then he dashed away.

Aurelia watched him until he disappeared over the ridge. Slowly, she sat down. The lamb stood up and nuzzled itself between her legs. She petted its head. But even the lamb could not dispel her terrible sense of aloneness.

"I don't understand," she whispered. She knelt down and hugged the lamb, burying her face in its soft, woolen fur. It leaned its head up and licked her cheeks. She squeezed it close.

"It's just a dumb old cave. It's creepy, but . . . it's no big deal. It's certainly not haunted or anything. I've been in it twice. Fell asleep there once." She shrugged. "Nothing happened to me."

CHAPTER VII

AT DINNER Aurelia told her father what Joey had said about the cave and the Holy Ceremony and his parents. Sam was not entirely surprised at what he heard. Holy places and shrines were not at all uncommon in different Christian sects, and fear seemed to permeate superstition; well, when kids started a rumor based on even the flimsiest of facts, especially rumors about haunted places, fear was the whole point. Like ghost stories around a campfire.

As for Joey's parents' disappearance in the cave, or being killed there, he suggested that perhaps they in fact had abandoned Joey, left the valley, and that no one had the heart to tell him. His not being able to cope with that feeling of rejection, of total abandonment could have made him need to believe more strongly in something like the superstition of the cave so that he could vent his anger, his hurt, his emotional confusion, on something else, in his case, the Blessed Mother and the children's rumors about the cave.

Kids everywhere, he reminded her, in every town, always had at least one haunted house to scare them. The rumors were always quick to spread. Sometimes an old woman who never left her home, especially if the place were a little dilapidated, would cause stories to circulate; that she was a witch, that the house was haunted. It happened all the time.

Aurelia knew what he meant. In Greenville it was old lady Kramer. On dares, her friends, mostly the boys, used to try to catch a glimpse of her by sneaking inside her house at night. It had been a real test of courage in Junior High School.

"Poor Joey," she said. "It's one thing to have a parent die. But to have them abandon you without a word. What a heartless thing to do to your own child."

"It's the only reason I can come up with. I certainly don't believe they were killed in an accident without anyone telling him. As concerned as the people here have shown us they can be, they wouldn't keep that from the boy, I'm sure. That's just too cruel to consider. And if his parents had left, who would have the heart to tell him if no one knew for sure where his parents were or whether they really had abandoned him for good? Who would want to be the one to suggest it when it wasn't substantiated? I wouldn't."

Aurelia nodded. Her father had a point. No wonder Joey had acted so strangely.

"I hope he can adjust. It'd be so hard, though. It's so depressing. Maybe they'll come back." Aurelia sighed. "Geez, when I told him I had been in the cave, he just freaked out. I guess I can see why now, but still . . ." She shook her head sadly.

Sam frowned. "You went in the cave?"

"I went there on my walk with the Blessed Mother. She said it was one of Mom's favorite places. I thought it was kind of creepy, myself." She didn't want to tell him about the other time, when she thought Richard had been following her, because of what Joey had said about snitching.

Sam looked across the table sternly. "I don't want you near that cave again. Caves are dangerous. And besides, if some of the people here believe in that superstition, it wouldn't be good for you to openly shun their beliefs, even if they are ridiculous, by going in there again."

"But I went with the Blessed Mother." Aurelia twisted her fork around on her plate. She did not like it when he ordered her not to do something. It was as if he were treating her like a child.

Sam shoved his chair away from the table and carried his dishes to the sink. He turned and waited until he caught her eye. The more he thought about it, the more he thought he should reemphasize the possible dangers. "I don't want you going there again. Got that?"

Aurelia looked down, sulking. "Yeah."

"What was that?"

Aurelia peered up at him, still mad at the way he was treating her. "Yes. I got it."

"That's better." Sam smiled. "Now how about another piece of Mrs. Throm's apple pie?"

Aurelia sighed. There was no reason to stay mad. She understood her father was just worried about her. "Sure. I'd love a piece."

Aurelia went to bed soon after dinner. Sam sat in the living room by the fire, reading M. Scott Momoday's *House Made of Dawn*, for the second time. He put down the book and stared pensively at the blue and yellow flames snapping up the black chimney. He had been reading the same page for the last twenty minutes. He didn't remember a word of it. He had been thinking about Joey and the cave and about Thomas' odd warning about the Blessed Mother.

Now, in the solitude of the fire and the night, Thomas' warning did not seem so ludicrously melodramatic. He tried to laugh it off as he had that afternoon, but he no longer could.

He believed what he had said to Aurelia about superstitions, and yet there was something wrong about the way the orphans seem so scared all the time.

There was also something odd about the Blessed Mother's taking Aurelia to that cave.

Sam leaned back and peered around the shadowed room. The firelight danced on the walls. He sighed and closed his eyes. Now the logical explanations he had offered Aurelia at dinner seemed too pat, and too pedantic without his having the credentials to back them up. He was certainly not qualified as a psychiatrist, especially after what happened to his wife, so what were his theories worth, actually?

Sam mulled the puzzle over again and again. What really had happened to Joey's parents? Could they truly have abandoned him without a word? It was hard to believe.

He didn't know why, but Sam kept thinking that the reason Joey's parents had disappeared and the reason no one knew who Becky's mother was, were somehow related. He couldn't explain why he felt that, but he did.

Maybe because no one in the valley could come up with any information about either matter, and they should have been able to.

That reasoning led him to only one conclusion. Some of the people had to know, but for some reason, would not speak up.

When Sam got up the next morning, Aurelia was already dressed and sitting out on the porch feeding the lamb milk from the baby bottle Joey had given her.

Sam leaned against the open doorway watching the lamb suck hungrily at the rubber nipple. Dark thick clouds sat heavily in the sky. A strong wind blew in from the northwest against the face of the house.

"A little cold today," he said.

Aurelia glanced up. "It's her second bottle."

"Hungry little devil." Sam knelt beside his daughter and petted the lamb.

"It's an albino," she announced. Sam lifted its head and looked at its clear pink eyes. It yanked itself away and went back to nibbling at the bottle.

"Guess it is." He stood and stared down the road, past the orphanage, at the low-hanging clouds that swirled, gray and black, down over the crests of the dark green mountains, hiding their soft-angled peaks. He decided there was no point in easing into the subject. He would ask Aurelia bluntly.

"The Blessed Mother seems to know a lot about Becky, doesn't she? I mean she acted so concerned about her when we met her, and then she took you to the cave because she said Becky liked to play there as a child. Did you two talk about her much?

The lamb slurped at the now empty bottle. Aurelia put it on the chair and stood up.

"I guess so. She certainly did like her a lot. I could hear the pain in her voice when she talked about Mom's leaving here." She glanced at her father curiously. "Why do you ask?"

"Just wondering. You like her?"

"Sure. She's nice."

"What about the other kids? Joey certainly doesn't like her."

"Well, the other kids are scared of Matthew—you know, the mute. And I told you Joey said the Blessed Mother hates the orphans. But I think we figured out why he'd say something like that. Or maybe the other orphans just told him that to scare him. I don't think she's mean. But the mute sure gets to 'em."

"Why do you say that?" Sam watched her curiously.

Aurelia shrugged. "He just scares 'em. When he walks into the hall, everyone shuts up and bows their heads." Aurelia thought for a moment. "But they do that when the Blessed Mother comes in to lunch too." She shook her head. "I don't know. Neither of them bothers me. Maybe that's just the way they show respect here."

Sam smiled. "Let's eat. I'll cook breakfast."

There was a knock on the porch door just as Aurelia scooped up the last of her eggs. She bolted out of her seat. "I'll see who it is."

"I think you already know," Sam laughed, but she was already to the porch and hadn't heard his comment.

"Daddy, I'm going now. See you in school," she called. "Is it all right if I leave the lamb on the porch? I'll clean up the mess."

Sam got up and watched from the window over the sink as they left. He was very concerned about the boy. It was a terrible ordeal Joey was going through, but he was handling it pretty well, all things considered.

As the two teenagers walked down the dirt road, the wind blowing hard against their faces, Sam could tell they were arguing. They stopped suddenly, and Sam leaned over the sink to get a better view. Aurelia gave Joey her books, then entwined her hand in his.

Sam grinned. So much for the argument.

He was glad to see they were getting along again and that yesterday's trauma was over. They needed each other, a lot, he thought, probably more than either of them knew.

"I checked thy desk and locker," Joey said. He was relieved she had accepted his apology for running away the day before and had not demanded a long explanation. She squeezed his hand and leaned her head on his shoulder as they walked. He didn't care if anyone saw them touching in public. Richard had already seen them yesterday. They could not punish him twice for one offense, he thought, almost laughing.

"Do you think he'll bother me again?" Aurelia said suddenly.

"I was just going to tell thee." Joey curled his fingers in hers. "The mute took each of us, one at a time, to the Blessed Mother's rooms last night. She asked everyone a lot of questions. The mute looked awful angry. She asked me where I went yesterday, and I told her. She actually said it was good of me, but . . ." He glanced over to his left, then stopped and stared.

"But what?"

Joey scrutinized the trees just ahead of them.

"Joey?" She shook his arm. "But what?"

"She told me not to seek thee out again." He was still staring at the trees. "I did not say anything. I just left."

They started to walk again. Joey kept glancing to his left.

"Well, it's none of her business," Aurelia stated emphatically. "She can't run my life."

Joey sighed. "She runs all our lives."

"You're here *now*. So she can't run yours that easily."

Joey grinned, feeling very brave then.

"So why did she question everyone?" Aurelia went on.

"She wanted to find out about the doll. Someone is going to get it. I think it is Richard. He is the only one who was not taken to her room by the mute. I could see he was scared at dinner. Even worse afterwards. Something is going to happen today, no doubt about it."

Aurelia was startled to discover she felt a twinge of pity for Richard. She wanted him to be punished, and yet . . .

Joey yanked her to a halt. Kneeling down, he picked up a fist-sized rock. "Someone's been following us." He gazed at a clump of thick bushes around five big maple trees behind them.

One of the bushes shook.

Joey reared back, his front leg lifting in the air like a pitcher's, then heaved the rock as hard as he could. It tore through the section of bushes that had just rustled.

Something squealed.

"Got him," Joey yelled proudly.

A raccoon dashed out of the bushes and hightailed it across the field.

Aurelia couldn't hold it back. She burst out laughing. Joey shook his head and began to laugh too. He had thought it was Richard again. They both laughed so hard their stomachs hurt.

Then they heard thunder over the western ridge of mountains. Big raindrops began to pelt their faces.

"We had better hurry," Joey said, pulling her hand. "It is going to pour any second now."

The rain turned into a downpour almost as he said it. They started running for the orphanage. It soon became a race. Joey was startled at her swiftness. She ran in long, lithe steps, like a doe. He had to run as fast as he could to beat her.

He never even suspected that she had let him win.

Soon after the class filed in and sat down, Sam entered the room. Aurelia immediately felt the anxiety permeating the classroom. Sam felt it too. Half the class stood up, but he quickly waved them down. Tension choked the atmosphere. No one could sit still.

He noticed Richard's seat was empty. "Is Richard sick today?"

He glanced around at the class. Most heads turned

towards Ruth. No one raised a hand or made any effort to answer.

Ruth moved her desk closer to the window. Sam could see she was upset. She kept brushing her hair back out of her face, and peeking out the window.

The others in the row by the windows kept shifting and stretching their necks, trying not to be detected as they watched outside.

"Did you all complete the math assignment I gave you yesterday?" Sam waited for an answer.

The huge front doors of the orphanage banged open. The whole class suddenly seemed paralyzed. The heads of the students by the windows jerked sideways. One boy partially stood out of his chair to see.

"Excuse me, class." Only a few even glanced his way. He raised his voice. "What is the matter with all of you today?" He decided to single someone out. General questions were being completely ignored. "Mary, can you tell me where Richard is, please?"

Mary slowly peered up at him, then glanced over at Ruth, never uttering a word. Sam edged near the corner window to see what was going on. Nonchalantly he looked outside.

The monstrous, scowling mute was dragging Richard by one arm towards the gray shed next to the barn. As the mute opened the door, Richard kicked him. Grabbing the back of his neck, the mute tossed him forward into the darkness. He glanced back at the classroom, as if, it seemed to Sam, to make sure he had everyone's attention. Slowly, he closed the door of the shed.

"Now what the heck is going on?" Sam questioned loudly.

Aurelia looked at Joey and raised her eyebrows. Joey nodded, and she knew. This was to be one of the punishments Joey had spoken about.

Sam was becoming frustrated, having been ignored once again. "I've had enough of this. Someone is going to tell me what's going on."

The class glanced at him, then at Ruth and the windows.

"Ruth?" Sam persisted.

She did not move.

"Ruth, I'm speaking to you."

Slowly, she tilted her face towards him, her thick hair hanging down over her eyes.

"I want you to tell me what is going on."

When she looked up, he saw her lips quiver as she fought back tears. He walked down the aisle between the desks and the windows.

Horrible, muffled cries exploded from the woodshed. Something whip-like cracked, then snapped again.

A scream pierced the air.

One of the youngest boys dashed to the window behind him. Sam spun around. The boy's whole body was trembling.

Another howl echoed from the shed. Sam could feel the class shiver as one. The boy gasped, covering his face with both hands, and began to cry. The older boy, whose desk he was next to, stood up and hugged him, gently pulling him away from the window.

"This has gone far enough. What the hell is going on out there?"

Sam leaned over Ruth's desk and gently lifted her face by the chin. She closed her eyes and bit her lower lip. She yanked her head away and put it down on her crossed arms on the desk.

Sam glanced at Aurelia. She was staring out the window too. He pushed the desks in his way aside and stormed out of the room.

As soon as he had left, the whole class piled against

the window. They watched Sam dash across the muddy grounds.

Sam tugged at the shed door, only to find it was bolted from the inside.

"Open up! You hear me? Open up!"

He banged his fists against the door.

"Open this goddamn door or I'll kick it in!"

Sam stepped back and kicked the door. It rattled. He could hear the latch crack, but it didn't break. He stepped back again and raised one foot.

The door flew open.

The mute stood in the darkness, staring. Sam could sense the mute threatening him, daring him to enter. Instinctively, he stepped back and looked around for a weapon. In that moment, he felt as if his life were in real danger, the same way he had when three migrant workers had surrounded him outside a small rural bar in Texas when his car had broken down during a spring break from college. He had had to fight them with a tire-iron. But there was nothing near him now that he could use against this giant.

Richard stumbled weakly out the door. The mute followed him, keeping himself between Sam and Richard.

"Are you all right, Richard?" Sam tried to push the mute back, but his massive body shielded Richard and wouldn't let him pass. "What did he do to you in there?"

The boy, head bent, his hair soaking with sweat, his clothes drenched, staggered toward the orphanage doors. It looked to Sam as if he were going to pass out at any moment.

Suddenly Richard's legs buckled and he fell forward on his knees. Sam dashed over to help, but the mute blocked his path again. Lifting Richard by the armpits, the mute carried him into the orphanage. His feet barely touched the ground.

Sam stopped at the bottom of the stairs as the doors to the orphanage slammed closed. He clenched his fists until they hurt. He glanced at the windows of his classroom. Everyone was watching. It began to drizzle, but he didn't notice. He was trying to assess his position. He felt very uncertain about his next move. His adrenaline was pumping fast, he thought he should do something. Exactly what, he didn't know. The rules here were not his rules. He tried hard to keep that in mind.

Sam made his way back to the classroom, and was about to enter when the mute stopped in front of him. Sam was determined not to move aside. He leaned all his weight into the doorway and shoved the mute to the side, then marched to his desk. When he glanced back, the mute was gone.

Sam spotted Richard slumped in a chair. Everyone's eyes followed him as he approached Richard's desk.

"What happened in there?"

Richard barely held himself up in his chair; he was swaying, his chin bobbing on his chest. "Richard?" The boy's head raised weakly. His eyes were blurry. They didn't seem to focus when he looked at Sam.

"What did he do?"

Richard slowly shook his head. "Leave me alone." His eyes finally focused. "Please?"

Sam backed away. He would only cause more pain now if he questioned him further. As he wearily walked back to his desk, he realized that the more he thought about it, the more certain he was that there was nothing to say. This was their religion, their way of life. If they accepted it, he had to as well.

But he didn't like it, not one bit.

● ● ●

The four hours of class dragged on dismally. Aurelia sat uncomfortably at her desk, watching the others try to act as if nothing had happened. Joey's warnings were no longer foolish misconceptions to her. There was no doubt the punishments meted out here were severe. She wondered if everything else he had said about the Blessed Mother and the cave were more true than she had thought.

Then she remembered how scared and how hurt she had been yesterday when Joey had lifted his desk top. Richard had deserved to be punished; after all. Maybe his punishment was unusually severe.

Aurelia inhaled slowly and looked at Joey. His head was bowed as he played with a pencil in his lap. Then she looked at Richard. He was slumped face-down on his desk. His body twitched suddenly. His head shot up off his desk. She could see the agony in his face.

No, she thought, even Richard didn't deserve to be beaten that badly. No one did.

Finally, class was over.

Sam had been having a hard time as he lectured about medieval superstitions, the inquisition and the Salem witch trials. He had thought those subjects, if any, would grab the students' attention today, but nothing seemed to interest them.

They were all in a state of shock. And yet Sam could tell it wasn't the first time such a thing had happened. The kids were scared, but they seemed to accept the fear, as terrible as it was, as part of their lives.

After the class filtered out the door, Sam walked over to Richard's desk.

"Richard?" Sam shook his shoulder lightly. "What happened in the woodshed?"

Richard slowly looked up; his eyes were glassed over. His sweaty hair clung to his forehead. Suddenly the boy winced and grabbed his wrist. Sam gently lifted Richard's forearm and pulled up his sleeve.

Sam stifled a gasp.

The skin on Richard's wrist was torn; blood was caked around it in a three-inch ring. Sam was reminded of an incident he had observed as a child living in Georgia. The sheriff had caught a black man in the alley by the hardware store, and to prove he was the one who had escaped from a chain gang, he tore the black man's pants leg to show the crowd his bloody, festering ankle.

Richard jerked his arm away and stood up. He fell backwards against a desk, then twisted upright and stumbled for the door.

"Richard. I'm sorry for what he did to you. I'm not going to . . ."

"Leave it alone," Richard mumbled, opening the door. "Just leave it alone."

Ruth didn't let anyone else sit in Richard's chair at lunch. As she ate, she kept glancing at it. Joey sat between Ruth and Aurelia. On Aurelia's left, Mary was scribbling on a note under the table.

The Blessed Mother entered when everyone had finished eating. Two girls got up to clear the table, but the Blessed Mother pointed at them with her crooked, black-gloved hand. They immediately scurried back to their seats.

No one spoke after she entered. They had been talking earlier because the mute had not eaten with them as he usually did.

When the Blessed Mother sat down at the head of the cross at one end of the room, all heads turned.

"The Devil," she said, her veiled face scouting the tables, "is at hand."

Aurelia felt the tension build. The younger children were too frightened even to fidget. Most held their breaths, waiting for her to continue. Aurelia glanced out of the corner of her eye at Joey. He sat, stiff-backed, watching and waiting too.

Under the table, Mary quietly folded her note.

"It is written that the sinful shall inherit the fires of Hell." Again the Blessed Mother scrutinized the tables. "And the fires of Hell shall tear at their flesh for all eternity. Those who sin shall never see the face of God. Their tortured bodies shall smoulder under the eyes of the Horned One. To disobey our ways is to sell thy soul to Satan."

The children uttered a frightened "Amen."

"One of thee, thy brethren, was a sinner. He dared defile our ways. I have fought for his soul with the Devil. His punishment cleansed him. Pain was his baptism. In pain, so shall he be saved. Blessed is our Savior. In his pain are we all saved."

The children again sang, "Amen."

Under the table, Aurelia felt Mary tap her leg.

"The Holy Children are truly blessed in the ways of salvation. The light is our father. Darkness, our mother—the darkness of the grave before Judgment Day. In that darkness, the hallowed darkness of our Holy Cave, shall we be delivered."

Aurelia reached down and took the note. The name Ruth was written across it. Aurelia wondered whether she should pass it to her or not. She decided it might be just the thing to break down some of Ruth's animosity towards her. Anyway, it wouldn't hurt to try.

"Know thy judgment and it shall cleanse thee. Truly that is a wondrous thing. Children, thy sinful ways can be purified as I have purified a sinner today."

Aurelia sneaked a glance at Ruth. She was the only one not staring, terrified, at the Blessed Mother. She was holding her hands in her lap, her eyes closed, rocking slightly in her chair.

Aurelia reached over Joey's legs and flicked the note against Ruth's forearm. Ruth's head jerked up.

Suddenly the room was silent.

Heavy footsteps pounded behind Aurelia. A huge hand fell on her shoulder. She flinched, clutching the note in her lap. The hand dropped down past her chest and grabbed it. The mute walked to the Blessed Mother and handed her the note. The Blessed Mother read it, crumpled it up and threw it on the floor.

Aurelia glanced at Mary. She would not look back at her. Under the table, Mary's hands squeezed her knees tightly.

"Who gave thee this?" The old woman's voice broke the silence like the quick fall of a guillotine. The children shuddered.

Mary's eyes caught Aurelia's, pleading, then she lowered her head again.

"No one," Aurelia said.

"Thee wrote it?"

Aurelia peeked at Mary. Her chin was pressed to her chest. She didn't move a muscle.

"Yes. I wrote it."

"Will thee tell me what thee wrote?"

Aurelia's heart fluttered. She swallowed and sat up straighter. Gathering her wits, she turned and met the Blessed Mother's gaze head on, never looking away.

"You have read it. You know what I wrote. It was not meant for the others. It was for Ruth."

Some of the children gasped. They had never heard anyone speak to the Blessed Mother like that before. A few whispers crossed the tables.

Aurelia lifted her hands from under the table, never taking her eyes off the Blessed Mother and folded them beside her plate. A long, uncomfortable pause followed.

"So be it." The Blessed Mother stood up and walked out, the mute close behind her.

A sigh of relief echoed throughout the room.

Mary glanced at Aurelia and nodded, too scared to speak. She tried, but no words came out.

Aurelia stood up and looked at Ruth. Even Ruth was shocked.

Aurelia smiled, then quickly left the silent, awe-stricken room.

Now they will accept me, she thought. I took the blame, I stood up to the Blessed Mother. What else could they want from me? I have finally proven myself, even to Ruth.

But she was wrong.

She had left the room too soon. She did not see Ruth's face slowly resculpture itself with humiliation and rage.

The children whispered among themselves, and Ruth listened. They were all very impressed. The same children who had always looked to Ruth and Richard for leadership now were praising Aurelia.

She had threatened Ruth's position of authority.

And Ruth was not one to forgive such an insult.

CHAPTER VIII

SAM HAD sat at his desk for a long time. The boy deserved to be punished, but not like that, he thought, shackled and beaten, humiliated in front of his peers, then made to come back to class. He slammed his fist on the desk.

After a half-hour of thinking, he had finally decided. He didn't care what their beliefs were, he wouldn't allow that kind of cruelty while he was a teacher there.

He tried to imagine his wife as a child, raised in the orphanage, living under the same fears, the same horror, wondering if she had ever been dragged to the shed like that.

Something had made her so terrified she had to run away, and try to make a new life in a world totally alien to her own, he thought. Whatever drove her away had to have been so awful, so frightening that it had forced her to give up everything—her religion, her friends, her way of life; so terrible that she had never even wanted to talk about the first seventeen years of her life.

Why she had left Paradise Valley suddenly became more important to Sam than why she had been abandoned as a baby and by whom.

His anger intensified the more he tried to picture the kind of horror Becky had fled from. Imagining her being beaten like Richard was almost more than he could stand.

His hands curled and uncurled by themselves. His teeth grinded loudly as he gnawed them together and stared down at his desk. His imagination had gone wild. His skull felt as though it were burning as each new horror exploded in his mind.

Then he heard the kids enter the hall after lunch. He did not want to see any of them now. He waited until the hall was silent again, then rose and walked out of the classroom. He stopped at the stairs and gazed upward. The cruel way Aurelia had been treated, Thomas's odd warning, the superstition about the cave, the constant fear, the awful beating, why Becky had run away—all these buzzed in his mind.

He stormed up to the fourth floor. He wanted answers and he wanted them now. He halted outside the sliding doors to the Blessed Mother's rooms and breathed slowly. He waited until he could think clearly, then slid the doors apart without knocking or being asked in.

The Blessed Mother was sitting in a big red chair facing the door. Sam had the eerie feeling she had been expecting him.

And she should have, he thought. The heartless bitch.

The Blessed Mother calmly poured herself a cup of tea. Without looking at him, she said, "Thee seems upset, Mr. Hill."

Sam turned, grabbed the doors and banged them shut. He marched up to her chair and stared angrily.

She peered up through her veil. "Would thee like a cup of tea?"

Sam almost laughed. It seemed like such an absurd,

almost obscene question to him then. Her calm air disgusted him.

"What the hell did you do to that boy?"

"He was punished. Because of what he did to thy daughter. It is our way."

Sam rubbed his forehead and shifted his weight to the other foot. "That's how you punish your children? You shackle and beat them?" Sam squinted at her. He wanted to slap that smug look off her face. "I won't stand for it. Do you hear me? Not to my students." He leaned down close and pointed in her face. "You call yourself the spiritual leader of a Christian people? Holy Children? Bull-shit. To beat children is not God's way."

The Blessed Mother pushed out of her chair angrily and pulled the red, braided cord dangling from the ceiling. Sam tried to regain his composure. He would get nowhere swearing at her. He had to control his temper. There were too many questions that had to be answered, and answered now.

"Thee shall not speak to me like that again. I will not permit it."

Sam ran his hand through his hair. "I'm sorry." He hated having to say that. It wasn't true, but it was necessary. "I have questions that must be answered . . . or you lose a teacher."

The mute suddenly drew back the doors. He looked questioningly at the Blessed Mother, then stepped towards Sam. Sam put his fists up, bending slightly like a boxer, and waited for the attack. He felt sure it was coming, and he was ready.

He knew he didn't stand a chance.

"It is all right, Matthew. I will not need thee." She waved at him. "Go."

The mute glared at Sam for a moment, Sam met his glare with one equally as mean.

The mute turned and left, closing the doors behind him.

"Was that a threat?" Sam walked across the room and slid one of the thick curtains open. He knew the light would bother her, but did not turn to see how much. He stared down at the shed.

Look at that, he thought. He couldn't believe his eyes. The orphans were busy doing their chores as if nothing had happened.

The poor bastards are that scared, he thought.

Or that used to it.

Either way, it turned his stomach.

"There are laws, you know. Laws against child abuse." Sam spun around to see how this tactic would work. "And you've broken them. And if Richard's not a minor, an assault and battery charge will do."

"Now thee threatens." The Blessed Mother walked back to her chair, sat down and calmly took a sip of tea. "Our ways are not thy ways. The outside laws do not apply here."

Sam stepped closer. "They sure as hell do."

The Blessed Mother slammed her cup back on the saucer so hard that it cracked. Sam watched the tea ooze out until it filled the saucer and spilled over onto the table. He was glad he had finally gotten to her. It made him think more clearly, knowing he had finally taken the upper hand.

"Is that why Becky ran away? Did you let him beat her too?"

"That is enough," the Blessed Mother hissed. Her skinny fingers trembled, dangling over the edge of the arm of her chair.

"No, it's not. Tell me why she left. If anyone knows, you would." Sam leaned down again, his face inches from hers. "Why did Becky leave? What did you do?"

The Blessed Mother swung her arm along the table,

scattering the teapot and cups across the floor. She pushed her chair sideways and stood up, then stumbled to the doors.

"I'm quitting this place," Sam warned. "And I'll bring back the law unless you tell me why she left. Who her parents were. Why they abandoned her. And why someone would want to warn me not to ask you about it because they were concerned for my safety."

"Thee has gone too far," the Blessed Mother screamed, pointing her black trembling finger. "It does not matter anymore. Becky is dead. She deserved to die. She fled her destiny. But now . . ." She smiled tauntingly. "Now her destiny will be fulfilled. Thee cannot stop it. Aurelia—" She laughed horribly. "Thy daughter shall inherit what thy wife shunned. No, Sam Hill, she was never beaten. It was fate that she fled. But the children could not let her go. They called to her." The old woman laughed loudly. "And she answered."

Sam knocked the chair over with one jab of his elbow, then started towards the old woman. He wanted to grab her skinny throat and squeeze the laughter right out of her.

Suddenly the doors slammed open and the mute stepped in front of her.

She kept laughing. It was obvious, then, that she was completely insane.

"Aurelia," she screamed, her arms stretched above her head. "She is mine! And the children's."

Sam pulled his right fist back and crouched down, shuffling heavy-footed, towards the mute. The huge man grabbed the iron poker from the fireplace and raised it above his head.

Sam stopped and stared. Facing the mute, his body taut, ready, he sidestepped for the door. The mute let him pass.

"I'm getting Aurelia and we're driving out of here

now." He pointed at the Blessed Mother. "If anyone tries to stop me, I'll run the bastard over. And I'm coming back. With the law. Your cloistered little hell has just come to an end."

"Thee are already too late," the Blessed Mother laughed. "Thee cannot stop the children. Did thee stop them from taking thy wife?"

Sam felt his heart surge against his ribs. He was not going to let her get to him now. He had to find Aurelia and get her out of this place. He backed slowly out into the hall, never taking his eyes from the mute.

He ran down the stairs and out the front doors, glanced around the grounds, then dashed to the barn.

"Joey, have you seen Aurelia?"

"No, sir. I thought she'd come to help me in the barn today. I guess she went home. Is something wrong, Mr. Hill?"

Joey had heard the anger and the apprehension in Sam's question. It frightened him. He walked to the barn doors and watched Sam run down the road towards his house.

Joey put down his pitchfork and quickly began to search the orphanage grounds in case she was still there. He knew then that what he had feared all along was true. Aurelia was in danger, grave danger. The Blessed Mother did want her.

Nothing was more terrible than that.

When Mary walked into the first floor bathroom Ruth was splashing cold water on her face. She did not dry it off, but picked up her brush and began to pull it through her hair. Mary glanced away and saw three of the older girls watching her. Despite their hostile looks, she walked on into the room. She was glad she had heard Ruth's voice from the hall and suggested that Aurelia wait there for her. The two of them had gone for a walk after lunch, so that Mary could thank Aurelia in private for what she had done for her.

The three girls were talking about the note. Mary listened, trying to act nonchalant as she washed her hands. She kept waiting for Ruth to speak again. Ruth had always been their leader. Even though the other girls didn't really like her, they feared her because of her closeness to Richard. And they did her bidding. Mary was sure that was all Ruth cared about. She sensed Ruth did not actually like anyone but Richard.

The reflection of Ruth's dark piercing eyes met Mary's in the mirror. Ruth had said nothing at all to her about the little note of consolation Mary had tried to give her, and now Mary felt like a fool for even thinking such a thing would matter to Ruth. Mary tried to smile while Ruth stared, but the smile faded quickly under that intense, chastizing gaze.

"I think she let her off so she could get her later, when she is not ready," Rebecca, the tall girl with a receding chin said.

"I was shocked when she just got up and left," Martha added.

Mary stepped back, outside their little circle. She had always been scared of the older girls. She tried to be accepted, but they had always made fun of her, left her out of their conversations, teased her about her weight to make her go away.

But now she had decided to speak up anyway. She felt it was her duty, an obligation she couldn't ignore, especially with Aurelia right out in the hall, waiting.

"I thought she was very kind and brave to take the blame," Mary blurted out nervously. The group turned towards her, startled by her sudden audacity. She stood her ground. "She didn't have to. She did it to protect me. It was the sweetest thing I've—"

Ruth turned from the mirror, scowling. "We should

get that little bitch. If it were not for her, Richard would not have been punished. The Blessed Mother hurt him to please her and her father. I thought I was going to get it after Richard. That was why I was so . . . worried in class.'' She looked each in the face. ''Even Richard knew better than to tell on me.'' She grinned.

Mary felt terribly alone again. No one had stood up for her. But she was tired of Ruth's cruel, dominating ways. This time she knew she was right and she was going to say so.

''I thought thee was almost crying in class.'' Mary held her head up bravely. Ruth's angry mouth twisted. ''And I still think Aurelia is nice. She did me a favor I could never repay. Thee should not call her names.''

''Crap,'' Ruth growlèd. ''That pink-eyed tramp knew she would not get in trouble. That is why she stood up to her. She knew that. The Blessed Mother would never dare punish her like she does everyone else. Never. And the bitch knows it.''

The three older girls murmured in agreement.

''You have never been punished either, Ruth.'' Mary could not believe she had actually said it. She stuck out her chin defiantly. One quick glance from Ruth, though, and she lowered her head.

''I never deserved to be,'' Ruth injected. ''Thee did. Everyone did, but me. I was her favorite until . . .''

The bathroom door opened. Heads turned. Aurelia walked in. She had heard it all from the hallway. I won't let her intimidate me, she repeated to herself. I won't. But seeing Ruth's sinister face made her want to turn around and leave. Well, at least I won't show it, she told herself.

Aurelia saw Mary behind the others and smiled. Mary smiled back. Ruth stomped forward, shoved Aurelia into the wall and kicked the door to the hall open. The older girls quickly followed. Mary tried to stop at the door to say something, but they pushed her out before she could.

Aurelia slowly walked over to the mirror. She rested her purse on the sink. Feeling inside it, she located her lipstick. They can't hurt me, she thought. But she was moving in slow motion, her muscles suddenly so heavy it took all her strength just to raise one arm. She uncapped the lipstick and stared into the mirror, examining the empty bathroom through its reflection.

Why had they shoved Mary out? All Mary wanted to do was talk to her. And why didn't she come back? Aurelia just couldn't understand—they didn't even like her when she went out on a limb for them.

She gazed back at her reflection. The silence in the room sickened her.

She remembered how, at Greenville High, there were always girls in the bathroom chattering and joking and she could joke with them. Sometimes they smoked cigarettes. Twice she had seen some of the senior girls smoking pot in the stalls and once they had offered her a hit. It was always fun, she thought. They might not have been her best friends, but at least they talked to her.

Aurelia stared at herself. She began to apply the pink lipstick. She stopped for a moment and peered hard at her reflection.

Suddenly she jammed the lipstick into the mirror and smeared it back and forth across her reflection. She felt the tears coming and didn't care. "I hate them. And I hate you and your ugly skin," she cried quietly, still smearing. "I hate it. I hate it."

Then she froze, peeking out the unmarked corner of the mirror. Mary was standing inside the door, watching sadly.

"What do you want?" Aurelia sniffed and rubbed her eyes. The lipstick had coated her fingers. When she wiped the tears, it smudged her cheeks.

"I wanted to thank thee again. I am sorry they pushed me out. I told them I did not like them and came back. It was very kind, what thee did for me."

"No one seems to think so."

"The girls my age do. The older ones do only what Ruth says, even if they do not agree. I told thee they were scared of her."

Aurelia sniffed again and dabbed at her nose, smudging it pink. Slowly, she turned to look at Mary. The short, chubby girl took out a handkerchief and walked up to her.

"Thee has something on thy face." She began to wipe it off. "What is it? A crayon?"

"Lipstick."

"To paint thy . . ." Mary dropped her handkerchief and spun around. The Blessed Mother marched through the door. Mary bowed her head and nervously scampered out the bathroom.

The Blessed Mother picked up the handkerchief, wet it in the sink and lifted Aurelia's chin to clean off the lipstick.

"Thee are sad?" the Blessed Mother asked. Aurelia shrugged. "Because thee are different?"

Aurelia squeezed her eyes closed and nodded silently. The Blessed Mother wet the handkerchief again and scrubbed Aurelia's nose.

"There. Thee are clean." She threw the handkerchief in the sink, then glanced at the smeared mirror. "They do not treat thee as one of them?"

Aurelia took one of the towels on the rack, dried her face, folded it and put it back.

"Maybe it's because I'm from the outside and they—"

The Blessed Mother held up her hand. "Do not make excuses for them. They have treated thee cruelly. There is no excuse for that."

"But still, maybe they—"

"There is no excuse. Do not stand up for thy enemies. Slay them."

"It's always been a little like this, but never so bad before." Aurelia looked up into the veiled face. "I hate being different." Her upper lip curled, then tightened as she tried to stop the tears. "I just feel so awful sometimes. So alone. They look at me sometimes like . . . like . . ."

The Blessed Mother hugged her. Suddenly Aurelia wondered if Richard's punishment had only been the mute's idea. This sweet old woman couldn't hurt anyone.

"It is good to be different." She held Aurelia close against her chest, the girl's head tucked into her shoulder. "Thee are blessed with a rare gift. Do not chastize thyself for it. The others are sinful. They have lost their souls. Thy soul is in thy face, thy eyes, thy hair. Thy soul is as pure and white as thy color."

"But why do they hate me? Why?" Aurelia pushed away from the Blessed Mother. Her black-gloved hand reached out and stroked the girl's wet cheek.

"Thee are not common. They are. They know that. They know thee are Chosen. They could never be. They are scared of thee. And jealous. So they are cruel."

"But I'm not—"

"Thee must know what it means to be the Chosen One. As thy mother knew. It is time for that understanding."

"My mother was—"

"Chosen. Just as thee are. We shall go to the cave. There thee shall learn of thy inheritance, thy destiny. No longer shall they harm thee. Thee shall be as the blessed children. None will dare hurt thee. Praise be to the children for they are the blood of the Valley, the soul of my people. Psalm 139:12, 'Yea, the darkness hideth not from thee, but the night shineth as the day, the darkness and the light are both alike to thee.' Blessed is the darkness that awaits thee, Aurelia. Blessed is the light of the children.''

"But Daddy said I can't go to the cave again."

The Blessed Mother pointed angrily. "Thy father cannot . . ." She lowered her voice. "Thy father said it would be all right this time. I explained to him that I know the cave well. That thee should see where thy mother liked to play. It would do thee good. The first doll Becky ever had is still there in the cave."

"Really?"

The old woman had thought that would capture her interest. It was a lie.

"I left it there for her. For when she returned. Now it is for thee. Come, I will show thee."

Sam Hill could not run full speed all the way home. A jabbing pain cut into his ribs. He had to walk, his big chest heaving, until the side-ache was tolerable again. Then he started to jog. In a few minutes he was at his house.

He bounded up the porch steps. "Aurelia?"

She was not in the house. Sam hurried out the back door, looked in the shed, then surveyed the fields up to the small hill on one side and the cliffs on the other. He ran to the front of the house and checked along the cliffs as far as he could until the woods blocked his view.

"Damn," he muttered, punching his open palm with his fist. He kept scouring the land, his hand shading his eyes each time the sun broke through the clouds.

He had to find her and get the hell out of the valley. There was no time to waste. The Blessed Mother was insane and she wanted his daughter. And whatever she wanted her for was the same horror that had driven his wife from this valley years ago.

He wiped the sweat from his eyes. A lone figure was running up the road towards him. It cut across the plowed field, bearing down on him in a straight line.

"Mr. Hill," Joey yelled, sprinting as fast as he could. Sam dashed towards him.

"Joey, what's wrong? Did you see Aurelia?"

Joey stopped, exhausted. Bending at the waist, he held himself up, straight-armed, by the knees. He shook his head quickly, then gulped in air, trying to regain his ability to speak. He had never run that fast, that far, before. He gulped again and swallowed. For a moment, he thought he was going to be sick.

Sam grabbed him by the shoulders. "Where is she?"

"With the . . . Blessed Mother," Joey spit out between breaths. "I . . . saw them . . . going to . . ." Joey anxiously glanced up at Sam. ". . . the cave."

"Why would she take her there?" Sam demanded.

Joey shook his head. "I do not know. But it is a bad place. A place of death. That much I do know. All in the valley fear it as they fear the Blessed Mother."

"I'll kill her," Sam mumbled. He dashed over to his car. He hopped onto the seat, took the flashlight from the glove compartment and checked its light intensity. Quickly he fumbled in his pants pockets for the keys. He yanked them out, and put them in the ignition.

Click.

Click.

The engine didn't even turn over. Two clicks, then nothing.

Sam jumped out and threw open the hood. The starter was smashed, the distributor completely torn out. He slammed the hood down.

"Was the mute with them?" he yelled.

Joey shrugged. "I did not see him, but . . ."

147

Sam ran to the woodshed, pushed aside the wheelbarrow and the hoes, and grabbed the big double-edged axe.

He hurried back to Joey and looked at him seriously, his hands constantly gripping and ungripping the axe handle. "Would she really hurt Aurelia? I mean . . . is she really that . . . crazy?"

Joey lowered his eyes and nodded.

"God help us all."

Sam started to run towards the cave, flashlight in one hand, the double-edged axe in the other.

CHAPTER IX

THE BLESSED Mother stopped inside the mouth of the cave and lit the lantern perched on the flat gray rock. The cold wind blew against their backs. They had not spoken since they left the orphanage.

Without a word, the Blessed Mother walked to the big tunnel and began to descend. Aurelia followed hesitantly. She was frightened of the cave, but her curiosity had been aroused. She wanted to see her mother's doll. The cool darkness of the cavern engulfed her. She thought that once they reached the place where her mother used to play, she would feel safe and secure again, lose the uncomfortable nervousness that had swept over her as soon as she had entered the cave.

The lantern's dim yellow light flickered ahead of her, dancing upon the wet, glistening rocks and the reddish brown dirt floor. The sound of rushing water echoed from the tunnel's depth.

They turned into another cavern. It was low-ceilinged at first, and both of them had to bend to walk. Then it opened up and in the light, Aurelia could see that crystalline deposits, white and sparkling, covered the high walls like frozen snowflakes. It looked like the inside of a great snow palace.

"It's beautiful," Aurelia whispered. Her statement reverberated into the far reaches of the massive yet delicate-looking cavern. "Is this where Mom played?"

The Blessed Mother shook her head and continued on, turning into another tunnel. Aurelia ran after her as the lantern's light disappeared. The sound of rushing water intensified. When Aurelia caught up with her, the Blessed Mother was standing on a small bluff above a stream. She pointed her crooked finger down at its clear, swelling water, bubbling white over the jutting rocks.

"It is full now because of the rain." The old woman lifted the lantern high over her head. "Look."

At the end of the cavern, there was a waterfall. It gushed out of the rocky ceiling, about twenty feet high, and crashed down into a foaming whirlpool.

"This is the blood of the Valley. The water of life." The Blessed Mother, still holding her lantern above her head, turned her shadowed face towards Aurelia. "This stream goes into the great lake deep within the cave. The lake pours into another stream that winds through the mountain and feeds the river that runs through the Valley. The lake is the heart of the land. The river and this stream are its arteries. All things in the Valley live or die because of it. It is sacred. It is to be revered. To worship the cave is to worship the water. Without it, my people would surely die."

Suddenly Aurelia was sure she should never have come.

The old woman walked along the banks, deeper into the cave. Aurelia followed the light. Her stomach began to twist with cramps.

"The cave belongs to the dead who never die. It is

eternal. Like Heaven. Like Hell. It gives life. It takes life away.''

The light passed a small, closet-like indentation in the cavern wall. Aurelia jumped forward against the Blessed Mother.

"What is it, my child?"

Aurelia held the old woman's arm. "I . . . I thought I saw bones back there."

The Blessed Mother kept walking.

"Nonsense." She quickened her pace. "Just an odd formation in the rocks."

Aurelia walked in cadence with the Blessed Mother, but she kept glancing back at the cavern. The old woman patted her hand. Aurelia backed away. She couldn't stand being touched by her then. Her hand was as cold as death. But she couldn't leave. Only the Blessed Mother knew where they were and how to get out again.

"Are thee afraid?"

Aurelia let go of the arm. "Yes. I want to go back. I don't like it here. Please? I don't feel good. My stomach hurts.''

"Do not be afraid. This is thy refuge now. Thy home. Come.''

They followed the stream until it flowed into a very low tunnel. Aurelia was too frightened to question the Blessed Mother's strange statements. She just wished she had listened to her father and never come.

Another cramp almost doubled her over. It felt as though something alive inside her was trying to get out.

The Blessed Mother climbed up a wall of rocks piled one over the other like stairs on a steep ledge. Aurelia waited until the pain lessened, then caught up with her. There was nothing else she could do.

They veered to the right into a high-ceilinged tunnel.

Where it ended, the shore of the great lake loomed before them. Its black water rippled slightly, splashing against the stony shore.

"Is this where Mom used to play? By this lake?"

The Blessed Mother rested the lantern on a wide rock, then sat next to it, ignoring her questions. She patted the stone on the other side of the lantern. Aurelia sat on it, too scared to disobey. For the moment she was at the old woman's mercy.

"The cave is our soul." The Blessed Mother arched her back and began taking out the pins that held the veil to her hat. "Only the Chosen are allowed in this Holy place. Only they may know its secrets."

Slowly she lifted her veil. Aurelia stared, paralyzed, as the old woman turned to face the light.

Aurelia's mouth fell open. Her eyes widened, shocked. "You're . . . an albino, too."

The Blessed Mother nodded slowly. Her face was barely wrinkled, but Aurelia could see the years in her eyes and the way her mouth twisted down in a permanently creased frown. The Blessed Mother took two pins and stuck the veil up on her hat.

Shadows from the flickering lantern danced upon her pale, shadowed face. Her eyes shone in the light. Her thin, tight lips looked white. "As Becky was, so shall thee be. It is thy fate. Because thee are Blessed, the others hate thee. It was so before, it shall be so again. It is man's way. It cannot be changed. To hate, as they have hated, is to see them revealed, to know their true nature, the color of their souls. Only then can thy destiny be fulfilled."

Aurelia was mesmerized by the face before her. She heard the words, but they didn't register. They were merely a hypnotically melodic sound emitted from a strange mask, a mask she could not take her eyes off of.

Suddenly the face reminded her, in the round, deep-set eyes, the high cheekbones, of her mother. The resemblance horrified her. Then the cramps cut through her belly again. She clutched her stomach and, curling into a tight ball, fell off the rock. The pain was overwhelming. Aurelia rolled over and over, screaming.

Suddenly, she lay still.

In the distance, echoing across the lake, voices began to chant.

Aurelia's throat was dry. She tried to swallow, but couldn't. Slowly she uncurled herself and sat up. The cramps were gone now, but her clothes were soaked through with cold, sticky sweat. She felt chilled and hugged herself as she listened to the voices.

"Does thee hear them?"

Aurelia glanced across the dark black lake. She felt oddly calm then. The chill subsided. Her arms dropped limply to her sides.

The voices were singing loudly now. Aurelia glanced back at the Blessed Mother. She was humming with them, her eyes closed, as if in a trance.

Unconsciously, Aurelia began to rock to the rhythm as she looked out over the rocky shore.

Five hollow-eyed, yellow faces stared back at her from the darkness between the big rocks. Aurelia glanced at the Blessed Mother. She was still humming, her eyes tightly shut. Aurelia glanced back at the rocks.

The faces were gone.

And the singing had stopped.

A hand fell on Aurelia's shoulder. Slowly she turned and gazed over her shoulder. Her eyes were only half open.

"What thee are to hear is for thy ears only. Does thee understand?"

Staring into the old woman's red, glowing eyes, like two burning moons in a black night sky, Aurelia nodded. A strange feeling of floating enshrouded her.

"For another to know what thee shall know would mean death. Know that in thy heart."

Again Aurelia nodded. Her eyes were blank, her mouth hung open limply. She could still hear, still feel with her limbs, but it was all as if from a great distance now.

"Then let it be done." The Blessed Mother snuffed out the lantern's light. Blackness instantly engulfed them. The Blessed Mother's gloved hand reached down and enclosed itself around Aurelia's, but she didn't feel it. She didn't feel anything.

"It began seventy-four years ago. At the time of my birth," the old woman began. "There were six of us born in one generation. All within four years of each other. Albinos. Eric Stutgard, the Holy Children's elder, went on a pilgrimage to discover why we had been born as we were. The Holy Children had never seen albinos before."

The words bombarded Aurelia from all sections of the cavern. They pounded in her head. Each word seemed to vibrate, then break up into little pieces.

"It was soon discovered how much the light of the sun bothered us. The youngest, William, was like a little brother to me. I took care of him. I was the eldest of the six.

"When we came of working age, no longer children to be tolerated playing, the people became suspicious. The other children would not speak to us. They were warned by their parents to shun us because we could not work in the fields. William's parents said he was a curse from God. They made him help plow the land in his tenth year. I was fourteen. He became almost totally blind. After that, the others thought we would ruin the harvest if we were allowed in the fields. They chased us away.

"The six of us stayed together, away from the other

children. They would call us names and throw things, hurt us. The adults did nothing. They would laugh as the children teased us and chased us out of the fields.

"That is when I began to explore the cave. It was my sanctuary. I brought the others there. We took chairs and candles and a table into the great cavern.

"Every day we awoke before the others and met there. The elder called the cave the Devil's Hole. He had warned his people not to enter it. But it was our place of safety. The other children would not follow us when we escaped into its sanctuary. It was always cool and dark and safe. We came to worship it.

"We had ceremonies there, as the others had in the big wooden church in town. I led the ceremonies. They were a great comfort to us in our time of need. Even our parents were turning against us. Eric Stutgard preached to the Holy Children, telling them that we were a burden, a punishment from God for their sins. Our parents felt the others shun them for what had come from their womb, their seed.

"It grew worse as the year of my fourteenth birthday progressed. By the time I became fifteen, my parents hated me. The other five also felt the anger, the shame, the stern retributions of their parents.

"The elder, Stutgard, proclaimed that only those who shared in the work of the fields could reap the rewards of their labor."

The Blessed Mother's thin, gnarled fingers dug into Aurelia's. She did not feel them. She was floating in a warm sea of blackness.

Sam Hill shone his flashlight into the main tunnel at the back of the cave. Muddy footprints on its dirt floor led down its darkened throat.

"Aurelia?"

He held his breath to listen. All he heard was the

distant echo of his voice. He gripped the axe tighter and descended, following the footprints until they disappeared at the edge of a rock-bottomed tunnel.

"Aurelia?"

He waited. He realized he could easily get lost if he kept turning into different tunnels. But it was a chance he would have to take, he decided. He didn't have time to go back and get some chalk or string. He knew Aurelia was down there somewhere and he had to find her.

He climbed a short, slippery cliff, then carefully edged along a narrow two-foot ledge. He directed the beam of his flashlight down past the ledge. It was a thirty-foot drop, at least.

The ledge slowly narrowed until it was a little over a foot in width. He leaned back close against the slimy wall and inched sideways towards the next tunnel.

Suddenly his lead foot slipped on a loose rock. The stone crashed down into the ravine. He spun around as the leg slid over the ledge. The axe flew out of his hand. He caught himself on a sharp, upturned rock just below the ledge. One foot dangling, he pulled himself back onto the ledge. He had not dropped the flashlight. He was grateful for that at least.

Carefully, he stepped up over a foot-high stone and entered the cavern in the wall behind the ledge. He sat in the dirt for a few minutes to catch his breath. His heart's pounding seemed almost to echo in the cavern. His left arm ached. Both hands shook badly from the quick exertion.

Sam Hill cupped the flashlight in both hands and prayed. He prayed he would find his daughter soon, before he got too lost to lead her out of there. His own life did not seem important then, except as a tool to save Aurelia's. He prayed not just to find her soon, but to get her safely out of the valley as well. After that, he didn't care what happened to himself.

He was trying to make a deal with God. His life for hers.

He soon found he couldn't stand upright as the tunnel became smaller. He hobbled, bent at the waist through the black twisting labyrinth.

In the distance, he heard splashing. It sounded like a stream gurgling over rocks. He followed the sound of the water.

Suddenly he realized just how futile his search really was.

Maybe I should go back, he thought. Wait at the entrance. I'll do Aurelia no good lost in this cave.

He stopped and sank down on his knees to rethink his strategy.

Then another sound echoed with the rushing water. Sam held his breath.

Voices. He could hear them in the distance. He leaped up and hit his head on the low ceiling.

"Aurelia," he yelled.

He couldn't tell if they had heard him or not. There was no reply. He hobbled through the small tunnel as quickly as he could.

There was no turning back now.

He could hear her. She was close.

He had to go on.

"It was then that it truly began," the Blessed Mother continued. "The 'falling disease' they called it. I could not stop it. I could feel it, like a great winter storm approaching. The ground would begin to swell and dip. The sky would whirl above me, and then both the sky and the earth would reach out together and interlock. I would begin to shake and foam at the mouth. No longer would I have control of my body. I would collapse and heave and choke.

"Once all six of us went to church together. We had not been for almost two years. But no one had ever declared our sin, as they would another who had missed but one Sunday. We went because I had had a fit during our ceremony at the cave and we were scared for our souls.

"When the elder started to preach, I felt it again. The church rocked. The roof swayed. I could no longer stand. I saw their dark, hating eyes watching me as I screamed and fell."

Aurelia felt others gathering around her in the blackness. She could hear their breathing close to her ears. She tried to reach out and touch them but her body would not respond. She felt as if her conscious mind had left her body and was trapped in the darkness somewhere beyond her grasp.

"I do not remember what occurred when I was in the fit, but William did. He did not have to see to know the fear. He could feel it, he told me later. The others also heard the murmurs and what the elder said.

"I began to flop about, crying, foaming at the mouth. Then suddenly I was still. The others circled around me to protect me as the parish approached.

"That is when I first spoke in tongues. The elder pushed his way through my friends' tight circle and hearing me, called out to God to save our tormented souls. He said it was the Devil's tongue I spoke. The word of the damned who could not toil in God's fields, but were condemned to the darkness of the 'Devil's Hole,' the mouth to Hell.

"He condemned us all that day. He told the parish that our white skins lacked the color of life and that this was a sign. He said that in the blackness of Hell, we would be Satan's shadows, pale and colorless, blind to the light of God, following the Black Angel as he rode upon his chariot of death to the world of man.

"The other five crouched down, terrified, then fell to their knees, praying in a circle around me, pleading as the crowd enclosed them.

"As the elder preached against us, I heard a voice. It was speaking through me. I stood up. The voice was deep and strange, not my own. I felt strong. The crowd stepped back. My friends held me, still on their knees about my feet.

"I warned the Holy Children that because of what was in their hearts, what they felt towards us, the river would run dry and a drought would prevail. Their crops would shrivel and die. Their livestock would grow sick and their stomachs would bloat.

"The others, seeing how the people stared, feeling their hot breaths bearing down on them, took me by the hands and led me outside while the parish was still too shocked to react.

"The elder followed, keeping his people behind him. He closed the doors of the church, never to be opened to us again. Then he preached even more terrible words. And the people called out, 'Amen', each time he damned us.

"We fled to the cave and hid deep in the tunnel. They came for us, but could not find us. We waited until they left.

"Soon the river turned to mud. The crops began to wither. There was no rain for weeks. The cattle bloated from drinking the little water left in the swamp.

"The people went to the elder, pleading with him to save them and their livestock. They, too, were becoming sick drinking the swamp water. There are no wells in our valley. The river is the only source of water.

"After that, we lived entirely in the cave and foraged at night for food, stealing what meager supplies we could. Each night all the Valley met in the church to pray for deliverance. It was then that we would raid their homes. If they had found us, we learned later, they were supposed to bind us and deliver us to the elder to be burned.

"But deliverance did not come. On Sunday night, we saw the torches. The people were marching from the church to the cave.

"We watched from the darkness of our tunnel. The elder called them together around the great rock in the mouth of the cave. We listened, horrified. William held my hand and cried silently. We huddled together, clutching each other, fearful for our lives.

"Eric Stutgard told the people that we had poisoned the Valley with our presence. Someone spoke up against him, saying that I had foretold their doom, that they were being punished by God because of what they had planned to do to us. Some murmured in agreement.

"The elder screamed out that we were Satan's children. His death-shadows. A curse upon the land. Only in our death could the Holy Children be saved, the Valley cleansed. William threw his arms around my neck when he heard the elder demand that we be burned at the stake as witches.

"One of our parents intervened, saying that it was against the commandments of God Almighty to kill a human being. Many agreed. Two of the oldest in the valley spoke up. They told of their homeland across the ocean and of their forefathers who had been tortured and killed for their beliefs.

" 'It is why we came here,' they shouted. 'We shall not become as our enemies. It is not our way.'

"For a long time they argued. We did not notice that some had left the crowd. They surprised us from behind and dragged us out into the mouth of the cave. William was so terrified that when he opened his mouth to scream, nothing came out. I held him close to stop his trembling.

"The elder quieted the people. Only the water dripping from the tunnel's ceiling could be heard. We wrapped our arms around each other.

"I will always remember his words.

" 'These children,' he said, 'are Satan's offspring. They shall die deep within the Devil's Hole. It will not be our hands that judge them but His. If they are the Devil's children, they shall die together in Hell, never to see the light of day again, the light they shun already, the light that blinds them. But if they are Holy Children and if it is His will that they live, if it was His tongue that spoke through the girl's mouth, then they will survive, led by His loving hand, back into the light of the living. If that comes to pass, we shall fall to our knees and worship the girl, for it will be proven that she is God's tongue, His word to us upon this earth. And even if they cannot share with us the burden of toil, which is our way, they shall be fed. So take these six deep into the catacombs of the cave, deep into the bowels of eternal darkness. Mark thy way with chalk, leaving a man at each new turn, each new tunnel, to call thee back when the task is done. Give each child one candle. The matter is in our hands no longer. It is in God's hands now . . . or the Devil's.'

"They took us crying, screaming for mercy, deep into the recesses of the cave, far beyond where we had explored. We marched for hours. They left us together, one candle each, and walked back with their torches, wiping off the chalk marks as they ascended.

"Luke, the oldest boy, tried to follow them, but they had torches and could move much more quickly. His candle went out as soon as he began to run. He called to us for help.

"We had to walk slowly, each cradling his candle, to find him. He was screaming for us, petrified of the darkness. We had no matches to relight our candles. We heard his screams echo about us, vibrating in the tunnel.

"We never found him. His screaming turned into choking gasps. Then we heard him no more. We tried to follow the people's footprints in the muddy corridor past the cavern, but the footprints stopped on a rocky ledge.

"William held my arm with one hand as we walked, his candle in the other. Anna, the next eldest to me, decided we should go through the big cavern with the lake. I told them we had never passed a lake on the way down, but she argued angrily.

"William began to cry. His candle fell and went out. He sat down on the rock and began to shake. I sat with him, but Anna told us we must hurry—our candles were burning down quickly. I said we had to wait until William was ready. I tried to lift him, but his legs were like jelly. He was too frightened to move.

"Anna said we should leave him. We had to go on. I got angry. She said she was only looking out for the group.

"I stomped my foot and, in my anger, told her to go on without us—I would catch up as soon as William was ready. They did not protest. I watched them leave. I never thought they would actually do it. Suddenly I knew I would never see them again. I called out to them to wait.

"I heard Anna's scream pierce the darkness like a child awakening from a nightmare. I cried out to her. No one answered.

"Later I heard them weeping, pleading to me for their deliverance, but I knew not where they were.

"I sat with William, speaking to him, holding him and rocking him. I told him we would save his candle until mine burned down, then we could go twice as far. Surely we would make it then.

"When I helped him up, he was finally able to walk. I

led. He followed, holding my dress. We turned many times into new caverns, new tunnels. We were lost, hopelessly lost.

"Then it happened.

"My candle began to quiver uncontrollably. Its light flickered all around me. The cavern seemed to grow and shrink. I couldn't breathe. I heard William screaming to me, but he sounded so far away. I tried to answer, but could not. I wanted to tell him to grab my candle before I fell.

"When I awoke, I saw him sitting in the mud, his back resting on a rock. His candle was lit, but the stub of mine lay dead, next to it. I pushed myself up on my knees and called his name.

"William? William?"

"His eyes were open but they never blinked. They just stared, wide and blank, into the yellow light. I crawled next to him and shook him. He fell over. I pulled him back up and caressed his face. It was so cold. He was not dead, but his body was rigid. He was no longer aware of anything. I tried and tried, but I could not even bend one of his arms.

"I stood up and attempted to lift him. He was too heavy. I pleaded with him, slapped him. Nothing helped.

"He had given up.

"I took the candle from the mud and stepped back. I thought he would follow the light if nothing else. He did not move. I sat down again and began to weep.

"I remember nothing after that until I woke up in a bed.

"They said I had come out of the cave as if in a trance and spoken to them. I had told them of a ceremony, the ceremony of the Chosen One, that had to be performed in order to atone for their grievous sins. God had commanded it of them."

The Blessed Mother relit the lantern. Its brightness hurt Aurelia's eyes. She looked at its glittering trail burn across the black lake. Slowly she arched her back. She felt very stiff. She rubbed her eyes. Her head ached badly. She felt as if she had just awaked from a deep sleep.

"I was blessed by God to carry out His commandments. All, including Eric Stutgard, did my bidding from that day forth. After we performed the ceremony of the Chosen One, rain came and water began to flow in the river from out of the mountain. Half of the crops were saved."

Aurelia stared at the old woman. She had no idea what she was talking about.

"I went to town and closed down the church. I told the people it was an evil place where they mistook the Devil's word for God's. The cave was the only true sanctuary of the Holy Children. It was to be a Holy place where none would be allowed except the Blessed who followed in God's path. The path he had chosen me to lead them on."

The Blessed Mother stood up. The lantern light glowed below her, darkening her eyes and hair. To Aurelia, her face suddenly looked like a skull's face, a horrible mask of rotting death. It made Aurelia's skin crawl.

"Thee, too, are blessed, Aurelia, as I was blessed. The children of the cave have chosen thee, just as they chose thy mother. It is a great honor." Aurelia tried to stand up, but the old woman held her down on her knees. "Pray, Aurelia, pray for thy enlightenment, pray for the light of Darkness to shine in thy heart." Her voice grew louder, echoing across the lake. "Pray for the gift of vision. Pray for the Word, for the Word is sacred. Pray thee shall be allowed to dwell for all eternity in this Holy place, our sacred temple. Pray, Aurelia, pray.''

Aurelia did not look up. She felt the skinny hands dig into her shoulders. She did not want to see that death mask of a face screaming above her, preaching words she did not understand, that fell upon her ears like hailstones.

"Please," Aurelia whispered. "I want to go home. Please."

"This is thy home, Aurelia. This is thy life. The life of darkness. The life of the Children. Of William and Anna and Luke."

"What are you talking about?" Aurelia cried. She rolled across the ground to break the Blessed Mother's grip and stood up unsteadily. "Let's go back now. I'm cold." Aurelia tried not to show how terrified she really was, trapped deep in a cave with what she now thought was a madwoman.

A warm breeze whispered over the lake. With it came singing, distant and haunting.

The Blessed Mother stood near the lantern, her veil once more covering her face. Aurelia stared at the lake, petrified.

The singing echoed until the echoes themselves became their own harmony. The melodious, soft-fingered notes floated inside Aurelia's head. She felt the singing then, rather than heard it.

She suddenly found herself swaying and humming with it. She felt as if a vast reservoir inside her were being tapped. She opened herself to it, letting its soft, swirling energy flood her mind. She felt as though she had become a part of the cavern, as if her body's molecules were breaking apart and fusing with the rocks and the darkness and the lake.

Suddenly her body quivered. A powerful spasm

knocked her to the ground. The cavern started to close in around her. Now she felt as if she were suffocating in a sealed tomb.

Then darkness.

And the singing.

And the awful stench of death.

The light from Sam's flashlight glimmered down the smooth path. The light followed the path to the small river. Sam leaned back and slid down the steep incline to the edge of the river.

"Aurelia?" He flashed the light up and down the stream. "Aurelia?"

He hurried upstream, listening for their voices. He had not heard them since he neared the end of the short tunnel. They must be moving, he thought. But he had heard them. He knew he had. They were close by. They had to be.

He jogged along the stream until he reached a waterfall.

How long have I been searching? he thought. I should have brought my watch. He sighed and rubbed his neck. And rope, and extra batteries and . . .

A dim sound echoed in the tunnel.

Sam spun around. "Aurelia?"

He flashed the light into the tunnel. Suddenly he could swear he heard giggling.

"Aurelia?" he screamed, running into the tunnel. "Where are you?"

The giggling grew louder. Sam halted and listened more closely. There was a hole in the tunnel wall about twenty feet ahead. He dashed for it and flashed the light.

"Aurelia?" His body tensed, as he prepared to scream as loud as he could. *"Aurelia!"*

Something rumbled, then crashed behind him. He

jerked around and flashed the light. The ceiling of the tunnel by the waterfall was caving in. Huge clouds of dust tumbled towards him. He jumped sideways into another tunnel and started running to escape the thick, choking dust.

Both feet flew out from under him on the moist, slippery rocks. He fell backward and cracked his spine on a sharp stone. The impact flipped him over. He began to roll, gaining momentum, unable to control his fall down the steep rock-strewn tunnel. Sharp ridges ripped at his flesh. The flashlight flew out of his hand, then his body smacked against a protruding boulder.

Darkness instantly devoured him.

The dust waves quickly followed. He tried to cover his mouth. He couldn't move. His hands, his arms, his legs, were all useless.

He was totally paralyzed.

Slowly, the dust settled, burying his face and body with a thick, dirty film.

In the shadowed darkness on the other side of the boulder, he heard that giggling again. He tried but couldn't even move his head sideways.

He knew that whoever it was must be close.

He spit the dust out of his mouth. "Aurelia?"

Suddenly he felt something pull at his hair.

He lay there, utterly helpless, not even able to see.

"Who's there?"

Whomever, whatever it was, it was panting just above his face.

CHAPTER X

IT WAS drizzling as Aurelia sat on the front steps of the orphanage late that afternoon. The children were done with their chores, but none were outside playing. She had walked back with the Blessed Mother and left her in her rooms. Coming outside, she had slumped onto the steps, trying to piece together the vague memory she had of their time in the cave.

She could remember something about albino children, and the cave and . . . and horrible darkness. But only quick, fluttering pictures, framed in confusion, drifted through her mind. They didn't make sense. Sometimes that horrible, yellow, skull-like face flashed in her head. She couldn't remember what it was, if it were just a product of her imagination or if she had really seen something so monstrous.

And she remembered singing.

And other faces—pale, hollow, almost translucent faces.

And cold, ghost-like hands.

Then a voice, a horrible voice, began to . . .

Aurelia lifted her head. The drizzle splattered on her face. She closed her eyes, letting it wash away her dream, her vague memory, whatever it was that now hid deep inside her, trembling, waiting.

Her body shuddered as if something within it didn't want her to know what she was trying so hard to remember.

Then it was gone.

She stood up and began to walk towards home. Her hands still shook badly. Something is happening to me, she thought. First, in the cave when I hid from Richard. And now, after going there again with the Blessed Mother. She didn't even show me the doll. Or if she did I . . .

She couldn't remember.

She brushed her hair back. The wind and the rain pelted her face.

Why can't I remember? What's happening to me?

She started to run. The rain bit at her skin. She had to jump or sidestep the puddles as they came upon her. Her heart pounded against her ribs. The questions kept echoing in her mind as she ran.

Then those faces reappeared, horrible, accusing faces. Like gray shadows, they flickered in and out of the heavy rain.

They were watching. Laughing. Taunting her. She ran even faster.

On a small hill above the road, Ruth and four of her cohorts were waiting. Aurelia did not see them as she dashed by.

But she heard them. They were laughing.

They began to chant, "Pink eyes. Pink eyes. Pink eyes." The chant kept getting louder. "Pink eyes. Pink eyes."

Aurelia slowed her pace. They yelled louder. She began to walk, trying to locate the voices.

Was it the faces in the cave calling her? Were the visions real?

She felt a cold mudball splatter into the back of her head. It knocked off her hat. She quickly bent over and picked it up. Another mudball smacked her on the rump. One splashed in the puddle on her left, soaking her leg.

"Pink eyes . . . pink eyes."

She recognized Ruth's voice. It was almost a relief to know her tormentors were real flesh and blood people. Aurelia walked even slower, her head high and proud. They were laughing harder now as they yelled. A mudball hit her on the cheek, stinging her badly. It had come from the other side of the road.

Aurelia couldn't pretend any longer. She started to run again, fleeing their awful chant. More mud splashed about her feet. They were chasing her. She increased her speed beyond her ability to control it.

Why won't they leave me alone? Why?

Slipping in a rut, she stumbled and fell face first in a deep puddle. She rolled out of it and closed her eyes. Bringing her knees up against her chest, she hugged herself into a ball.

Suddenly the chanting stopped. It was frighteningly quiet. Only the noise of the raindrops in the puddle interrupted it. Aurelia lay in the mud, not wanting to open her eyes, only to hold herself close.

Two huge hands reached her arms and lifted her. Aurelia's eyes flashed open.

It was the mute.

He wiped her face with a handkerchief and smiled that distant, rock-hard, awkward smile she had seen in the hall by her locker. It felt strangely reassuring. Aurelia threw her arms around his neck and wept. All the horrible vague memories, the fear, the mud, the taunting voices, the terrible laughter, flooded out. The mute caressed her hair and stared up at the hill. His nostrils flared as his cold gray eyes scanned the tree-studded summit until he spotted where the girls were hiding.

Aurelia squeezed against his chest. He looked down and shook his head as if to tell her not to worry. She buried her face in his massive shoulder and closed her eyes. She felt oddly safe in his powerful arms. He gently stroked her back and began to walk.

He carried her all the way to her house, and set her down on a chair on the porch.

"Thank you," she said, "I'm sorry I . . ."

He shook his head to let her know words were not necessary.

Aurelia pushed out of the chair and hugged him around the waist. He lifted his arms, letting them hang in the air, not knowing what to do. Slowly he wrapped them around her, feeling her small, wet body against his.

Aurelia heard him sigh. She took a step back.

"That was very kind." She smiled.

A tear ran down the mute's wide, sharply chiseled cheek. Stretching up on her toes, she wiped it off.

The mute shifted his weight and grunted, turning his head away from her. Quickly, he backed out of the porch door and trotted away.

When he glanced back, she waved. Then she hurried into the house. She needed her father now almost as much as she had needed him after her mother's death.

"Daddy?" she called, checking his room. The house was empty. She dashed out the kitchen door and cupped her hands around her mouth.

"Daddy?" she screamed. "Where are you?"

Thomas Borg bent over, balancing his hefty bulk by leaning one arm on the wooden workbench, and checked the copper coils of his still.

It was running well. He had just corked another full

clay jug. The rain pelted the roof and washed down in waves across the one window of his tool shed.

Something had not felt right to him all day. It was the same empty, dark feeling he had each spring. The feeling of death riding, black-cloaked, sword in hand, across the valley, its masked face almost glowing with the dread and horror of its mission.

Thomas pulled himself back up and uncorked the half-full jug he had been carrying with him all afternoon. He took another big swallow. It no longer burned. The burning had ceased hours ago.

His body swayed and he grabbed the edge of the table. Today he couldn't drink away the horrible feeling as he had done so many other times.

Slowly he stumbled over to the window. The glass was fogged on the inside. He wiped off a section and stared out at the hard-driving rain.

He saw a boy emerge from its fog-like grasp, running toward his house. Thomas felt his guts tighten ominously as he walked out of the shed into the rain.

"Mr. Borg," Joey yelled, banging on the front door of the house.

"Joey?" he called. "Is that thee?"

Joey spun around. "Mr. Borg." He waved and ran over.

"Come in out of the rain." Thomas put his arm around him and led him back inside the shed.

Joey was breathing quickly. "Mr. Hill . . . he went to . . ."

"Catch thy breath first." Thomas pushed him towards the old wooden chair in the corner. "Sit. Then tell me why thee has come."

Joey took two deep breaths. "Mr. Hill went . . . to the cave . . . after Aurelia." Joey inhaled again, wiping the rain from his eyes.

Death, Thomas thought. He rides back to his lair.

"Why did Mr. Hill go there?"

Joey jumped out of his seat. "The Blessed Mother took Aurelia to the cave. Mr. Hill . . ." He gulped quickly. "Went after her."

"When?"

"Hours ago." Joey waved away any more interruptions. "But Aurelia came back. The mute . . . I saw him carrying her home. I do not know if she was hurt." Slowly Joey's frightened eyes looked up into Thomas Borg's. "Mr. Hill has not come back. I waited for him at their house. Then I waited by the cave. I . . . She . . ." Joey opened his mouth, but the words were lost. His lips were trembling.

Thomas put his arm around the boy and patted his shoulder. "Does she know about her father?"

Joey shook his head. "Unless he met her in the cave. But *he* would have been with her then, not the mute. He must still be in the cave. I tried to warn him, but . . ."

Thomas pulled the boy closer and hugged him. Joey held tight to the old man and cried briefly, trying to hold back each fitful sob.

"Only the Blessed Mother can find him if he is lost within the cave." Thomas looked slowly out the window, pensively, almost without seeing. "Unless the children . . ."

He stopped when he saw the horror on Joey's upturned face. Mr. Borg sighed, trying to smile reassuringly.

"I will go to the Blessed Mother and tell her of this. I want thee to go to the Throms' house. Tell Mrs. Throm that Aurelia's father is missing, but no more than that. Tell no one he has gone to the cave. Does thee understand?"

Joey stepped back, wiped his tear-streaked face and nodded.

"Good. Then go. She will help comfort the girl. Thee

will too, I suspect.'' Thomas smiled teasingly.

Joey did not smile back. "I shall comfort her."

"Do not tell her of her father. No need to worry her unnecessarily. Just say her father must be at the orphanage. I will come later. If it is necessary, I will tell her then."

Joey nodded and ran out the door.

The Black-Faced One, Thomas Borg thought as he walked to the barn to hitch his horse to the buggy. He has heard His children crying.

They call him home once more.

Thomas Borg coaxed his old horse into a fast trot. The red sun was low above the western mountains. The heavy, broken clouds barely held above it, glowing orange and gray as the sky between them turned a dark purple.

The buggy tilted into the long evening shadow that rippled out across the grass from Aurelia's house. A cold wind rustled through the budding branches of the big oak in front of the house.

Joey, Gertrude Throm, and Aurelia were sitting on the porch chairs. Two other women were there too. They had all brought food. It was spread out on the small table between the chairs.

Mr. Borg leaned back into the shadow of his buggy and took one more swallow of his home-brewed whiskey. Then he ambled up to the porch. Gertrude Throm caught his eye, questioning him silently with a concerned glance. He shook his head slightly.

She slapped her big thighs and rose out of her chair, looking at the other two women. "Come, it is time we saw to our own children. The sun is nearly down. I will give thee a ride."

She ushered the women down off the porch to her buggy. Thomas would tell her where Mr. Hill was later.

She knew that whatever he had to tell Aurelia was best not done in a group of concerned old women.

They waved good-bye from the buggy as it turned and headed up the hill. Aurelia and Joey waved back.

Aurelia had watched Thomas and Mrs. Throm exchange glances. She knew then that something had happened to her father. It had been a long, terrible day already. She could not stand much more. She tried to draw on the last of her ebbing courage as Thomas Borg sat next to her. Looking at Joey solemnly watch the old man, her fear grew. Joey had been acting unusually formal for the last hour. Now he was sitting like a statue, too nervous even to meet her eyes.

"Thee went to the holy cave today with the Blessed Mother?" Thomas Borg asked.

Aurelia slowly peered over at him. "Yes."

"Thy father was greatly concerned. He went after thee. Into the cave."

Aurelia shuddered. All the feelings, the horrible flashes of memory that she had tried to piece together earlier, flooded back into her mind. She reached, trembling, for her glass of lemonade. It slipped out her hand and crashed onto the floor. She did not move. She just sat, shaking, staring, empty-eyed, as the liquid seeped down through the cracks in the wood.

Joey wanted to hold her and tell her that everything would be fine, that he would take care of her, that she did not have to worry; her father would be home any second now.

But he knew it was a lie.

"Why hasn't he returned?" she asked in a quiet, nearly defeated voice.

Thomas leaned over the arm of his chair. "The cave is deep. There are many tunnels. He may have gotten lost."

"Daddy's too smart for that. I'm sure he . . ."

Aurelia locked her jaw and blinked rapidly to hold back the tears. She took several quick, short breaths. Her fingers encircled the edge of the armrests and squeezed them until it hurt enough to stop the growing numbness in her limbs.

Thomas patted her hand. "Do not be worried. The Blessed Mother has gathered our best men together. They have already gone into the cave after him. She knows the cave well. She will find thy father and bring him back." He smiled reassuringly. "Do not doubt this."

Thomas let go of her hand. He was hoping he sounded more convincing than he felt.

"But the cave . . ." Aurelia rubbed her eyes. Her lower lip quivered. "The cave is horrible. There are things there. I've heard them. I can't remember. But they're there. They are." She began to weep uncontrollably. Thomas glanced at Joey. The boy was near tears too. He pointed with his chin to the door. Joey nodded and went into the house. He couldn't stand seeing Aurelia hurt. He sat in the kitchen, alone, and cried. He felt so utterly helpless.

Thomas pulled his chair closer and gently squeezed her arm.

"First Mom, then Dad . . ." Aurelia could hardly form the words. Her whole world seemed to be caving in around her. It felt as though a whirlpool were sucking her down and down. She ached so inside. Everything was spinning, twisting . . .

"Let it out," Thomas coaxed, "until the pain has lessened."

The sun sank below the mountains. Darkness swept over the valley.

"Why did we come here? Why?"

Aurelia tried to stand. Her legs wobbled and she fell against Thomas's shins. She covered her face with both hands and rocked against his legs.

"Daddy? I need you. Daddy?"

Thomas felt the sorrow and the fear well up into his throat. He reached down and pulled her to him to hold her as she rocked and cried and called to her father.

"He will return," he kept whispering, hoping it might be possible. "He will, Aurelia. He will."

He waited, but she did not quiet down. He let go of her, hurried to his buggy and returned with the jug. He poured some whiskey into a half-full glass of lemonade.

Aurelia sucked in what air she could between sobs, but was not able to get up off her knees. Thomas lifted her back onto her chair.

"Drink this." He held the glass out for her. She tried to grasp it, but her hands shook too badly. Thomas enclosed his hands around hers and tilted the glass towards her mouth. "Drink. Drink it all."

When she was done, he refilled the glass with whiskey and lemonade. He placed it on the table next to her.

"Thee must drink. It will make thee feel better." She sniffed, then wiped her eyes and cheeks. Mr. Borg handed her his handkerchief. She blew her nose weakly. "That is better. Now drink some more."

Aurelia nodded. Already the whiskey was taking its effect. It warmed her trembling stomach and loosened her throat. She drank half the glass.

"Good," Thomas lifted her face and smiled. "This is our secret. When thy father returns do not tell him I gave thee whiskey. And, please . . ." His smile broadened when he realized he had finally caught her attention. "Do not tell the Blessed Mother or anyone else. It is not allowed. No one knows I make whiskey. It's between thee and me. Our secret."

Aurelia half smiled and nodded. "Daddy let me drink screwdrivers in Florida."

"Then it is good I brought it. Thy father will not think ill of me."

She sipped some more, then glanced up at Thomas. "Do you really think he'll be all right?"

Thomas Borg braced himself for his next lie. "Thy father is strong and smart. He will be just fine."

Aurelia heard the creaking of a buckboard coming closer, and with it, the splashing of horses trotting in the mud. Aurelia peered through the porch screen. The lantern on the wagon seat illuminated the mute and another man as they drove in front of the house.

"They found him," Aurelia cried, leaping down the porch steps. "He's all right."

Thomas Borg closed his eyes and prayed she was right. He grabbed the jug and slipped it behind his chair, then followed her out.

Aurelia was silently staring into the back of the wagon as he approached.

"Daddy?" She reached out slowly to touch her father's face. He was strapped to a cot, covered to his neck with a blanket. He did not move or speak. He just kept gazing blankly up into the darkness.

Aurelia touched his skin. It was damp and cold. She jerked her hand back. Her pleading eyes flashed up at the mute. The other man with him, Mr. Grotten, jumped down. He was the valley's closest thing to a doctor.

"We will carry him into the house." Mr. Grotten looked sadly at the girl. "His spine has been hurt. We found him like this. He is in shock. That is why he does not recognize thee."

Aurelia backed away from the buggy. It had happened. Her life had just collapsed around her. Nothing was left. Her body swayed backwards. Everything started to spin and spin and spin. She squeezed her eyes closed and a sensation of falling, as in a dream, over-powered her.

She fainted.

Thomas wrung out the cool wet towel and placed it on her forehead again.

She kept moaning and twisting her head. Thomas was glad Joey had had to go back to the orphanage. He was concerned about the boy, but did not need to have to comfort him as well as Aurelia. The towel fell off again. Thomas put it back on and held it.

She had been unconscious for over thirty minutes. The mute and Mr. Grotten had carried Sam in on the stretcher and carefully placed him in his bed, after Thomas had shoved the boards they had brought under the thin mattress. At Mr. Grotten's command, they had rigged pulleys from the bed and ceiling, then roped through them and hooked the leather straps. Together, they harnessed Sam's hips, shoulders, legs and chin with the straps. Mr. Grotten told Thomas that now that they had his spine in traction, it would be critically danger-ous if Sam were to be moved again. His spine must be held tight, and movement now that his spine was stretched would probably kill him, or leave him per-manently paralyzed from the neck down.

"Daddy?" Aurelia moaned. Her eyes opened slightly.

Thomas wiped her sweat-soaked face and neck with the cool towel. "He is in bed, Aurelia. In his room. He is resting."

After Aurelia drank another quick whiskey and lem-onade, Thomas told her what Mr. Grotten had said. She wanted to see her father right away. Thomas agreed and helped her to his room. She was still very weak and dis-oriented.

She sat on the chair next to her father's bed and

stared, sometimes at him, sometimes at the ropes and the straps. She never said a word. Thomas decided to leave her alone. He went out to the porch to drink from his jug.

At least he got out alive, he kept telling himself. Mr. Grotten said that the wagon ride, one wrong jolt, could have killed him. He was lucky they had even found him.

Thomas looked out into the dark-shadowed night. The sky was clear now and thick with stars. He could see the orphanage in the distance, cold and stark in the moonlight. His gaze wandered over the rock cliffs near the cave.

"He escaped Thee, Thou Black-Faced One. He escaped Thy Lair," Thomas whispered to the darkness. "Perhaps the girl truly is our savior as some have said. Perhaps she will end our curse."

The words did not hold any comfort for him then.

"What?" Aurelia asked, slipping out the front door to the porch.

Thomas spun sideways, almost dropping his jug. He had not expected the darkness to answer. "Nothing. I was just thinking out loud."

"Oh," Aurelia walked to the end of the porch and turned. "Will he get better? He didn't even know I was there."

"I cannot say. It is in God's hands now."

Aurelia felt numb, almost empty inside.

Thomas walked to the table and picked up a black box.

"The mute came back while thee was asleep. He brought this for thee."

Aurelia took the box and opened it. Inside was an intricately carved and painted wooden doll, dressed in a fluffy blue dress with pale yellow flowers and a white, ruffled blouse. Her hair was whitish blond, her skin white, her huge eyes closed. When Aurelia lifted her upright out of the box, the doll's eyes opened wide. They were pink.

Aurelia smiled. Thomas's heart lightened, seeing how pleased she was. It was difficult for him to admit the mute had brought it. It was the only kind deed he could remember Matthew ever doing.

"I'm tired," she sighed, "so tired."

"Come." Thomas led her to her room. "Sleep. Sleep away the fear and the hurt. I will stay here tonight. I will be in the living room if thee awakens and needs me."

Aurelia hugged the old man softly, then looked up into his eyes.

"I'm scared," she whispered. "Please help my father get better. Please."

Thomas nodded as he patted her hair. There was nothing more he could do for her father, except pray.

Pray to the Lord that this girl was their Blessed Savior, chosen by God Almighty to lead His people from their terrible bondage.

A bondage that had turned His eyes from them many years ago.

A bondage that had led the Holy Children to the gates of Hell itself.

Aurelia awoke in the middle of the night, feeling warm and slightly queasy. She kicked the quilt off the bed. The cold night breeze made her shiver, and she crawled to the bottom of the bed to retrieve the quilt.

She had been having a dream. She couldn't remember it now, only a hollow, empty feeling remained. She put on her robe and slippers and stood by the window next to the doll the mute had brought. She looked out at the mountains, dark and rolling in the moon's dim green light.

Suddenly something inside her clawed at her belly.

She doubled over, clutching her stomach as the pain ripped through her torso.

"Stop. Please," she moaned. She gasped when her body shot upright of its own accord. She tried to grab the windowsill, but her body twisted and threw her, wheeling, against the dresser.

"Pl . . . . . ease," she coughed. A low, angry cry howled up from her throat. Her mind shuddered as she flew forward, smashing against the wall next to the window.

Her throat tightened, and her body felt as if it were being stretched until her joints were ready to explode.

Her eyes opened wide, then snapped tightly shut. Saliva dribbled out of the corner of her mouth and down her neck. Her body heaved itself against the wall.

Slowly, her eyes opened again. Her body began to move. It shuffled to the window, opened it, then picked up the doll and cradled it clumsily in its arms.

She stared at the cave glowing in the moonlight.

A gnarled, tortured grin spread across her once pretty face.

She began to remember.

She sneaked into the living room. Mr. Borg was snoring loudly. Quickly, she gathered the things she would need.

It was clear now. She understood.

It had not been a dream.

She picked up the candle and went back into her room. She climbed out the window, taking her new doll with her. She was not thinking of her father now. He didn't seem to matter.

Nothing mattered now but the voices.

She walked slowly towards the cave. The wind screeched down through the cliffs, crying out to her.

But she heard only the voices.

Inside her.

Telling her what must be done.

A raccoon, hearing her footsteps, froze, its yellow eyes caught in the light of her flashlight. She stopped and stared at it.

The raccoon hissed; the hair on its back stood up straight, and its hind legs flexed. It hissed again, then ran into the bushes, terrified.

Aurelia entered the cave. The voices were strong now, moving her the way a puppeteer controls his marionette. They melded together and beckoned her into the tunnel.

Each cavern flickered in her mind before she entered it. The visions cleared the black void before her like memories from another time, another place, leading her forward with each new image.

"Don't be scared," she said to the doll, caressing it. Aurelia stopped and held her breath. She heard someone calling from far away. She started to walk again.

She edged sideways along a steep ravine, then climbed down where the rocks opened up into a path.

This was the place. The voices had told her.

She walked into the cavern. It was smaller than her bedroom. Her head almost scraped the moist, low ceiling.

"Sit." She bent the doll's legs at the hip joints and sat it on a rock. She took the candle out of the pocket in her robe, jammed it into the hard, semi-dry mud and lit it. The candle flickered across the wide-eyed, wooden-faced doll as it stared blankly at the opening of the small cavern, its arms outstretched stiffly, its little red mouth open slightly, the yellow light dancing erratically upon its pale white face.

Aurelia knelt down, straightened out the doll's fluffy dress, and kissed it on the forehead. Then she stood up and walked out of the cavern.

Darkness engulfed her.

...Aurelia...

Instinctively, she criss-crossed through the jutting rocks, following the voices.

...Aurelia...

She stopped at the edge of the huge lake. She could hear it lapping at her feet.

...Aurelia...

Slowly, she unbuttoned her shirt and slid it down over her shoulders.

...Aurelia...

She stripped off the rest of her clothes and stood naked in the darkness.

...Cleanse thyself...

She stepped into the lake. It was cold, but she didn't feel its icy chill.

...Aurelia...

She waded out into the black murky depths of the lake.

...We baptize thee...

...In the name of the Darkness, and of the Cave, and of the Children...

"It was a good lesson for the girl," the Blessed Mother said, sitting by the fire, crocheting. "It will strengthen her will, kindle the flame that sparks her destiny. Her time is near, now that her father is dying."

The mute yanked open one of the thick red curtains that hung down to the floor, and glared out the window. It was late at night. The moon was high above the black rolling mountains. The wind blew hard against the back of the orphanage. He listened to it pound and cry, trying desperately to seep into any open pores of the huge house.

He could not contain his anger. The Blessed Mother watched him out of the corner of her veil. He worried her tonight. He was not the same.

He had never gone against her will before.

The mute spun around suddenly and waved his huge hand, shaking his head. He pointed downstairs, then outside, his other hand clutching at the air as if he were grabbing someone by the neck.

"It is not for thee to punish without my command." The Blessed Mother put her crocheting down and lifted her veil. The mute grunted and pointed downstairs again. "It was good for Aurelia. She must know their hearts and hate them as I hate. Now her soul will be opened to me. She will fill her heart with hate."

He grunted loudly and paced the room. He would not listen, and that the Blessed Mother would not tolerate.

"Thee are mine, Matthew, to do my bidding," she warned. "It is why thee has been passed over. It is thy duty to obey me. Thee owes me thy life."

The mute stopped pacing and stared defiantly at her. The Blessed Mother rose out of her chair. Her hands trembled.

"I will not stand for this. The girls did what they did because they are like their forefathers, filled with the same prejudice and hate that destroyed the children. She must learn their ways quickly, before her father dies."

The mute stomped his foot. His stony face reddened. His eyes narrowed into slits. He did not care about Aurelia's father; it was the girls he had seen teasing Aurelia who filled his mind with fury.

The Blessed Mother approached him, bent shouldered, her head cocked sideways, never taking her eyes from his.

"Thee shall not do that again," she hissed. "Does thee understand? Never disobey my will."

The mute growled back.

"Never," she yelled, slapping his face. He peered

down at her, silent and determined as she had never seen him before.

Her shoulders quivered. She could not continue to look at him. She turned and walked to the fireplace, purposely keeping her back to him.

"If thee thinks it must be done . . . ." She turned to face him. The fire outlined her black attire with a reddish glow. She lowered her veil. He grunted and pointed at the floor again. "Thee loves her. That is good. Then so be it. I should have realized. Thee has my permission. It will cause their hate to grow. Perhaps it will help. Do what thee must."

The mute walked up to her and put his hand on her shoulder. She backed away into the shadows.

"But remember thy task, Matthew. It is not for thee to question the ways of the children. Not even for one of thy blood."

The mute awoke Ruth and the other girls he had seen hiding on the hill. He pushed them downstairs and out the front door. The two youngest were crying quietly, holding hands to comfort each other, too terrified to make a sound.

The cold wind blew up through their long nightgowns. Ruth clutched her chest with both arms and shivered. Then she felt his huge hand shove her forward into the shed.

The five girls huddled together in the darkness of the cold shed. None of them had ever been in it before, but they had all heard the screams that came from behind its closed doors.

The mute lit a lantern and turned up the flame. The orange light illuminated the small shed. He put it down on the workbench in the corner and approached the girls. They clung to each other, too frightened even to look at him.

He yanked Ruth out of the circle and dragged her to the far wall. The others watched, horrified, wondering what their fate would be. They were too scared to cry now. The shed filled with shadowy silence.

The mute reached up. They could hear the rattling of chains. That terrible clanking, squealing noise sent chills over their skin. One girl began to sob again, unable to control herself any longer. Urine dribbled down her leg. Her body convulsed and she went limp. The others held her up.

The mute put Ruth's wrists into the cold manacles, then took the rope tied to the wall and tugged it. Ruth gasped and bit her lip to keep from screaming as her arms were pulled high above her until she could barely stand on her toes.

Half dangling, her back to the others, she felt as if the earth had just opened up and swallowed her.

Thick, cold fingers grabbed the back of the collar of her nightgown and ripped the gown downward, into shreds.

She screamed. The other girls stood paralyzed, staring. Their moist eyes glittered in the dim light.

The mute took the long, thick, black leather strap from the wall. Ruth, her nightgown torn and hanging from her hips, her bare breasts heaving in the cold yellow light, closed her eyes and prayed for deliverance—prayed to God for His forgiveness, promising Him never to be cruel to the girl again, if only this horror would be taken from her.

The mute yanked the taller girl out of the huddled circle. Rebecca was the closest thing to a friend Ruth had. No, Ruth realized, that wasn't true. She had no friends, only accomplices who did what she wanted out of fear.

Rebecca swallowed to keep from getting sick. She wasn't sure she could stand without the support of the others. The mute led her into the middle of the shed, facing Ruth's naked back.

He handed her the strap and pointed at Ruth. The girl slowly peered up at him. Her eyes pleaded with his, not wanting to believe what she knew he meant.

He pointed again and grunted.

She shook her head. "No. Please. I could not."

He undid his big, black belt and wrapped it once over his fist. Then he pointed again.

The girl turned her head away and stared down at the dirt floor. She could not do it. It was too horrifying even to consider. He could never make her.

Then she heard the crack of his strap and felt its stinging tongue lash across her shoulders. The searing pain sent shudders throughout her body.

He whipped her again across the small of her back, cutting through her nightgown. She screamed, then she felt the warm blood trickling down over her buttocks.

Head bent, she cried quietly. "I cannot. Please. Not that."

That awful, tearing pain cut through her again. She screamed. This time, the pain lingered horribly. Another lash or two and she would surely die, she thought.

Slowly, she lifted the heavy leather strap that dangled down from her thin hand. She flicked it out weakly. It barely slapped against Ruth's back.

Ruth squeezed the chain above her manacled wrists.

The mute growled and pointed at Ruth. He lashed the girl again, across her buttocks. She choked on her scream. Her legs and back were on fire. He stood above her, growling, pointing.

She lifted the belt again. This time she swung it hard.

Ruth cried out. Her body spasmed, dangling from the manacles. The other girls clutched together, crying pitifully.

The mute growled and kept pointing.

This was merely the beginning.

CHAPTER XI

FOR THREE days, the people came. From every house in the valley, the Holy Children traveled to visit Aurelia and express their condolences. They came in buggies—whole families—and they came on foot. It was obvious that their concern and their sincerity was real. They were so kind; Aurelia felt as though they were all her distant relatives.

They came with gifts, with food, with words of sympathy. Those who had lost loved ones before, spoke about the hurt and the anger openly to show they understood and shared in her grief and to tell her how lucky she was that her father still had a chance. They helped her immensely to get through each day.

Thomas Borg was proud of his people then. Prouder than he had been in years. For those three days, he stayed with Aurelia, sleeping on the couch, cooking, helping her spoon-feed her father, always ready to lend his shoulder for her to lean on.

Sam Hill remained in shock. He never moved. Mr. Grotten came each morning and stayed till sunset. He sat with Aurelia for hours in her father's room, waiting, observing. He told her that her father was seriously injured, but, if he was kept still and the traction worked, and if no other complications arose, there was a good chance he would recuperate. Whether he would regain full movement of his limbs was impossible to predict. It was the most optimistic diagnosis he could give her without lying outright. He did not tell her the main reason he came each day was that he was expecting complications to develop at any moment.

Gertrude Throm came every day as well, and Joey always showed up after chores in the afternoon. Together, they gave Aurelia strength, and the feeling of family, of caring that she needed desperately.

On the third day, in the afternoon, Aurelia was sitting on the chair next to her father's bed, reading Steinbeck's *Of Mice and Men* to him. It was one of his favorite books. She had been reading it out loud for two afternoons while her father lay as still as death. She did not know if he heard her or not, but she wanted to let him know she was there.

Thomas stood in the doorway, watching and listening. He smiled sadly. When she noticed him, he quickly grinned.

"Mr. Grotten and I are going to my farm for a while. Joey is here. He is out back by the shed, chopping wood."

Aurelia accompanied him to the porch. The lamb met her at the door. She bent down and patted it. It also had been a great comfort to her; it was always so happy to see her. It licked her face and tried to crawl into her arms. When she scratched under its ears it baaed happily.

"I think thee should try to go to school tomorrow," Mr. Grotten said, standing outside the screen door. "I will come in the morning and remain with thy father until thee returns. It will be good for thee to get out for a while. Mr. Borg agrees."

"The children at the orphanage are concerned. They want to see thee," Thomas added. "Besides, it is not healthy for thee to sit inside day after day. If anything happens, word will be sent to thee."

Aurelia stood up and wiped her hands on her jeans. "All right."

Thomas glanced at Mr. Grotten. They shared a look of relief. They had discussed making the suggestion to Aurelia yesterday, but had put it off until she seemed ready. Thomas was relieved that she had agreed without an argument. The girl had to get back to living her life—what was left of it—to maintaining a schedule that might later help keep her strong during the trials to come. For Thomas did not think her father would live, and even if he did, there was no doubt he would be paralyzed.

That burden would be easier for her now that she knew everyone in the valley would share it with her, he thought. But he knew there was no hope for Aurelia's father unless what the people were hoping, praying for, turned out to be true. Only if Aurelia really was their savior, the one chosen by God to stand against the Blessed Mother and end her reign of death, only then would it matter what happened to Aurelia's father. For if she could not stand up to the Blessed Mother, Sam Hill's life was worth nothing anyway.

That burden, Thomas thought, seemed so heavy to put on the shoulders of such a fragile young girl, one who had already faced terrible tragedy.

But she had been to the cave, alone and with the Blessed Mother, and had heard the children and had come back unscathed, to tell of it. No one had ever done that before. It was a true sign.

A sign neither he nor Aurelia could ignore much longer. Soon he must tell her of the people's hopes. But not tonight, he thought. Tomorrow she would go back to school. If she was strong enough, he would tell her tomorrow.

It was something she had to know quickly, though. Time was running out.

The Blessed Mother's plan, whatever it was, was imminent. Aurelia must understand her position and be ready. The others had already agreed.

Her life, her father's, those of everyone in the Valley, depended on it.

In the morning, Joey came over and walked Aurelia to school. The children were very receptive when she entered the orphanage. Ruth and the four older girls who had taunted her were not in school. Richard was there, but stayed in the distance by himself. Many of the kids her age had come with their parents over the last three days to visit Aurelia and every one of them came up to her before class to greet her. Most of the younger orphans did the same.

After class, Aurelia talked with Joey in the hall. Lunch was going to be late and he had to sweep the chicken coop. He told her he would be done with his chores quickly and was going to skip lunch. He asked if she would meet him in the barn in a little while. Aurelia agreed.

As soon as he left, Mary approached. She gestured with her hand for Aurelia to follow her. They went upstairs to the girls' bedrooms. Scanning the empty hall, Mary waved Aurelia into her room.

Aurelia closed the door behind her. It annoyed her that Mary still felt she had to meet with her in secret, not talk downstairs in front of the others, especially since Ruth was not there today and she seemed finally to have been accepted by the others.

"They were punished four nights ago," Mary whispered. She eased around Aurelia and leaned against the door, listening to be sure no one was outside it. Aurelia sat down on the corner of the bed.

"Who was punished? Ruth and the others who were missing from class?"

Mary nodded, one ear still pressed to the door. "The mute took the girls who teased thee. We all heard them. It was horrible. They were in the shed for hours. We were not allowed to see them afterwards. None of them came to breakfast the next day. Ruth is still in her room. Glynne took her breakfast to her today. She said she looked terrible. Could hardly even speak. Just lay there, staring at the ceiling. The only thing Ruth said was something about thee. And it was not nice. Ruth hates thee now more than ever. She blames thee for what happened to her." Mary walked towards Aurelia and touched her arm. "Be careful. She can be awfully mean."

"I appreciate the warning." Aurelia opened her purse. "I can take care of myself, though. I'm not scared. Look, I've got something to show you." She pulled a small radio from her purse and turned it on. Mary watched, puzzled. The radio crackled. Turning the dial, Aurelia found a country-rock station.

"Music in a box?" Mary slowly shook her head in wonder, fascinated. She forgot all about listening at the door.

"A radio. It picks up stations that play music. Everyone has one. All the cars have them too."

"The metal buggy thee arrived in?"

"A car."

"With no horses?"

"An engine. Runs on gas. But the way gas prices are going we may be back to horses real soon."

Mary smiled, not really fathoming her words, but knowing it was some kind of joke.

Suddenly Mary's head spun back towards the door.

Three of the orphan girls, about thirteen, shyly entered. Mary exhaled, relieved.

Aurelia held up the radio. It was playing Linda Ronstadt's "Desperado."

Aurelia put the radio on the dresser. The three girls encircled it, whispering.

Mary leaned towards them and pointed. "A radio."

They looked at her in awe.

"Do you dance?" Aurelia scanned their faces.

Mary frowned, confused. "Dance?"

Aurelia laughed. She began to dance, disco-style, to the music. The song was a little slow for disco, but she improvised. The girls started giggling.

The littlest, a girl with curly blond hair and big, innocent blue eyes, began to imitate her.

"It's fun," Aurelia laughed, twirling in a circle. She began to lower her body, knees bent, moving her hips sensually to the slow rhythm.

Another girl clapped with excitement. The little blond tried to follow her descent but lost her balance and fell against the bed. The others caught her and lifted her back up, laughing.

Aurelia stopped and reached into her purse. She had decided this morning before leaving for school that the other kids should learn about teenagers in America. She thought it would help her make friends. And they were responding just as she'd wished—they circled her, giddy with curiosity. She pulled out a rolled up *Teen-Fan* magazine.

She showed them different rock stars and movie stars. They kept stopping her from turning a page, pausing to point out a young, handsome face and to sigh wistfully. Aurelia explained who each one was as they cooed and giggled. Each soon had a favorite picked out. Questions began to zing at her all at once.

Suddenly Mary jumped over to the door.

"Shhh!"

Aurelia quickly turned off the radio. They could hear heavy footsteps pounding down the hall. Everyone froze. The little blond girl hid behind Aurelia, holding onto her blouse.

Aurelia grabbed the radio and shoved it back into her purse, along with the magazine. Slowly, the door opened. Mary backed away.

The mute's stony face peeked in.

Aurelia stepped forward. "Hello."

He glanced around, almost smiling. The other girls grabbed each other's hands, shocked. His head disappeared and the door closed gently.

They waited until his footsteps faded down the stairs before starting to chatter again. They couldn't believe the mute had almost smiled or that Aurelia had actually walked over and spoken to him so casually.

Aurelia was a star. They questioned her with great respect after that, remembering, as well, how she had stood up to the Blessed Mother at lunch four days ago. All the commotion made Aurelia feel wonderful.

"Do you want to see my other magazines? I have a lot. I also have records. I mean . . ." How did you explain records? she thought. "A music player."

"Tell us about John Travolta," the little blond asked, tugging Aurelia's sleeve. Aurelia smiled and glanced at Mary as she took out her radio. Mary opened the door slightly and peered out into the hall. Then she closed it and nodded at Aurelia.

"All right. I'll tell you. But only if you all try to dance next time a good song comes on."

Giggling, the girls agreed.

Joey was watching out the barn door as Aurelia approached. He beckoned her to the far end where the sheep were kept.

"Did thee ever go fishing?" He reached behind a rusty scythe and extracted a pole. It was handmade, without a reel—just a long stick with a wooden bobber, line and hook. "I already got the worms. I know a good place on the river." He realized he had not given her a chance to answer. "Has thee?"

"No. But you can teach me."

He grinned. "Come on. Morning and night are best, but sometimes they bite around noon too. Mr. Borg said it would be all right. He is watching thy father."

They hurried out the barn door and headed towards the cliffs. They climbed a grassy embankment to get above them. Joey was determined to avoid walking by the cave.

Aurelia told him about the girls dancing with her and showed him the radio. He was more interested in fishing. He did not tell her that Mr. Borg had asked him to take her along.

"We will climb down where the river comes out of the rocks. There is a big pool off to one side there. It is the best place in the Valley to fish. Mr. Borg showed it to me two years ago. I used to fish there with him when the sun was going down. That is the best time, usually."

Aurelia smiled and took his hand as they walked. All the attention she was getting felt good, but she was glad to get away from everything and be alone with Joey.

"Look. There is Mr. Borg outside thy house." They stopped and watched. "Does thee want to tell him where we are going?"

"No," Aurelia said. She had other plans. She squeezed Joey's hand and leaned her body against his arm. He stared down at her awkwardly. She stroked his cheek and, stretching up, kissed him quickly. She felt very grateful to him for this pleasant escape from reality. Joey had been so sweet and thoughtful for the last few days. He had made her feel loved. She felt closer to him than she had felt towards any boy she had ever known.

She had been trying to figure out how to let him know how much he meant to her, but the kiss had just sort of happened. Afterward Joey stared at the ground awkwardly.

Aurelia liked his shyness. He lacked the conceit of the boys she knew at Greenville High.

She smiled and tugged his arm. "Let's go fishing."

The river poured down out of the rocks into a swirling blue whirlpool. It circled out and down a small incline, gurgling over the smooth white rocks. On one side, a deep, still pool, like a miniature pond, lay quiet under the two hanging willows that shaded it. The woods were dense and a layer of last year's leaves, soft and thick, carpeted the ground. The sun filtered through the trees in bright patches, dabbing their half-grown leaves like an unfinished impressionist painting. Further down, the sun's glare twinkled on the river like gold.

"It's beautiful," Aurelia sighed.

They climbed over the rocks above the escaping river, then circled through the clump of white birch to the small pool. Joey placed the can of worms against the trunk of the bigger willow, whose long, slender yellow branches dripped down over them into the clear water.

Aurelia leaned against the trees. Joey sat next to her. As he proceeded to hook a worm, Aurelia curled her lip in disgust.

"Doesn't that hurt it?"

"No." Joey laughed, flipping the line into the middle of the pool. "They do not have feelings. That is what Mr. Borg said." The line sank until the bobber was tight above it on the water. Joey balanced the pole so the line was taut, and stuck it between two rocks. He put another stone at the end of the pole to secure it.

"All thee has to do now is wait and watch the bobber.

It will dip if a fish is nibbling. When thee sees that, yank the pole quickly to hook it.''

Aurelia smiled, trying to look interested. She was hoping no fish would bite. She felt sorry for the drowning worm. Besides, she had other plans. She was alone with her first real boyfriend.

And today she felt sure she was in love.

She cuddled up against Joey's chest and massaged his neck. She leaned up to stare into his eyes as she had seen so many of her favorite stars do in the movies. But he didn't stare back right, not like he was supposed to. She sighed and pulled him down to meet her lips. They kissed slowly and awkwardly. Aurelia placed Joey's arms around her waist.

This was not going the way she had planned. She sighed noisily and sat back up straight.

Joey checked his pole. She watched, making sure he noticed her annoyed look.

"Is it not fun, fishing?"

Aurelia rolled her eyes and looked away. Joey watched her, confused, not really wanting to take his attention from his fishing pole.

She decided not to give up so easily. She sat on the rock that steadied the pole.

"Thee might disturb the—"

She kissed him before he could finish his sentence, pushing her body against his. They fell over onto the soft leaves and banged teeth.

Aurelia sat up, rubbing her lip and shaking her head.

"Haven't you ever kissed anyone before?"

Joey stood up defensively. She watched his expression turn from stubborn indignation to embarrassment. He looked down at the ground, flicking a pebble into the water with his shoe.

"No."

"Didn't you like it?"

He glanced over at her and cocked his head sideways, the way a puppy does when it's confused.

"Yes, but . . ."

"But what?"

"It is a sin."

Aurelia stood up and tried again. This time she put her whole body into the kiss and held his face with both hands.

"Did that feel sinful?"

He shrugged, then grinned. "No."

"There. Then that's settled."

They sat under the willow, holding each other, kissing, staring into each other's eyes and into the clear blue pool. They talked sometimes, but not often. Not until Joey brought up the subject of his parents to stop her from talking about her father again. Mr. Borg had told him to keep her mind off her father's condition.

"And I hate the orphanage," he continued. "It is not like home. My mother always laughed with me. We . . ." He did not want to seem childish to Aurelia, but he couldn't help it then. He could tell she understood by the way she squeezed his shoulder gently. "We could talk. I could tell her my dreams and . . . and my fears."

"My mother too." Aurelia snuggled closer against his chest, her arms tight around his waist. He began to caress her long, smooth white hair. Touching her soft body was so wonderful it was almost overwhelming. He had never felt sensations like he was feeling now. He never wanted them to end.

Then he felt the tears soaking through his shirt. He lifted her face to his. She looked so small and helpless, so fragile suddenly, and he felt strong and protective. He would fight to the death for her if he had to, he decided, after looking deep into her wet eyes.

"I miss her so much," Aurelia whispered. "I need her now. Now that Daddy . . ." She sniffed, then looked at

Joey. "But you're here. You've been my strength. You've helped me so much."

Joey leaned back, slightly embarrassed. Aurelia rolled over next to him. Feeling her warm body mold against his, looking up into her beautiful face, he felt a strange surging, an almost painful swelling in his chest.

He kissed her then, and she clung to him, molding her body against his. She did not want to talk anymore about pain or grief or death or anything else.

"Please, Joey," she whispered, kissing his ear. She curled one leg over his and took his hand. "Touch me. Please."

She lifted his trembling hand and cupped it gently over her small, firm breast, then kissed him deeply.

Joey's heart fluttered. Those terribly wonderful feelings, those thoughts that kept him from falling asleep at night, were actually happening now. Joey could barely believe it.

Nothing else mattered to either of them that moment.

Only the touching.

And the love.

As the sun began to set, Aurelia watched the black-curtained buggy approach her house. When it stopped, the mute got down and reached up to help the Blessed Mother to the ground. Aurelia walked out to meet them.

The Blessed Mother hobbled up to her, holding the mute's huge arm for support.

"I have mourned for thee," the old woman said, putting her gloved hand on Aurelia's shoulder. The bony fingers dug into her flesh. It felt as though a skeleton, raised from its clammy earthen grave, had just touched her. Aurelia shivered.

They ascended the steps and sat on the porch chairs.

The mute quickly went back out to wait in the buggy.

For too long a time, they sat in silence. Aurelia shifted her weight, uncomfortable now at even being near the veiled woman. She listened to the heavy cracks of the axe behind the house and felt slightly more at ease knowing Joey was there, cutting wood.

When she had come home from fishing, Mr. Borg had told her he had chores at his farm that had to be completed before he could come back tonight, so Joey had volunteered to stay until then.

"Thank you for rescuing my father." Aurelia poured cold water into two glasses and handed one to the Blessed Mother. The words had sounded too formal, but she had to break that horrible silence somehow.

"I have prayed for him often. And for thee." The Blessed Mother put the glass on the table between their chairs. "I am happy to see that thee came back to school today."

Aurelia nodded. Seeing the old woman again triggered the awful pictures in her mind once more: the skull-like face, the eyes, the horrid blackness. Aurelia brushed her hair back nervously. The strange visions had not bothered her for the last four days, not even when she was sleeping. At least not that she could remember. But now they came back to torment her. Aurelia knew they were connected to the Blessed Mother then and hated her for it.

Aurelia held her hands together in her lap and squeezed them. The visions kept coming.

"Thee looks pale," the old woman said.

Aurelia tried to smile. "I always look pale." She did not want the Blessed Mother to know how frightened she was, and the joke gave her confidence.

The Blessed Mother reached across the small table. Aurelia recoiled in her seat. The old woman sat up straight and adjusted her veil. She was obviously insulted and Aurelia was glad. The visions were weaker now.

"Thee are afraid . . . of me?"

Aurelia peered at the woman. Why pretend? she thought. I don't even like for her to be in the same house with my father . . . or me.

"You told me about a doll of my mother's. You took me to the cave to show me it. I can't remember being there. I can't remember anything about it. But there was no doll. I know that. But something else was there. Something horrible. When my father went there, something hurt him badly. Something in the cave. I don't believe my mother ever went there, not of her own free will. It is a dark, evil place. My mother was kind and good."

The Blessed Mother folded her arms on her lap. "And thee blames me for thy father's accident?"

"Yes."

"The cave is sacred. He knew not to go there."

Aurelia pushed up out of her chair, marched to the screen door, then spun around, "But you took me there. Why?"

"It was my duty."

"What do you mean, duty? What's in that cave? What is everyone in this valley so scared of?"

"They are scared of their own sins. The cave is merely a reminder of those sins. We are born sinners. Since Eve we have been cursed with the plight of sin. The sins of man are his heritage. We must constantly make acts of retributions. The cave is our Holy temple. Our sins are cleansed within its hallowed ground. The people merely fear themselves. The sins in their hearts cannot be hidden there."

Aurelia stared angrily. "I don't believe any of that crap."

"Thee will . . . in time." The Blessed Mother stood up to leave. "I have come to express my sorrow for thy father. I will pray for him again tonight."

The old woman slowly shuffled to the buggy. Aurelia's eyes followed her, but her head did not move.

She realized that she now feared the Blessed Mother as much as Joey and the others did. She couldn't say what exactly the old woman had done to her or to her father to cause that quick rush of anxiety when she came near and tried to touch her, but it was real . . . and deserved.

That evening, after dinner, Aurelia told Thomas Borg that the Blessed Mother had visited her and how she had felt about it. Thomas was building up the fire in the living room as he listened. It burned loudly, crackling in the silence of the house.

Aurelia checked her father once more before settling down again with Thomas, then sat next to him in front of the roaring fire. He could tell by her uneasy expression that she was still not finished talking.

"The night they brought Daddy back, when the mute brought the doll . . .?"

Thomas nodded, waiting. Aurelia closed her eyes and rubbed her forehead. She didn't know how to begin.

"I went to the cave that day with the Blessed Mother. I told you that. What I didn't tell you was, I can't remember what happened while I was there. And the next morning, I found my nightgown and slippers all full of mud and . . . and the doll was missing." Aurelia cocked her head. "But I know it wasn't stolen. I can remember putting it somewhere, or giving it to someone or . . ." Aurelia sighed and shook her head. "Things keep flashing in my head, Thomas. Terrible things. Faces. And I hear voices. And I see horrible dark places. And death. I feel death come near me, all sticky and cold. I feel it." A tear pushed out one eye. "Thomas, something is happening to me. Something I can't control. I was all right for a few days but ever since *she* came over, it's been happening again. Weird things in my mind. I can't stop them." She wiped her eyes, then looked helplessly at Thomas. "I feel like I'm going crazy sometimes. That terrifies me. I . . . I don't want to do what . . . what my mother . . ."

Her head dropped down on her arms and she wept.

Thomas waited until she stopped, then gave her his handkerchief. She had to be told now. For her own sake, he thought, as well as the others'.

"The rumors you heard from the children about the cave are true," he said. His face grew grim. Aurelia was looking deep into his eyes, and he wished he didn't have to do this. "There are things in the cave. Unexplainable, evil things. Lost souls, I believe. Tormented and wandering, looking for salvation." Thomas sighed. "No one knows for sure, except the Blessed Mother, what is in the cave. The cave has no end to it. It goes deeper and deeper into the earth. There are many who have disappeared in the cave. The dead who do not die. Devil's children. I believe the cave is Satan's door to Hell. Thee has heard His children. They call thee back. They want thy soul. Those are the visions thee sees, the voices thee hears. The lost children. They call thee, for the Blessed Mother has shown thee to them. Thee are white-skinned, the same as them. Their cries are strong within thee."

Aurelia leaned back in her chair, clutching her quivering hands in her lap, and stared, horrified, at the fire. She did not want to believe him, but she felt the truth of his words deep in her heart and in the fear that overwhelmed her when the visions came.

"How can I stop them?" she asked, trying to remain

calm in the face of a terror whose dimensions she could not begin to fathom.

"I am not sure." Thomas pulled his chair closer and touched her arm. "But I believe that if thee let their powers grow within thee, if thee opened thyself to their cries, then, only then, would thee have the power to stop them." He squeezed her arm. "Thee must use the power given to thee, by them, for their own salvation, the power to end the Blessed Mother's evil reign of death. In this way, thee shall be saved, as their souls shall be saved. My people look to thee, Aurelia. They see thee as their only hope. Their . . . Savior. Only thee can battle the Blessed Mother, for the Children of the Cave have called to thee. I believe they want thee to end their own horror as well, and that is why they will give thee the power to destroy the Blessed Mother. Then their tormented souls can be released from that black hole of Hell in which they are trapped."

"And my father? Do they also—"

"The Blessed Mother brought him back to keep thee here. It can be the only reason he survived the cave. The Blessed Mother is responsible for his accident, as she was responsible for thy mother's death."

Aurelia looked through the window at the darkness that covered the valley. "But I never told you . . . I never told anyone about my mother."

"We were told by the Blessed Mother as a lesson to those of us who might disobey her. I am sorry to have to tell thee. But I know it is her insanity which thee fears the most." Thomas Borg reached behind the chair for his jug. "The children have the power to torment another's soul. To drive them . . ." Thomas gulped at the jug. "Insane. To possess their hearts and minds until nothing is left but fear, total and unrelenting fear."

It was all so incredible, so shocking that it did not

seem real to Aurelia. She felt totally drained.

"Will it happen to me?"

"I do not think so. The power that is being given to thee is not to drive thee insane, but to give thee that power over others. Perhaps even the Blessed Mother. But it seems to be what she wants as well. That is the only thing I do not understand."

"How do you know all this is true?"

"I do not. Not for sure. But I know how thy mother was affected. I know how the power can eat away a person's reason. It can be slow or it can happen all at once. I have seen it before, fifteen years ago."

He gazed at Aurelia. She could see that it hurt him to remember. His glassy, half-drunk eyes looked through her, back to a past that was still tearing him apart. A cold breeze washed over them. Aurelia hugged herself tightly and waited.

"We tried to stop her then too. Beth, my wife, was a strong woman, a woman a man could depend on as well as love. She had all the courage, not me. She led the people against the Blessed Mother. She stood her ground and ordered the Blessed Mother to leave the Valley." Thomas sighed and rubbed his eyes. "The Blessed Mother had one of her falling fits. When she arose from the orphanage steps, Beth began to scream. She was choking. Voices, horrible, howling voices surrounded us all. Beth clutched her head, pleading for them to stop. They just kept getting louder. When I tried to hold her, she pushed me down and ran. Before I could get up, the mute had me by the arms. The Blessed Mother asked if anyone else wanted to question the sacred ceremony of the Chosen One. No one spoke." Thomas bowed his head. "Not even myself."

He coughed, trying to hide his quiet weeping. Aurelia sensed that and did not look at him. She did not want him to feel she was judging him.

"The crowd ran after Beth. They caught up to her near the cave. They told me she was growling and clawing at herself, tearing her own flesh from her bones."

Thomas stood up and threw the jug against the fireplace. It crashed into pieces.

"Damn," he muttered, trembling.

Aurelia wrapped her arms tighter around her chest and stared deep into the fire. Then she looked back up at the old man.

"Why didn't you just leave the Valley? Leave the Blessed Mother and her cursed cave? Why do the people stay?"

"Our farms are our lives. We cannot change our ways. We are a part of this valley as it is a part of us. We are inseparable. The land was blessed by our founding father. His sons, our elders, blessed it also. All of them are buried here. The land is sacred to us. Thee would not understand. Thee has not lived with the land, prayed to it, been fed by its grace and goodness. This valley was chosen by our spiritual father. We could never leave."

Thomas Borg knelt down next to her. "Kneel with me. Let us pray for our deliverance. Pray to God Almighty, for the salvation of His people has come. Pray for the children, that they may hear thy words, and know thee are their salvation as well. That thee shall use their power to free them forever from the Hell in which they are bound, free them forever from the Blessed Mother and Satan's black door. Pray with me."

Aurelia knelt beside the old man, facing the fire. The flames grew huge in the fireplace.

"Our Father," he began, "Which art in Heaven."

She spoke in unison with his words.

"Hallowed be thy name. Thy Kingdom come . . ."

The fire roared, its glowing red shadow coloring their

solemn faces. Its heat began to scorch their flesh.

"Thy will be done . . ."

Suddenly, Aurelia felt sick. Her stomach heaved as if something had turned over inside her. She swallowed hard to keep it down.

"In earth as it is in . . ."

Aurelia forced herself to concentrate. It was no use. She could no longer remember the words.

CHAPTER XII

LOW OVER the eastern ridge of mountains, the morning sun caused slender blue shadows to elongate far from the trunks of the trees. The shadow of the orphanage extended onto the side of the red barn. Only a few pink-gray clouds stretched above the sun in thin, wispy lines.

Richard stared at the bright orange ball until his eyes stung. He had not seen Ruth for days. She had never come out of her room since the night of the punishment. It frightened him to try to imagine why.

Turning from the window, he decided to go to her, even if it were forbidden. He did not know what to do without her. She had always made the decisions for him. The last few days had been empty and directionless without her.

The hall was quiet on the third floor. Richard listened carefully for any sounds as he descended the stairs.

They had never hurt her before. Not like the others, he thought. She had always been the Blessed Mother's favorite. She was privileged. She did not have to work like the others.

She had been . . . special.

Now Aurelia was special and the mute had beaten

Ruth. Richard had to see her. She would explain it all and he wouldn't be so confused or frightened anymore.

Richard sneaked along the hall of the second floor, his big muscular body light-footed, totally aware, like a mountain lion stalking its hunters.

Slowly, he twisted the knob of the door at the end of the hall. It was unlocked.

He eased through the narrow opening and closed the door silently.

Ruth was lying in bed, sleeping. She groaned and twisted over onto her back. The sheet was caught between her legs, exposing her body above her waist. Richard crept forward, staring. She was naked. Her large, heavy breasts pressed together as she rolled back onto her side.

Richard tiptoed around the bed and peered out the window at the sun. It shone bright yellow now, its gold flames igniting the bed, illuminating the long red-brown welts across Ruth's bare back.

Richard's insides twisted, remembering the sharp-tongued sting of the belt. Flashes of the agony tore through his body like a hot, searing iron. He shuddered as he bent over and touched her shoulder.

She cried out. He muffled her scream with his hand. She felt the burning on her back as she awoke and fought away the tears.

She had cried enough. Now was the time for vengeance. Richard had come. She had known he would.

"Hurt bad?"

She nodded and sat up, her naked torso orange in the sunlight. She watched him stare at her breasts and smiled slightly.

"She did this to me," Ruth whispered. "Aurelia. She made him do it."

Richard looked at her, puzzled. He sat on the side of the bed and caressed her arm.

"They never dared punish me before," she said.

He raised his eyes from her breasts and faced her.

"Never. Now they have whipped me. Because of her."

Richard nodded, saddened at the pain in her eyes.

"We must get rid of her," Ruth said. "Then it will be the same again."

Richard's eyes widened. He shook his head no. She grabbed his chin and held it still.

"We must, or she will hurt us again. Thee cannot let her hurt me, Richard." She took his hand and held it in her lap. "Thee cannot. Not again. Ever."

Richard pulled his hand away and gazed out the window.

"I'm scared," he mumbled in his deep growling way, "of the Blessed Mother." He kept looking away from her. "Thee has been beaten. Thy place is gone. To hurt Aurelia again would only bring the Blessed Mother's wrath down upon us once more."

Ruth had never heard him admit he was scared before. She had always been able to manipulate him anyway she had wanted, but he had never been scared. She had gotten him to put the rat in the locker. When that didn't work, she had convinced him to steal the doll, and when she was done with it, nail it to the desk. His attitude made her wary.

Perhaps she would finally have to let him do it.

She pulled him closer, pushing one of his big hands down between her legs.

"What scares thee?"

Richard looked into her eyes. "Everything has changed. Thee has lost thy position, thy protection."

Ruth sat up and kissed him. "No, Richard. I'll protect thee. Have I not always protected thee before?"

Richard pulled back, shaking his head, remembering the shed.

"Yes, Richard. I will." She drew him to her. Her hand slid up his thigh. "Believe me, I have the power. Not her. I will show thee tonight. I will."

He felt the throbbing begin to build.

"Tonight, Richard. Do my bidding and I will protect thee. After that it will be like it used to be."

She began to unbutton his pants.

"Thee wants me, does thee not? Thee has always wanted me."

She pulled him down on the bed.

"Thee may have me now. But only if thee are with me."

Aurelia had not slept much that night. There had been too many questions. It all seemed so absolutely absurd, so totally impossible. And yet, after thinking about all that had happened already, it didn't seem nearly as ridiculous as it should have.

Thomas Borg could tell Aurelia was deeply immersed in her thoughts during breakfast and decided to leave her alone with them. He had said enough last night. She needed time to consider.

The poor girl, he thought, watching her barely eat, just push the eggs and sausages around on her plate. Perhaps he should not have overwhelmed her with so many revelations last night, but there was no other way.

"I'm going to take the lamb for a walk," she said suddenly. "First I'll check on Daddy, though." She arose and walked into her father's room. His eyes were open, but he still did not move or speak.

But he could eat solid food now, she reminded herself. That was a start. A good start.

She sat on the edge of the bed by his feet and smiled at him. She could have sworn she saw his eyes change slightly, almost brighten when she smiled.

"I don't know what to do anymore, Daddy." She squeezed his ankle, never taking her eyes from his. She thought for sure he could hear her then. "I'm scared. Please, Daddy, wake up." She shook his leg slightly. "Please. Help me. Tell me what to do. Thomas says I have some kind of power from being in the cave. That I got it from some lost children, or something . . . I don't know . . . the same as the Blessed Mother. But if she has a power I haven't seen it. And even if it is true, why me? Why not someone like Ruth? Or Joey? Someone who lives here and is part of their religion? Thomas says my albinism is the cause. The Blessed Mother, she's . . ." Aurelia squinted, trying to remember how she knew. It wasn't clear. "She's albino too, like the other children in the . . ." She rubbed her forehead. What other children? She didn't know what she had been about to say. She sat up straight and let go of his ankle. "Maybe I can help these people. I like them. Since you got hurt, they've all come over and been so kind to me." Aurelia smiled, embarrassed. "And I love Joey, Daddy. I really do. And Thomas, too."

Aurelia rose and walked to the door, then turned. Her face flushed with a quick surge of anger. "If she is responsible for hurting you, and for Mom's death, I'll . . . I'll get her. Nothing will stop me then. I'll do whatever I have to, but I'll destroy her." She squeezed the doorknob. "If it's true, I'll kill her if I have to."

After feeding the lamb, Aurelia tied it to a hemp rope, like a leash, and took it for a walk. Thomas watched her from the house. He decided to chop wood out back by the shed. They had enough wood for a few days, but he wanted the exercise. He needed to relax, and the exertion would help. He had been up all night, watching the windows and pacing through the house.

The axe descended with all the force he could muster.

It split the thick log like balsa wood, sending up chips like exploding shrapnel.

Perhaps he had pushed too hard, he thought, balancing the next log on the stump. What if his theory was wrong? If there was nothing the girl or any of them could do?

Thomas heaved his shoulders into the swing and the axe snapped through the log. Sweat poured over his face and down his body.

Perhaps, he thought, he was still taking the coward's way out. Like he did with Beth. It was she who had had the courage to stand against the Blessed Mother. He had not even gone after her when they took her into the cave and left her to die.

He lifted another sawed piece of wood onto the block. Now he was letting a girl fight his battle for him. *No*, he thought, *our battle. Beth's and mine.*

The axe cracked through the log.

But Aurelia had the power. He knew it. The cave had chosen her. The Blessed Mother knew it too. It was part of her plan. But could they turn the Blessed Mother's plan against her? The girl was willing. She had seen her mother's mutilated body. Lived with her father's paralysis. She certainly had the anger needed to stand against the Blessed Mother. But did she really have the power?

And did the Children of the Cave want to be saved? Or were they truly the Children of the Black One?

He heaved the axe, his arms flexed and tense, down through another piece of wood.

And did the people deserve salvation? They who had stood in fear for so long, feeding the cave its human sacrifices without doing anything to end such horror, such ungodly practices? Did they?

He slammed the axe into the stump and ran his thick fingers through his hair.

Or would their own sick fears and their terrible sins destroy them still? And in doing so, would they destroy an innocent girl as well?

Aurelia stayed with her father all evening. Thomas sat by the fire, drinking. He had opened the jug after he came in from chopping wood and had not put the cork back since, not even during dinner. And he had not spoken to Aurelia since breakfast, not even when he knew how disappointed she was that Joey had not come over that afternoon.

But no one had come today, not even Mr. Grotten or Mrs. Throm.

Something was going on, something bad, Thomas thought, swallowing another large gulp of whiskey. His mind was reeling. He could barely keep a thought long enough to absorb it.

He had felt the tension all day today. It was in the wind. The valley had been swept with a cold, ominous fear. It was everywhere.

Thomas leaned closer to the fire. He hadn't been able to get warm all day, even with the whiskey. But he did not want to tell Aurelia what he felt. There was nothing they could do to change things anyway.

Thomas's head began to grow heavy. It slowly sagged down until his chin rested on his chest. The whiskey spun him quickly towards unconsciousness.

Just before he passed out, he had the awful feeling that something was in the room with him, watching and waiting until he blacked out.

Aurelia awoke, kicking at her covers, sweating, the horror of the dream still fresh in her mind. She could still see one chilling vision.

A black-hooded shadow, blurred and distant, beckoning with its white, skeletal hand.

Was it beckoning her?

Or was she the eerie shadow beckoning another?

She couldn't decipher the vision. She wiped her forehead with the sheet and got up out of bed. The dark sky was cloud-ridden, hiding the moon. A gray fog churned, low and heavy, across the valley. It buried the land, hiding its life underneath it, fuming up like smoke, as if something were burning beneath the soil.

Aurelia stood at the open window. She glimpsed the lone figure from her dream standing in a field, its hollow eyes blank and unfocused, staring at her as the fog hungrily engulfed its form.

Then it was gone.

Suddenly she heard footsteps. Someone was near the house. She leaned sideways to peer out the top corner of the window.

A black shadow, bent low into the fog, disappeared into the trees. Aurelia wasn't even sure she had really seen it. It had happened so quickly and the night was so dark and foggy, and her dream had seemed so real.

She tiptoed to the door and opened it, wincing as it creaked. She slipped through its partial opening, adjusting her eyes to the darkness of the living room.

Thomas was asleep in the chair by the fireplace. She stepped around him and looked out through the porch towards the orphanage.

She could see that the barn was alight; a glow seeped the cracks in its walls. She wondered what could be going on so late at night. What horror, what punishment had the Blessed Mother concocted?

Quietly, she hurried back to her room and closed the door. Standing by the window, she searched the fog-heavy night.

In the dark, foreboding distance, she saw the figure in her dream again, watching her.

It beckoned her with a sweep of its black-cloaked arm.

"No," she moaned, backing away from the window. "Please, no."

The visions came at her again. Dark, shadowed faces flickered outside her window. Her body began to sway off-balance as if it were being shaken by an earthquake.

Aurelia spun around as the sharp pain shot through her stomach and down her thighs. She grabbed the bed post for support. Her body jerked in spasms again and again as if it were trying to regurgitate some wretched foulness from deep in her belly.

She squeezed the bed post, trying to fight whatever it was that churned through her body, so unrelentlessly mean and unforgiving.

"Please," she cried.

Suddenly her throat tightened and she couldn't unlock her jaw.

A howling swept through her mind.

Slowly, she let go of the post and stood up.

She walked to the window and climbed out. Her legs sank into the swirling gray mist.

Her mind was quiet then. There was no more pain.

She marched through the cold fog towards the cave.

Joey lay in bed, staring at the ceiling. He could not sleep. The wailing and chanting from the barn trembled throughout the orphanage. No one was sleeping. No one had been out of the orphanage all day. Fear clung to the halls like a cold greasy film.

Richard, fully clothed in the bed across the room, quietly arose. Joey did not move. Only his eyes followed Richard. The huge boy sneaked to the door, listened, then opened it and peeked out.

When he had closed the door behind him, Joey got

out of bed and put on his pants. He could hear the stairs creaking as Richard descended. It was the second time tonight Richard had sneaked out of the room.

Carefully, knowing where the sturdy floor boards were, Joey followed.

Halfway down the stairs, he stopped and crouched. Ruth came out of the shadows to meet Richard. She whispered something to him and he nodded. The pair, holding hands, hurried down the stairs to the first floor. Joey followed.

He watched them leave out the back door in the kitchen. They left it open. He edged to the doorway.

Lights flickered in the barn. Low, moaning chants pounded like drums in the night. Strange, slapping noises kept beat with the heavy chants.

Joey crept outside. The clouds darkened the night. The fog slithered up the back steps. Slowly, he entered the swirling mist. The black night engulfed him, hiding him, making it seem safe enough to walk across the grounds without being detected.

Squinting, he saw Richard and Ruth disappear around the barn, following the cliffs.

The Blessed Mother's voice rang out. Joey sucked in a breath and didn't move. He waited. No one had seen him.

She was preaching in the barn.

"Thy doubts have fouled the blood of our fathers, the blood of our children. Surely, thee must repent thy sins. Thy Redeemer has come, as I have foretold. In my likeness shall she guide thee. Cry out before God Almighty."

The people in the barn repeated her words. The dull whacking thuds continued.

Cold sweat trickled down Joey's ribs. He knew he should go back inside. But he had to see. He had to know what the terrible pounding was. Staying low in the fog, he sneaked to the far end of the barn where the small door to the lambs' pen was.

The chanting grew louder. The thuds turned into biting snaps. Joey peered over the grounds. No one was keeping watch outside.

Carefully, he opened the small door. Most of the people of the valley were inside. The Blessed Mother stood above them on a wooden platform, her arms outstretched, calling to them to repent.

Joey's mouth fell open. The people were naked from their waists up. Short leather straps with hard leather-bound balls, dangled from their hands.

"For the sin in thy hearts," the Blessed Mother cried out, "repent. There is no other salvation from thy wickedness. Thy sins are with thee still."

The people repeated her words. Then they swung the leather-balled whips over their shoulders, flagellating their naked backs.

Joey muffled a scream and stepped away, stunned.

"The Children of the Cave demand thy sacrifice."

The whips flew again, snapping against the people's spines.

Joey stared, mesmerized by the horror.

He did not see the huge shadow move behind him.

Ruth shoved her torch into the mud. It lit up the cave with dancing light.

"Tie it there." She pointed.

Richard lifted the frightened albino lamb onto the short, flat stone. It kicked wildly, its pink eyes darting from Ruth to Richard and back again. It could smell their hatred and knew by instinct it was doomed. It must flee or die.

Then it felt its feet yanked together. No longer could

it kick its hind legs. They were useless.

Richard tied the front legs to the hind ones, then backed away.

The lamb was sprawled helplessly on its side. Its wide, terrified eyes watched Ruth.

"Cave spirits," she called. The gray mist outside washed into the mouth of the cave curling around their knees. "Choose me, as I was chosen before. I offer thee this sacrifice to prove my worth, my faith. With this blood, shall I be delivered. Let thine eyes see my devotion. Know that I believe. That I am the one to follow thee. To do thy bidding."

From her robe she removed a long curved knife.

"I have been sorely punished," she cried. "Let the blood of the lamb cleanse me. Let thy vengeance be mine. Praise be to the spirits. Glory to the cave."

Ruth plunged the sharp blade into the lamb's belly. It kicked fitfully and cried out. The knife slit through its chest and up its neck. Blood boiled out in a pool across the rocks.

The lamb was still. Its guts flopped out, gray and purple, into the warm, red pool.

Ruth put the bloody knife back into her robe and knelt down in the mist before the rock.

"Anoint me tonight," she cried. "Thy kingdom has come. Thy will be done." Scooping up a handful of blood, she poured it over her upraised head. It spilled across her face, dripping down her shoulders and breasts.

Suddenly, from the big tunnel behind them, a screeching howl erupted into the mouth of the cave. It was as if the cavern itself had been stabbed and was screaming in agony.

Richard clutched his chest with both hands, backing away.

It howled again.

Ruth's face turned ashen. The blood still dripped from her cheeks as she fell, petrified, into the thick gray mist.

"No," she moaned. "I came to please thee."

Again, the cave howled like a wounded animal.

Ruth screamed. She began to crawl through the mist.

Richard dashed outside and tripped over a rock in the fog. He was shaking so badly he couldn't get up.

A putrid stench, like rotting flesh, blew out from the tunnel. It made Ruth gag.

The cave howled again. The horrid stench seemed to cover her, sticking to her like the lamb's blood on her face.

"Please," she cried. "Please, no."

She crawled frantically. Vomit heaved up into her throat. She tried to choke it down, but couldn't.

"Please," she moaned, between gut-twisting spasms. "Do not . . ."

Her arms and legs shuddered. She fell on her belly and began to claw at the mud to escape the horror.

"Richard," she cried, weakly. "Richard."

She dragged herself through her own vomit toward the mouth of the cave.

Joey gulped, unable to fathom the terror before him. Suddenly he realized the danger he faced if he were discovered. He backed away from the small door and looked into the darkness surrounding him.

The Blessed Mother cried out again. With each terrible thud, Joey shuddered.

He backed far away into the mist. Carefully feeling the ground before each step, he circled towards the back door of the orphanage.

He was grateful for the mist and the black-clouded sky. The only lights near him were the long yellow slits coming from the cracks in the barn.

He eased between two big trees. It was open ground from there to the door. Joey held his breath and listened.

Suddenly a huge hand dug into his shoulder.

He screamed.

The chanting stopped. Cold, deathly silence enveloped him.

He twisted to free himself and tried to run. Another hand grabbed his hair and yanked him off the ground. Searing pain shot through his head.

The front doors of the barn banged open. The light from inside spread out to the trees, illuminating his dangling body.

The Blessed Mother shuffled towards him. He felt her staring at him through her black veil. He kicked once but was squeezed even tighter. He went limp, hoping to ease the pain.

"I . . . I was looking for . . ."

She raised her hand in front of his face.

Suddenly he was yanked higher in the air. He felt as if his hair were being torn from his head.

CHAPTER XIII

JOEY HUNCHED down in the blackness of the small closet he was locked in. He had no idea how much time had passed. Each horrifying second was an eternity. His imagination overwhelmed him. In his mind he kept hearing Richard's terrible screams from the shed. He pictured in gruesome detail what the mute must have done to him.

Then he heard something. Distant whispers. Soft, shuffling feet.

Thunder boomed again. He clutched himself, curling tighter into a ball on the hard floor. The heavy pelting rain splattered against the walls. The storm had grown furious.

The children had been awakened early. They knew, without speaking, that something horrible was going to happen. Their whispers quickly faded as they dressed, each too frightened to voice his fears.

They gathered in the first floor hall. Many exchanged glances, peeking constantly at Richard and Ruth who stayed at one end, close together, away from the others. The orphans could see their apprehension by the way the couple openly clung to one another, and they wondered if Ruth and Richard were the ones to be punished.

The Blessed Mother descended the stairs. The children bowed their heads and waited.

The mute strode towards them. They parted quickly to let him pass untouched. He was not dragging Ruth or Richard with him. The children gulped, almost as one, their small hands clutching at their clothes. If it was not Richard or Ruth, who was it?

It could be any one of them now.

The Blessed Mother opened the big front doors. Lightning cracked above them. Thunder bellowed, shaking the ceiling. One small boy screamed, then covered his mouth, as startled by the sound as the others were.

The Blessed Mother pointed her skinny, black-gloved hand outside. The mute herded the children towards her. Falling into each other, grabbing limbs to regain balance, they pushed forward.

The rain splashed down so thick it looked like a wall. They couldn't see the barn through it. They shuffled down the front steps and walked, tightly grouped, towards the shed. Then they halted. Dawn's dark twilight was just beginning.

Remaining in the doorway, the Blessed Mother held up her hands. Lightning flared. This time its long, skeleton-like white fingers darted at the cliffs and exploded into a tree. Smoke puffed out into a cloud. Half the tree cracked, twisted, and fell to the earth.

Then they heard the desperate, pleading cries.

The mute yanked Joey by the arm, around the Blessed Mother, into the rain. The smaller children grabbed each other's hands instinctively. The rain oozed down their faces. They huddled closer, needing to feel the warmth of other wet bodies against their own.

"He has sinned against us," the Blessed Mother

shouted over the heavy pounding rain. "Like the Devil, the snake of Eden, he has slithered in the darkness to spy upon a Holy ceremony. For this, he must be cleansed or forever lose his soul to the fires of the Horned One. Glory to God's forgiveness. In his punishment, so shall he be delivered."

She pointed at the gray shed. The mute dragged Joey towards it.

Once inside, he knew there would be no escape. All the horrible tortures he had imagined in the choking blackness of the closet flashed through his head. He had to try something . . . anything.

Please Lord, he prayed, give me strength. Help me escape. Surely, this is not Thy way.

Joey felt his shoulder nearly being ripped from its socket.

He screamed as loudly as he could and clutched the arm the mute was pulling. The huge fingers loosened. The mute glanced back at the Blessed Mother, startled by the scream.

Joey's body went limp. He closed his eyes. The mute felt the dead weight and let go. Joey fell like a rag doll into the mud. One eye opened slightly.

The mute stared down at him, puzzled, then looked back at the Blessed Mother. Seeing the confused look on his face, Joey decided it was then or never. His trick had worked so far. The mute, thinking he had broken the boy's arm, that he had passed out from the pain, kept staring at the Blessed Mother apologetically.

Joey rolled away and leaped up. The mute jumped forward and grabbed the tail of the boy's shirt. Joey tumbled forward. The shirt ripped and he dashed for the forest. He could hear the Blessed Mother screaming and the splashing of the mute's footsteps behind him in the mud. Joey did not look back. He ran for his life, his heart stabbing at his ribs.

He did not stop running until he crashed through the thick bushes before the woods near the cliffs. He could not hear the mute anymore. He glanced back and tripped over a rock. The mute was twenty yards behind him and slowing down.

Joey yanked himself up and leaped over the rock, then zigzagged through the trees. He kept running until he reached the edge of the cliffs.

There was only one way to go now. He began to climb.

He would be safe if he could scale the cliffs. He could hide in the dense woods of the mountain above and no one would find him.

The steep rock wall was wet and slippery. Twenty-five feet up, between two rocks, his foot slid on a muddy crevasse. He clutched the sharp hump of the rock above him as his feet flew out from underneath him. Dangling, holding on desperately with the last of his ebbing strength, he glanced down.

Directly below, the mute stared up at him, waiting for his fall.

Aurelia did not awaken at the usual time in the morning. Thomas decided it was good she could sleep and left about noon to feed the livestock at his farm. He was worried, though. The feeling he had had yesterday had not gone away.

And again today no one had come to Aurelia's. Two days in a row the people had avoided the girl. It was a bad sign.

He stopped at Ezekiel Throm's farm on his way home. None of Throm's children or even Ezekiel were in the fields planting. That was not like them. They were always hard-working and conscientious about spring planting.

He pulled back the reins and got out of the buggy. It was still raining hard.

"Hello," he called, ambling up to the house.

Mrs. Throm hurried out of the front door and put a finger to her lips to quiet him.

"What is the matter?" Thomas whispered.

"Ezekiel is with the children. They have gone to the old church to pray. Others are there too."

"But why?" Thomas wiped his wet hands on his pants. His head was still clouded and pounding from yesterday's whiskey. He could smell its stale, sour odor in his sweat. His shirt was soaked under his jacket. It was not because of the rain.

"The Blessed Mother called the people together last night for the Act of Cleansing and Redemption."

Thomas brushed the rain off his forehead and took a deep breath. He felt dizzy, and apprehensive of what she said.

"But that is only to be performed before the Holy Ceremony. The ceremony of the Chosen One."

"I am frightened, Thomas," Gertrude Throm said as she walked him back to his buggy. "Thee was not asked to go. Nor I. Nor any of those who have spoken as thee has about the girl."

Mr. Borg shook his head, staring down at the wheel sinking in the mud. "I have stayed close to her. She is strong. She believes what I told her."

"I hope that it is true."

It was then that Thomas Borg realized he was doing the same thing he had done fifteen years ago. Here he stood, as terrified as one of the orphans of being punished. He would not let himself fall that far down again. He had had a hard enough time living with the memories of his earlier cowardice. He would not endure that again.

Thomas clenched his fists. "The girl has been chosen. Already the cave speaks to her. It calls her. If we are ever to end the horror in which we live—or should I say, grovel—it is now. Now, Gertrude, or we may never again hold our heads up with pride, hold up our eyes to heaven to pray to our God, the God we have forsaken for so many years."

"That is dangerous talk, Thomas."

"Those are the only words I have left. I speak them for my Beth."

"Bless her dear soul." Gertrude bowed slightly. "Perhaps thee are right. I will stand by thee. But not alone. Tomorrow, at the old church, I will tell those who have lost a loved one, who will not avert their eyes at such talk, to meet us there." She took a deep breath and stared over the hill at the pointed roof of the orphanage. "Perhaps the time has come."

"The girl shall bring us salvation. It must be so. She has the power, although she understands it not. Perhaps, finally, the children have forgiven us. Aurelia will set us free."

"I pray thee are right, Thomas."

Thomas Borg pulled himself up into his buggy. Mrs. Throm backed away. Her clothes were soaked from the rain. A cold wind blew over her and she shivered.

"And if not, Gertrude, what has changed? At least the girl brings us hope. Without that, what is life worth?"

She nodded. "Thee has a point. It will help give the others strength. It is easiest to be brave when one has nothing more to lose. Go with God, Thomas. I hope Beth's dream has finally been answered."

Aurelia awoke in the middle of the afternoon. Her head felt empty. She rubbed her temples in tiny circles.

She had had another nightmare about the cave. She

had felt a great surge of power, a sheer terrifying energy emerge from within her very being.

And a terrible hate.

Hate for those who had cruelly destroyed that which she loved. In her dream, she had brought the wrath of the cave down upon them and sent them slithering away, begging for their lives.

But who were they? What had they done? She could not remember.

Aurelia shoved the covers off and sat upright, placing her feet on the cold wood floor. As she started to stand, a stinging feeling shot up her legs. She fell back on the bed.

Her feet were dirty and cut and bloody. Her nightgown was mud-caked and torn.

Aurelia's head sank into her hands. She closed her eyes. It had happened again, she thought. But where had she gone? What had she done?

And the nightmare, was it really a dream?

Aurelia limped to the bathtub. Thomas had filled it hours ago. The water was barely tepid. She took off her nightgown and underwear and slipped into the water.

It was cold and felt awful, but she was too tired to heat more water. She took the rag, lathered it and began to scrub her feet over and over again as if that act would somehow cleanse her of the terror she now felt.

She scrubbed her feet until they stung. The pain felt good to her. It cleared her head of the strange, haunting visions.

What could be worse than this? she wondered. Worse than having pieces of your own existence lost forever in a dark, forboding realm of the unknown? An unknown where nightmares and reality become as one and cannot be separated even by the light of day?

Joey ran, hunched low behind the bushes until he

reached the edge of the woods beyond the cliffs, by the road that led back towards Aurelia's house. He checked the open fields past the road. No one was in sight. From the cliffs, earlier, he had seen that the fields were empty of workers. But how could that be? The farmers worked, even in the rain, he thought. That scared him. He felt as if the whole valley was hiding, waiting for him to appear so they could pounce on him and drag him back to the shed and the mute and the whip.

Joey crawled on his hands and knees through the grass, his head constantly darting like a cat's, watching for any movement.

He had pulled himself up on the wet rocks of the cliff after he had slipped, but the mute had not followed. For a long time, he had watched the mute sneak along the bottom of the cliffs. But then the mute had left. Joey had waited until he was out of sight, then ran along the bottom of the steep mountain above the cliffs until he had neared the river and the heavily wooded hill that edged back down to the valley floor.

Joey stood up when he could see no one was around Aurelia's house and ran across the open fields. He knew he had to chance it. Even crawling in the long grass, he could have easily been spotted, the grass was matted down so from the wind and rain.

He ran to the back of the house and checked in the windows. He didn't see anyone, not even Mr. Borg. Pressing tight to the wall, he slipped around the corner and peeked in Aurelia's room. The blankets were flung down on the bed. The room was empty. He edged further along the house and looked in her father's room.

Aurelia was sitting on the bed, feeding her father something from a bowl.

Joey lightly tapped the glass. Aurelia gasped, almost

dropping the bowl. He waved and she quickly opened the window.

"What are you doing out—"

Joey held up his hand. "Is anyone else here?"

"No, but—"

"I ran away." Joey was breathing hard. He gulped. "They were going to beat me. I . . . I saw the people last night, half-naked . . ." Joey's frightened, tired eyes peered up at Aurelia's. ". . . whipping themselves. And chanting. I saw them."

"Get in out of the rain." Aurelia pushed the window further open. Joey threw one leg over and pulled himself inside. He was soaking wet. When he stepped onto the floor, his shoes squished loudly.

"I have to hide." He rubbed his arms hard. For the first time today, he realized how cold he was. His body ached all over.

"Put on some of Daddy's clothes. You'll get sick like that. I'll wait in the living room."

Aurelia closed the door after her and put more wood on the fire.

Somehow what Joey had told her did not seem strange to her. Nothing seemed strange anymore. Her world had fallen apart and now . . .

Now, she thought, stacking the logs back into the flames, I live in a world so bizarre that I don't even doubt, for one minute, that I have been wandering around at night, although I can't remember where or what happened, and I don't doubt the crazy things Thomas told me about the cave and the children's spirits and the power.

Aurelia flipped the log over. Flames lapped at it hungrily. The fire crackled as the moist bark was consumed.

What the hell was wrong with her? Aurelia paced

back and forth by the fireplace. She couldn't believe what she was doing—simply accepting everything people told her . . . spirits, people whipping themselves, possession. . . .

Joey opened the door and walked into the living room. Her father's pants were belted tight to keep them up. The legs ballooned out below the waist like clown's pants. The shirt hung like a tent from his thin frame. The sleeves had to be rolled up just to free his hands.

Aurelia stopped pacing and stared. Suddenly it all seemed so ridiculous. Seeing Joey standing there in those clothes, his hair wet and matted on his head, his frightened, questioning face becoming embarrassed because of how she was looking at him—it just seemed so damn funny. Ridiculously, hysterically funny.

Aurelia started to laugh. She couldn't stop. She just kept laughing. She had to bend over, her stomach hurt so much from laughing.

But it really wasn't funny. She had tried to make it so; hoped, to God, something about it was. But it wasn't. The laughter choked in her throat.

And then she was crying.

It was a dark afternoon. The storm clouds collided, low and heavy, in the sky. Rain pelted the roof of the house. Joey sat by the front window, watching the road and the fields.

Aurelia warmed up some milk, put it in the baby bottle and went back into the living room. The big fire kept the room warm and bright in the oppressive afternoon.

"I hope Thomas fed the lamb this morning," she said, opening the porch door. "I forgot until now. Usually she lets me know when she's hungry. Thomas fixed a little pen for her in the corner of the porch yesterday."

Aurelia walked out to the wire-mesh pen. The hay

was pushed up into a little nest, but the lamb was gone.

"Joey," she called, searching the porch and the grounds outside.

He stepped out the door. "What?"

"The lamb's gone." Aurelia looked at him frantically.

"I will check out back. Maybe it is in the shed. Maybe Mr. Borg put it there because thee was sleeping."

"My father has a raincoat. I'll get it for you." She returned and he put it on. His hands disappeared in the sleeves.

"It couldn't have gotten out by itself. The chicken wire was too high and the door's still latched."

Joey could see the pain growing in her eyes. He wished he could do something to stop it. She did not need this. She was at the breaking point already. He wanted to say something positive, something reassuring, but he knew if the lamb was gone, it had to have been stolen, just like her doll. He tapped the screen door for a moment, then hurried around the house to the shed.

Aurelia checked all the rooms in the house.

Ruth had taken it. She was sure of it.

Aurelia felt sick as she walked into her father's room. She couldn't even cry. She had cried herself out. An awful numbness crept over her. She sat on the end of her father's bed and breathed deeply, staring at him. At that moment, she was past caring about his condition. It was easier to block out all her emotions, than to let them overcome her again.

What else could they do to her?

The growing numbness prickled underneath her skin. She welcomed it. It brought a strange relief to feel that nothing mattered anymore. She couldn't be hurt then. That was the only thing that mattered.

Joey hurried into the room, shaking the rain off the coat.

"It's not out back," he said. Aurelia did not look at him. She just sat, slumped over, holding herself up limply with one arm, staring at her father.

Joey quietly backed out of the room and put the coat on the hall tree by the front door. He stoked the fire and added another log. It was best to leave her alone then. He paced the living room, keeping watch out the front and back windows. The depth of his dilemma sank in as he paced. He had nowhere to go. He couldn't return to the orphanage. The punishment would be even more severe. But what else could he do?

Run away, he thought, out of the Valley.

The idea petrified him. Aurelia and Sam Hill were the only outsiders he had ever met. How would he live out there, in the other world? He would be alone, and no one would care what happened to him.

Joey leaned forward, a hand on either side of the front window, and watched the gray, stormy sky.

I cannot hide here forever, he thought. I have no other choice but to run. Run away. Far from this valley and the Blessed Mother's cruel influence.

And Aurelia should go with me. If she does not, something even more terrible will happen to her. It is destined to be so if she remains.

Joey pushed off the window frame and marched into Sam's room.

"We have to get out of here," he announced. "There is no time left. We must go. Now."

Aurelia stroked her father's foot as she slowly looked back over her shoulder. "I can't leave Daddy. When he's able to move, we'll go. Not before."

"It will be too late." Joey gently put his hand on her shoulder. "We cannot help thy father by staying. We will come back for him. Mr. Borg and Mr. Grotten will care for him as they have already."

"I can't, Joey. I can't leave him."

"Yes you can," a low voice muttered.

Aurelia's head snapped towards her father. "Daddy?"

Sam's eyelids half-closed, then opened. "Listen to Joey." His words were barely audible. His mouth hardly moved when he spoke. "You must leave."

Tears of joy streamed down Aurelia's cheeks. The prickly numbness was gone instantly. She jumped up and sat close to his head, caressing his face and hair.

"Daddy, how do you feel?" She bent down and carefully hugged him, then kissed his forehead. "Oh, Daddy, I'm so glad you can talk. You're all right now. You're going to be fine." She wiped away the tears as her face lit up in a huge, quivering grin. "Can you move?" She tapped his forearm. "Can you feel that?"

"Yes." Using all his willpower, Sam smiled. "A little. And I can move my fingers. That's about it, though."

"You'll get better real quick. Mr. Grotten put you in traction because you hurt your spine. You're all strapped in, that's why you can't move. But you'll be fine. Just fine."

"I don't think so," Sam whispered.

Aurelia leaned down, her ear to his mouth. "What?"

"I said, I won't be well soon." He knew it wasn't the straps that keep him from moving or even feeling his legs. "You must go. Get out of the valley at once."

She slowly shook her head. Tears poured down her face again. "I won't leave you. I won't."

"Aurelia," he whispered.

She kept shaking her head. "I won't. I won't."

"Aurelia." He said it as loud as he could. She leaned closer. "The only way to save me is to get help. Go with Joey. To the next town—the last one we were in before we came down out of the mountains. Get the police. And an ambulance. It's the only way. You must do it."

Aurelia sat up and stared at her father. "But—"

"No buts. It's the only way. Go. Now. Please. It's the . . ." Sam's eyes slowly closed. ". . . only . . ."

"Daddy?" Aurelia held his cheeks with both hands. "Daddy?"

He did not answer.

Joey reached down and lifted Aurelia from the bed.

"He is right," he said. "We will bring back help." When she just kept staring at her father, he turned her around and held her shoulders until she looked up at him. "Thee must do as thy father said. He knows best."

Slowly, she nodded in agreement.

Joey wrapped up some sandwiches and fruit in one of Sam's shirts. He filled a bottle with water, fastened a cord around its top and tied it to his belt.

Aurelia put on her hiking boots and raincoat.

"I'm going to leave Thomas a note."

"No," Joey barked.

"He has to know. So he'll stay here with Daddy."

"If someone else finds it, they will follow us. We need time to get away before they realize we are gone."

"I have to, Joey. We'll take that chance. I'll put it in the pen, in the straw. Thomas will find it. No one else will look there."

"If thee must." Joey tied the bundled shirt, containing food, with a cord, and looped it over his head and under one arm. "Let us hurry. It will be dark soon. We must get to the main road in the mountains by then. The one thee came down on."

Joey put on Sam's big raincoat. Aurelia quickly wrote a note and placed it in the pen.

"I have some rain hats," she said. She ran to her room and brought back two shiny, plastic, wide-brimmed hats. She handed him one, then picked up the big flashlight from the table next to the hall tree.

"We will head for the woods to the north. Keep inside its perimeters until we get to the east end of the valley. Then we will cut over the hill to the base of the mountain and follow the road from there." Joey hurried to the kitchen door. He opened it and looked back at her seriously. "It will not be easy. I know not how far the next town is."

"About twenty-five miles through the mountains," Aurelia said. "Let's go."

The real storm hit right after the sun set. The night was pitch black except when the lightning struck. For a moment their surroundings would flare into light, and then they would freeze, scanning the woods ahead.

It took two hours to get to the hill in front of the mountain. Rain poured down its slopes, coming together in small rivers between the trees.

It was hard walking. The ground was slippery. Climbing the hill, they fell often, slipping down the steep slope, then pulling themselves back up using the small trees for support.

"Are thee tired?" Joey helped Aurelia up the last muddy incline. They were on the top of the hill.

"I'm all right." She brushed the mud from her coat and pants. Joey untied the water bottle and passed it to her. Before she could unscrew the top, thunder exploded just above them. Lightning instantly flashed down in a branch-like line only fifty yards behind them. Aurelia dropped the bottle when the lightning struck.

Joey picked it up and held it for her as she drank. He tied it back on his belt and checked the downward slope of the hill with the flashlight.

"It will be easier going down. It is a gradual decline. Then we will be by the road at the base of the mountain. It will be easy walking from there."

At the bottom of the hill, they turned east and soon

arrived at the muddy road below the mountain. They stopped there and sat on an old fallen tree. Joey turned off the flashlight and watched Aurelia in the darkness. She had been breathing heavily for the last half-hour. Her whole body was trembling now.

"Are thee all right?"

"A little cold, I guess." Aurelia shivered and hugged herself. Joey put his arm around her. He could feel her heart beating hard and fast against his side. He decided to wait until her pulse slowed before going on. He squeezed her shoulders and wiped a drop of rain from the tip of her nose.

She looked up at him and he smiled. She put her arms around his chest and leaned her head on his wet, slippery coat. He did not move until her body stopped shaking.

"Are thee ready?" He adjusted the shirt full of food under his raincoat.

"Let's go." She jumped off the fallen tree. Her knees buckled, but she caught herself on an upturned branch, hoping Joey hadn't noticed.

She had been fighting that familiar sick feeling inside ever since they had gotten to the top of the last hill. It had begun to cause cramps in her stomach again. The pain almost doubled her over when she finally let go of the branch.

The dizziness had been coming in spurts. But it was happening more frequently now as the cramps had gotten worse. Twice, coming down the hill, she almost blacked out from the searing pain.

Aurelia adjusted her hat and looked at Joey. He had just turned on the flashlight and was shining it up the twisting road ahead. A stream ran down its low side. It was getting wider by the minute. He glanced back. She tried to smile as another cramp tore through her belly.

Joey smiled back and headed up the high section of the muddy road.

Aurelia coughed. She could only breathe in short gulps before the pain hit. She threw her shoulders back and hurried along at his side.

They walked up the mountain road. The storm was getting even worse. The cold wind howled through the trees, blowing down the road into their wet faces. The rain felt like small stones as it hit their skin.

Another cramp ripped through Aurelia. She grabbed Joey's arm to keep from falling. He stopped and held her as she bent over, gasping for air.

"Are thee sick?"

"I'm all right." She pulled herself upright by his arm.

"We will rest after the next bend."

She nodded, too weak to speak.

With the crying wind and the branches, like monstrous fingers, constantly grabbing at them, she began to imagine things again in the darkness—eyes watching from the woods, and horrible, screaming voices in the wind.

Joey supported most of her weight as they turned the next bend. He felt her body stiffen often, then quiver badly. He stopped and looked at her.

"No," Aurelia moaned. "We must go on. Get out of here quickly, before they . . . they . . ."

She covered her face with her arms and screamed. Joey caught her before she fell into the river by the road. He kept hold until she straightened up on her own.

"I'm fine. Just a stomach ache." Clutching her belly, she started to walk. She waved at him. "Come on."

Joey shined the flashlight past her, down the road. Two glowing yellow eyes peered back at them in the light.

"Aurelia. Wait." He ran next to her.

"We can't stop," she said.

"But . . ." Joey shined the light where he had seen the eyes.

The bloody head of the lamb was impaled on the top of a stake in the middle of the road. Its black sunken eyes stared back at them in the bright light.

Aurelia's body twisted slightly, then dropped onto the road. Joey sat her up. She felt as limp as a sack of cotton in his arms.

"Aurelia?" He shook her anxiously. "Aurelia?"

She flopped about in his arms, her head bobbing loosely on her chest. She did not respond.

Joey heard a buggy approaching in the storm. Lifting her under the arms, he dragged her off the road into the trees.

The buggy slid around the bend and headed towards them.

"Joey?" a voice cried out. "Aurelia?"

It was Mr. Borg. Joey sat Aurelia against a big tree trunk and ran out to the road.

"Mr. Borg," he shouted.

Thomas pulled the reins back and leaped out of his buggy. "Where is Aurelia?"

Lightning cracked bright above them on the mountain top.

"She fainted." Joey pointed the flashlight up the road. Thomas saw the lamb's head.

"God forgive us all," he muttered under his breath.

Joey ran back to the woods, scooped Aurelia up in his arms and brought her to the buggy. Thomas lifted her up onto the seat.

Joey jumped up and held her. Saliva dribbled out the side of her open mouth. Her body twitched like a dying animal's. Joey hugged her tight against his chest, squeezing her each time she convulsed.

"We must get her to a dry, warm place," Thomas said, turning the buggy around.

"But we have to keep going. Her father told us we must leave the valley. We must go and get help."

Thomas flipped the reins and the horse began to trot towards the valley.

"We have to get her home," Thomas cried, trying to speak over the howling wind. He looked down at the girl. Lightning flashed, and the road lit up. Her pretty face contorted in an agony only she knew, an agony deep inside her soul.

"Too late," Thomas whispered. Joey couldn't hear him over the storm. "She should have known it was too late for this."

CHAPTER XIV

AURELIA RAN a finger lightly across her father's forehead. His skin was hot to the touch. He did not open his eyes. She had been waiting all morning for him to awake, to speak to her again, but to no avail.

Joey and Thomas were in the living room, discussing Sam's condition. Thomas had fed Sam early, while both teenagers had slept. Sam was getting worse. He had had a fever since late yesterday. It was rising, but Thomas had not told Aurelia. It hardly seemed fair to burden her with more, after what she had been through last night, especially since she thought Sam was recovering so well after he had spoken to her.

Aurelia heard them whispering outside the door, but couldn't make out their words. She leaned down and kissed her father's cheek, then arose and walked to the doorway.

"I am sending Joey for Mr. Grotten. I know it is dangerous for him to go, but thy father must be checked on again." Thomas nodded to the boy. Joey quickly glanced at Aurelia and left. He knew why he was going. Thomas had just told him about the fever and about Aurelia's mother's death. Because of what had happened last night, he had thought the boy should know.

Aurelia walked over to the front window and peered out through the screened porch. The morning sun shone bright on the wet grass and the budding leaves of the trees. Again, no one was working in the fields.

The deserted valley, in its glistening beauty, only looked eerie and cold to Aurelia. It was like a painting, well-drawn, with good strong colors, yet totally lacking warmth or any artistic spark, leaving it bland and empty in appearance.

"He's getting worse, isn't he?" Aurelia turned from the window to face Thomas.

"He has a fever. It started last night. That is why I went after thee."

"But why did he seem better finally?" She bowed her head and rubbed above her eyes, then peered at Thomas again. "He spoke to me yesterday. That meant he was getting better."

"Perhaps the fever brought him out of his shock when it began. It could have jolted his system. I do not know. Only God knows why these things happen." Sam wondered how the girl had stood up to all that had happened to her since her mother's death. He was in awe of her courage, her inner strength, but he wondered how much more she could take. He hoped her strength had not yet reached its limit. There was something else he had to explain to her before she attempted something foolish again as she had last night.

Aurelia opened the front door. A warm breeze blew across her face, circling in through the living room. She breathed in its freshness.

"Thee should not have run away," he said to her back.

She looked over her shoulder. "Daddy wanted me to."

"He does not understand. Thee does not either. I had thought thee did."

Aurelia walked to the big chair near the fireplace, put her hands on its high back and leaned forward, straight-armed, as she stared at Thomas.

"Go on."

"I think thee should sit first."

Aurelia's arms tensed. She shifted her weight to the other foot. "I don't have to sit. Please, go on."

There was no subtle way to put it. Thomas decided to be blunt.

"Thy mother tried to run away."

"And she succeeded." Aurelia's fingers dug into the top of the chair.

"Did she?" Thomas glanced sadly at the girl's pleading eyes.

Aurelia stepped slowly around the chair and sat down, staring pensively at the cold, gray coals in the fireplace.

"In sixteen years, she never returned here. She married Daddy. She had me. She . . ." Aurelia's head sunk down into her hands. Her fingers began to go numb while they cradled her face. She had felt as if nothing more could hurt her. But it could.

"Thy mother had been taken to the cave by the Blessed Mother just as thee was. She, too, was Chosen. She, too, felt the pain. Had the visions. Heard the voices. She, too, tried to run away from the valley. But what was inside her, she could never run from. It drove her insane. Killed her, as it would have thee if thee had gone."

Aurelia felt her last remnants of hope being dashed like storm-driven ocean waves against a rocky cliff. Thomas watched the girl's head sink lower between her shoulders. She was beyond crying. She sat still and silent, staring blankly at the dark fireplace.

Thomas put his thick hand on her shoulder. She did not respond.

"All is not lost, Aurelia." He waited, but she would not look up. He knelt down in front of her and turned her face towards his. "The spirits of the children call to thee. They have chosen thee to succeed the Blessed Mother, to end her reign. She killed thy mother. She has murdered many in the valley. Thee can destroy her. They have given thee that potential. We shall all be set free."

Aurelia's weary eyes searched Thomas's. "How do you know that?"

"There is no other explanation." Thomas stood up so she wouldn't see the doubt in his eyes. "It must be so. We have no alternative. There is no other escape."

Aurelia rocked in the chair on the porch. Mr. Grotten had been with her father for a long time. It must be bad, she thought. The chair squeaked. She rocked even harder, staring across the fields and road at the orphanage.

Her sorrow had ended. Her knuckles turned whiter as she held the arms of the chair.

The old woman had killed Aurelia's mother. Crippled her father. Killed Joey's parents. Thomas's wife. Her eyes narrowed in the bright glare of the sun reflecting off the front walls of the orphanage. What Thomas said was true. She had no choice. Almost all that was dear to her had been destroyed. Somehow she must end it before all that she loved was gone.

If she didn't stop the Blessed Mother, what would the old woman do? She had already tried to have Joey beaten. She would come back and attempt to take him away from her. Aurelia was sure the Blessed Mother prayed for her father's death. She wanted to leave Aurelia nothing, no alternatives. She believed, in that way, Aurelia would have no choice but to obey her.

She does not understand me, Aurelia thought. If she takes all that I love away, I will have only hate left. Hate for her and nothing to lose. Not even my life, for my life is worthless without love.

The chair cried out under her as she rocked. Mr. Grotten walked out onto the porch. She immediately stopped rocking and searched his face for any clue as to her father's condition.

"Thy father has a high fever. It is a complication I had hoped would not happen. Perhaps there are internal injuries. There is no abdominal swelling or discoloration, but . . ." Mr. Grotten sighed, walked to the porch door, then turned. "We can only wait and see. The fever may break." Aurelia stared at him. He tried to meet her gaze, but couldn't. He fiddled with his bag of medicines. "It is in God's hands now. I will pray for thy father. He has the prayers of many in the Valley. God will hear them."

Aurelia, her lips drawn tight, said nothing as she watched him leave. There is one who prays against it, she thought. Prayers alone are not the answer. It is time to act.

She could feel Thomas and Joey watching her from inside the doorway. She slammed a fist down on the arm of the rocker and got up. She did not look at either of them. The way was clear. There was only one thing to do. She stomped to the door and swung it open. It cracked on the porch's wooden frame.

Without turning, she spoke. "I'm going to the cave. I must know what they want of me. How I am to destroy her."

Before Joey could voice an objection, Thomas grabbed his arm and shook his head.

Terrified, Joey watched in silence as Aurelia marched towards the cliffs.

It was night when Aurelia came out of the mouth of the cave. Sitting alone in the black-draped buggy, the Blessed Mother watched. Slowly her gloved hand drew back the curtain.

"I have heard the children," the old woman said.

Aurelia stopped near the buggy.

"Thee has gone to them on thy own. It is good."

Aurelia stared, her face solemn.

"Does thee remember now? Does thee know thy destiny? Why the children have called thee?"

Aurelia gazed into the veil, her jaw clenched.

"I know what they want," Aurelia said. She stepped closer to the buggy. The brass lantern on its side shone orange across Aurelia's face, making her eyes seem red in its dim light. The old woman's gloved hand crushed the bottom of the curtain and held it back. Aurelia leaned into the buggy, "You deserted them."

"It is not the children's words thee speaks."

"It is what they said."

"Liar," the old woman barked. She yanked the curtain back so hard that it ripped, falling into her lap. "Did they not tell thee? Thee knows not of thy destiny?"

Aurelia ground her teeth and said nothing, only stared, her eyes glowing like coals under the light.

"Thee are to be their voice, their instrument of vengeance. As I was, so shall thee be, Aurelia." The Blessed Mother's laughter echoed with the night wind, howling across the valley.

Aurelia stood erect. Slowly, she smiled. The Blessed Mother recoiled into the darkness of the buggy, startled at the strange, almost challenging look on Aurelia's face.

"The children speak to me even now," the girl said as her face pushed further into the buggy. "They said you deserted them. That you could have come back and saved them, but you didn't. You left them there to die. You sacrificed their lives, their souls for yours. They say you spoke with Hell itself to save your life. They say your falling fit was Satan's mark. That you made a pact with Him and delivered their souls for your own salvation."

"Do not threaten me with lies. I know their voices well. I have listened to their cries for too long. They are my children still. Why does thee lie?"

The lantern's light flickered across Aurelia's face as she stepped away from the buggy. Her smile disappeared. She did not answer.

"Thee will follow me, Aurelia." The old woman grabbed the reins tight against her withered chest and leaned out boldly. "It is in thy blood. Do not blaspheme. Do not twist the children's words."

Aurelia backed farther out of the lantern's light until she was only a shadow in the darkness before the cave.

"Does thee not hear me?" the Blessed Mother cried. "Thee are mine. Thy destiny is mine. Thy blood, Aurelia. Thy blood is mine."

Only the girl's glowing eyes could be seen from the buggy. The horse whinnied nervously, kicking his front hoofs. The Blessed Mother jerked on the reins.

"Step forth, Aurelia. Do not hide in silence now. Thee are not one of them, to slip always into the shadows."

The shadow disappeared. Aurelia was gone. The Blessed Mother's head darted out the window, anxiously searching the buggy's perimeter.

"You expect me to learn from you?" a voice cried out behind her. The old woman twisted in her seat to see near the back wheel. Aurelia walked back into the lantern's pale light. "That I will be as you? That I will come to destroy the ones I love?"

"Does thee not fathom what I said, girl?" The Blessed Mother yanked up her veil and held it. "Thy skin, girl. Thy blood. It is my skin. My blood."

Aurelia grasped the big wooden wheel. The cold wind blew against her back, flinging her long hair across her face.

"I am thy mother's mother, Aurelia. Thee are my granddaughter. My blood runs in thy veins. As does the mute's. The blood of the cave. For in it, thy mother was conceived."

"No!" Aurelia screamed, banging her small fists into the wheel. "The children stand with me. You lie, old woman. You lie to protect yourself." She spun away from the buggy, clutching herself in the darkness.

"Thy destiny, Aurelia, is in thy blood!" The horse bucked and the buggy jumped forward. "Tonight I will prepare thy silent one, thy right hand. Thy fate has come. Tomorrow thee shall stand by my side."

Joey saw Aurelia stumbling in the meadow near the woods. He ran to her and helped her back to the house. Thomas grabbed one of her arms to support her as Joey led her into the living room.

In the firelight, Thomas saw the terror etched onto her pale, innocent face.

"Fetch the tea," he ordered. Joey ran into the kitchen and brought back a hot mug. "Drink, Aurelia, to calm thyself." Thomas held the mug for her. She was shaking badly.

Joey glanced questioningly at Thomas, who looked at

the boy as he put down the mug and shook his head to keep him from speaking.

"She was waiting for me," Aurelia sighed, leaning back in the big chair. Her eyes flashed up at Thomas. "She told me she was my grandmother. Is it true?"

Thomas looked at Joey. The boy had frozen in midstep when he heard her question. Thomas glanced back down at the girl.

"I do not know. Why did she tell thee that?"

Aurelia pushed herself up in the chair, trying to think.

"I went into the cave. The voices . . ." Aurelia peered into the bright fire. Its warmth comforted her slightly. "They told me to help them. That I was their savior." She looked up at Thomas. "As I am all of yours. They said the Blessed Mother must be brought to them. That she will be the last. The ceremony will die with her. She has the power no more. They have given it to me. I told the Blessed Mother what they said. She called me a liar. Then she said she was my mother's mother."

"To scare thee," Thomas added quickly, putting his hand on her shoulder. He was greatly relieved. He had been right all along about what the Children of the Cave wanted. "She wanted to turn thee against them. She wanted thee to feel responsible for her, so thee would not destroy her in the name of the children."

"But why?" Aurelia peered deep into the flames. "Why would they have done her bidding all this time if they hated her so?"

"Perhaps it was always the other way around. Perhaps she did their bidding, was their pawn all along."

Aurelia slowly shook her head. She felt extremely tired suddenly. She could hardly keep her eyes open. She was trying to remember everything the voices had told her.

She lowered her head down on the arm of the chair. It

was so hard to interpret all that was in her mind then. It had been so clear before, but now it was blurred and hard to piece together again.

"She said I was her granddaughter," Aurelia mumbled, closing her eyes. "She's wrong. She is a murderer. She deserted the children." Her voice was barely audible. "And made a pact . . . a pact with . . . the . . ."

"Let her rest," Thomas whispered, putting a blanket over her. "Stay close to her. I will leave my buggy here. If she needs me, come quick. I must go to the old church. The people are waiting. I will tell them our fears are at an end. Our Deliverer has come."

What the Blessed Mother had told Aurelia confused Thomas Borg. He could not believe it. What the children's spirits had said had to be the truth. They had given Aurelia their power and turned against the Blessed Mother. They cried for the salvation of their souls just as the people cried for their own deliverance.

God has finally answered our prayers, he thought. He could not let us live for another generation in fear and in sin, ruled by the evil lurking in the depth of that cave. Our debt will finally be paid.

Thomas turned his buggy towards the church. Lantern lights filtered through the cracks in the boarded-up windows. He heard the people's voices inside arguing as he walked up the old creaking stairs.

Immediately, the voices hushed. He opened the doors. There were more people in the pews than he had expected. Almost half the Valley's adult population filled the church.

Thomas threw back his shoulders and marched down the aisle to the altar. He felt their questioning glances follow him. Suddenly he realized he had not had a drink in two days. It was the longest he had been sober in fifteen years. He felt strong and proud then. But when he turned to face his people, saw the fear in their faces and how they looked to him for hope, he wished he had brought a jug.

Thomas leaned on the pulpit and cleared his throat. It was parched. It is up to me now, he thought. As it was for my Beth fifteen years ago.

"We must stand together," he said loudly. The words scattered through the church. They seemed to bounce off the walls to be hurled back at him. He wiped the sweat from his neck. "The evil, the fear, the hate that has ruled our lives must end. We must look again to God for he has heard our prayers. The God of our fathers, taken from us by the Blessed Mother, has returned."

The people half-heartedly said, "Amen."

One cried out from the back. "And will thee lead us, Thomas? Remember thy wife and beware."

Thomas tried to swallow, but there was no saliva left in his mouth. He remembered all too well. He wanted to run out of the church then and find his whiskey. He literally held himself to the pulpit and waited until he could speak without his voice quivering.

"I will lead us," he announced. He looked over the crowd until he found Gertrude Throm. She looked up at him and smiled, nodding for him to say what must be said. Seeing her strong face, her encouragement, helped him swallow his fear. He cleared his throat. "All of us have asked why the girl, Aurelia, was brought here. And we know what the Blessed Mother can do if disobeyed. We have all lived to watch a loved one die for a sin most of us had never been a part of."

The people whispered to each other in agreement.

"Now the girl is one of us. She stands against the Blessed Mother and against her vile hatred. She stands against the Blackness that has enshrouded us on these many years."

"But what can she do?" a voice yelled. "She has no power against the—"

Thomas held up his hand. "She has the power. She has been to the cave and come back to tell of it. The Children's spirits have chosen her to be their salvation as well as ours. They have turned a deaf ear to the Blessed Mother. She is bound and shackled to the Hell she herself created. Now the Black-faced One calls her to His lair. When we bring her to Him we shall all be saved."

"How does thee know these things?" another called out. "The cave and the Blessed Mother are one. The girl is hers, to do her bidding. If the cave let her enter and live, she, too, is evil."

"Not so," Thomas cried. "Not so. She weeps for those who have been hurt. We have all seen her grief, her sadness, the way of her heart. She is her mother's child. Remember that. Her mother would not do the Blessed Mother's bidding. Neither shall Aurelia. It was she who told me what the children have said. It was she who listened to their voices and lived. It is she who has the power now. She who will protect all of us from the Blessed Mother's vengeance."

"I do not believe thee," an old woman in the front pew said, standing up. "Thee only wants to avenge thy wife. Would thee sacrifice us all to do that?"

"Thee are wrong," Gertrude Throm yelled, pushing her way to the pulpit. "I have been with the girl. She has her mother's heart. She would die rather than harm one of us. As for Thomas, know, all of thee, what it means if he leads us and is wrong. It is not thee who will be destroyed. Only Thomas. He speaks with faith and with courage."

The crowd murmured, still apprehensive.

"And if I am wrong, what will thee lose?" Thomas said. "Only me, friends. Only me. It will change

nothing. Beth's death threatened not thy lives. But . . .''
Thomas threw up his arms and stared from face to face
until the church was totally silent. "If I am right, if the
voices the girl hears speak the truth, if the children's
souls want deliverance from their dark abyss, if God has
sent us a Redeemer, then we shall be free at last.''
Thomas slammed his fists onto the pulpit. The
pounding echoed in the church. He closed his eyes and
turned his face upwards. "Oh, to see the face of God
again! To look upon Heaven without fear and without
guilt!''

The people in the church rose out of their pews and
cried for the salvation of their souls.

Gertrude Throm began to chant loudly. "The Lord is
my shepherd; I shall not want.

"He maketh me to lie down in green pastures: He
leadeth me beside the still waters.''

The people began to chant with her.

"He restoreth my soul: He leadeth me in the paths of
righteousness for His name's sake.

"Yea, though I walk through the valley of the
shadow of death, I will fear no evil . . .''

The Blessed Mother prepared the table in the woodshed.
Soon the girl will understand, she thought. She will
come to me, ready for what must be done. The lies she
spoke were the last vestiges of the outside world calling
to her. But they were weak. Her mother's lies. Now she
must be given a Silent One. Then she will obey. She will
be mine forever.

The mute kicked the shed door open and threw
Richard inside, onto the dirt floor. The door slammed
closed. Before Richard could get back on his feet, the
mute backhanded his jaw. Stars blinked around him.
When the dizziness ceased he was lying on a table.

"Let me go," the boy cried. "I have done nothing."

The mute strapped his arms onto the table. Richard lifted his hips and kicked him in the ribs. The mute grabbed his legs and strapped them down. Richard heaved his body against the leather bindings. His torso rose hard, then collapsed.

"Now his head," the Blessed Mother commanded.

The mute's massive hands grabbed either side of Richard's head and held it still. The Blessed Mother strapped his forehead tight against ·the table, then yanked a leather strip over his chin. The mute began to pull it. Slowly the pressure forced Richard's mouth open.

His eyes darted up at the two black-shadowed figures outlined in the eerie reddish hue. He heaved his body again. The straps held him taut. Straining, he could not budge his head or close his mouth.

The Blessed Mother stood above his face, blocking the light. She pointed.

"Thee went into the sacred cave. Performed an unholy ceremony. It was blasphemy. But it was not thy fault."

Richard couldn't shake his head. He tried to deny it, but with his mouth strapped open, he could only grunt.

"Thee knows it was against our ways. And thee took the girl's lamb. Know now that it was thy destiny that made thee do it."

Richard groaned and twisted his bound body.

"Thee has been chosen for a sacred duty. Thee shall inherit the ways of the Silent One." She pointed at Matthew. "Look to thy master and know thy place. Thee shall be Aurelia's strength as he has been mine."

Taking a step back, the Blessed Mother reached into her jacket. Richard watched out of the corner of his eye. The yellow light caught the glistening steel blade of the knife and reflected it into his face. He grunted and tried to break his chin strap. It was impossible.

The knife was long and thin and curved. The Blessed Mother held it up in front of her face. Its blade flashed like a mirror in the sun. She grinned.

The mute whined, holding up his hands to block the knife's reflection, stepping back away from its glittering horror.

The Blessed Mother slowly raised it above her head and held it by the blade, like a cross.

"The children have chosen thee, as they had chosen Matthew. Never again shall thee utter a word. Their secrets are safe with the Silent One. Their secrets shall be forever locked within thee. Truly, this is a great honor."

She lowered the knife into the three-legged iron bowl. It sizzled in the hot coals. As she turned it, the blade began to glow.

Suddenly a wide, flat, metal object was clamped onto Richard's tongue and it yanked the tongue out of his mouth.

Richard watched the red, glowing blade descend towards his face. He tried to cry out but couldn't.

The mute turned away, drenched in sweat. He remembered the pain well. It still haunted him in his dreams.

Richard heaved his body as the heat neared his mouth. The hot searing blade cut into his tongue. The mute heard its terrible hissing. His heart cried out against this abomination. Richard screamed as the excruciating pain exploded in his mouth.

The mute felt Richard's scream tear through his soul. It was his scream too, his horrifying, unyielding agony. He slumped down against the wall, his huge body limp from an agony he still felt, even now, forty-one years later.

Richard passed out. The mute stood up weakly and approached the table.

"In the morning, thee will take him to the girl," the Blessed Mother said. "She will nurse him. He is hers now, forever."

CHAPTER XV

"DADDY, I'M scared." Aurelia felt her father's brow. It was burning. His body was drenched with sweat. "Please, Daddy, don't get sicker. Please?"

He moaned and his head moved slightly on the pillow, yanking at the traction that held his chin tight. Rain splattered against the window. The wind pounded the walls. It was a dark, cold morning.

Thomas brought some chicken broth into the bedroom. Aurelia tried to spoon-feed it to her father. It would not go down. His throat gargled, and the broth drooled back out of his mouth and down his hot, sweating cheeks.

Aurelia peered helplessly up at Thomas.

"He won't swallow anything. I've tried all morning. Not even water." She rose from the bed and stared out the window. "Thomas, he's going to die." She crossed her arms and leaned stiffly against the edge of the window. "I know it. He's going to die."

Thomas Borg looked back at Joey. The boy was standing in the doorway. Thomas pointed outside to tell him to close the door and leave them alone. Joey obeyed, close to despair after hearing the terrible anguish in Aurelia's trembling voice.

Thomas walked to the window and hugged Aurelia from behind, trying to think of what he could say to comfort her. Sam Hill was getting worse by the hour. His fever had risen drastically during the night, but Thomas had decided not to awaken Aurelia. There was nothing she could have done.

Aurelia turned around in his arms, close against his barrel chest. Thomas patted her head. Her body heaved against his as she sighed. Thomas kept expecting her to break down and cry, but she didn't. That worried him too.

"He will come out of it," he lied. "Do not fret. Thy father is strong. He is far from dying." Lying seemed less sinful than the truth to him then. He stepped back and held her shoulders. "Try the broth again. Mr. Grotten left us herbs to break the fever. I put them in it. He will be better as soon as he drinks even a little of it."

Aurelia closed her eyes and nodded. She walked to the bed, picked up the bowl from the table and sat by her father. Thomas could see she did not believe him.

"Daddy, drink. Please, just a little." She forced a spoonful down his throat. He gagged and spit it up. "Daddy. You must drink it." Again she tried. This time the liquid went down. She wiped the perspiration off her face with one arm, then glanced at Thomas. "He drank it."

Thomas smiled. "Keep trying. It will help." He walked out of the bedroom. He could not stand seeing the pain in Aurelia's face any longer. He knew Sam was dying. If he had remained one more minute with the girl he would have broken down and she would have known the truth. Thomas did not think she could face that now. She was tottering on the brink of a total emotional breakdown already.

"He is much worse," Joey whispered as Thomas approached him. The old man rubbed his eyes and shook his head in agreement.

Joey opened the front door and stared out at the storm. The top of the big oak bent with each powerful gust of wind, its black branches shaking like the limbs of a corpse. The cold, damp breeze washed across him and into the living room.

"Thomas!" Joey cried. He pointed down the road. "She is coming!"

The black-curtained buggy, driven by the mute, bounced through the gray, heavy rain. Joey slowly backed into the house, his face taut.

"I must hide." He was barely able to form the words. He stumbled around the living room like a blind man, tripping over the furniture.

"The shed," Thomas said. "Get thee to the shed. It is cluttered with tools. Crawl in behind the wheelbarrow."

Joey glanced briefly at Thomas for reassurance, then dashed into the kitchen and out the back door. Thomas peered out at the approaching buggy, then stepped into Sam's room.

It begins, he thought. At the worst possible time for the girl, it begins.

"He drank more of it," Aurelia said. Thomas smiled, but could not disguise the apprehension in his eyes.

"The Blessed Mother is coming," he said. Aurelia slowly put the bowl down on the table. Thomas waited for some kind of reaction to what he had said, but none came. The girl just sat there, staring at the bowl.

"Thomas, the things you told me this morning . . . about what I had said after coming back from the cave?" She looked up at him. "I don't remember any of it." She held her hands in her lap and sighed, looking back at her father. "I want to help. I want to be strong. I want to end all the horror." Her voice suddenly cracked. "But I can't remember. I don't know how I can stop her, or what I'm suppose to do. I don't."

Thomas put his arm around her small shoulders. "Thee has the power. Do not worry. The children's spirits are with thee. God is with thee. When the time comes, thee will know what to do."

Aurelia arose and walked to the front door. The black buggy pulled into the yard. She did not want to tell Thomas that she had been terrified by what he had told her that morning. How could she not remember it? All she could remember was the excruciating pain, the awful, tearing cramps. The only other flashes of memory she had of the cave were full of death and torment, and screaming, agonizing horror. There was no comfort in any of that, no sign of God or forgiveness.

Aurelia watched the mute get down from the buggy and lift a body off the seat. He held it in his huge arms and waited for the Blessed Mother.

Aurelia hugged herself as the chilling wind spun, howling, through the porch. It reminded her of the tormented wails she had heard in the black depth of the cave.

There was nothing about what was happening to her, what was torturing her body, her mind, her soul, that could be interpreted as a sign of salvation.

But my words, she thought, trying to regain some courage, some hope. He said I spoke of deliverance, of an end to the killing and the fear. But how am I to do this? If he tells me I said it, it must be true. But how?

The mute carried Richard to the porch. The Blessed Mother opened the door. Thomas and Aurelia watched, silent and wary.

"Richard needs thy care." The old woman said, stepping closer. Aurelia squeezed her arms and backed into the house. "He has been purified. He will be thy strength, girl. He will protect thee."

The mute carried the boy into Aurelia's bedroom and laid him on her bed. Thomas inched next to Aurelia.

"What did you do to him?" Aurelia asked. If she must stand up to this old woman, she would do it now. She hated her for coming here, where her father might be dying. It was not right that the old woman should be in the same house with him. Aurelia gratefully let her anger grow. It gave her strength.

The Blessed Mother stared through her veil at Thomas and said nothing. The old man put his arm around Aurelia. The Blessed Mother waved at the mute. He started to search the house.

Aurelia gritted her teeth and sidestepped to block the mute from entering her father's room. He halted and looked back at the Blessed Mother.

Aurelia held her ground. "What are you looking for? I do not like for you to be in my house."

"I want the boy. He has disobeyed me." The Blessed Mother pointed. The mute went into the kitchen. Then they heard the back door slammed open.

"Leave us alone," Aurelia growled. She surprised herself with her own intensity.

"Us? And who is us?" The Blessed Mother hobbled to the fireplace and warmed her hands. She looked back over her shoulder. "Is Thomas the one who feeds thee with these lies, the lies thee spoke yesterday?"

Thomas let go of Aurelia. He did not want her to feel the tremors that raked his body then. He tried to meet the Blessed Mother's stare, but couldn't.

Seeing his fear, the old woman smiled and walked towards him, stopping by Sam's bedroom door.

"The Holy Ceremony takes place tonight, Aurelia. Thee shall prove then, to all who doubt, that thee are my daughter's daughter, blood of my blood, ready to receive my sacred gift. I am weary. Thy time has come. Richard has been silenced forever to keep thy office holy. He shall be thy hands, thy strength. His life will be lived for thee and thee only. His soul has been branded. He will do thy bidding.''

Aurelia glanced at Thomas. She needed some kind of reassurance now more than ever. Thomas's head was bowed. He was staring at the floor.

The old woman looked in at Sam. Aurelia pushed her away and yanked the door closed.

''I will stand against you,'' she said, tensing the muscles in her arms. ''You can't make me be like you. You're disgusting and cruel and . . . and completely insane.''

The old woman burst into a mocking laugh. It sent shudders down Aurelia's body. She looked at Thomas helplessly.

He lifted his chin. ''Get out of here,'' he warned. ''Now!''

''Thee has no choice, girl,'' the Blessed Mother said as her black-robed figure swirled out the door. ''Thee shall know that soon. And thee shall . . .''

Suddenly Joey's cries drowned out the old woman's words. Aurelia dashed to the porch. The Blessed Mother stood in the storm, silent now, as she gloated over her victory. She had come for the boy and she had found him. The girl could not stop her. This would teach Aurelia how futile it was to stand against her.

''Aurelia,'' Joey screamed. ''Help me!''

''Leave him alone,'' she yelled, stomping her foot.

The mute carried Joey looped over both shoulders, the way a hunter carries a deer. Aurelia had hoped the mute would listen to her, as he had before, but he just kept walking.

Aurelia dashed towards the buggy, grabbed the mute's arm with both hands and yanked. It was like trying to move a boulder.

The Blessed Mother climbed in the other side of the buggy and took the reins. The mute heaved Joey up next to her. The boy flopped onto the seat, dazed.

"You can't·take him. You can't." Aurelia held the mute's arm. His big hand gently pushed her away. He lifted himself up into the buggy and grabbed the boy securely.

"Aurelia!" Joey screamed, reaching out to her. "Aurelia!"

The horse bucked and the buggy shot forward down the road.

Aurelia stood in the rain listening to Joey's muffled cries grow fainter and fainter.

Aurelia pressed the cool, wet towel against Richard's parched lips. She couldn't believe what the Blessed Mother had done.

Thomas had sterilized what was left of Richard's tongue by washing his mouth with whiskey and an antiseptic herb of Mr. Grotten's. The wound had already been cauterized by the hot blade the Blessed Mother had used. It was a clean cut and had burned immediately to lessen the bleeding.

When he had come to earlier, Aurelia had held Richard's head while Thomas made him drink the herb-laden water, making sure that he swallowed it and did not choke. His sheets were drenched with sweat and he was beginning to moan.

Suddenly he cried out. The pain was monstrous. He stared at Aurelia, his eyes bulging, his mouth twisted in agony as he tried to speak. He couldn't.

He knew then that the terrible nightmare had been real. Tears streamed down his cheeks. He closed his eyes, hoping to pass out again to relieve the pain.

Aurelia took the damp towel and wiped his brow. In

his mind, he could see the flashing glow of the blade descend towards his clamped tongue. He squeezed his eyes closed and tried to speak. Only a horrible, muffled squeal erupted from his throat.

His eyes flashed open. He needed to know he was not still strapped to that table, waiting for the next horror to begin. Weakly, he lifted one hand. It rose a few inches under the blanket and fell.

Aurelia watched, wiping his face and shoulders with the wet towel. Its coolness dulled the burning agony that scorched the inside of his head and mouth.

"Do not move. Rest."

Aurelia pushed his sweat-soaked hair out of his eyes. She took a glass of warm water and held it to his lips. He turned his head. Softly she pulled his face back.

"Just a little. It will hurt, but you must drink. Just a little. Come on." She lifted his head and poured the water into his mouth. He spit it out and turned his head. "All right. Try again." His throat spasmed. His weeping turned into tormented sobs. She held his head and caressed it, whispering to him reassuringly. When it subsided, she lowered him back against the pillow. "You'll be all right. Thomas has herbs to deaden the pain. Drink a little of the water. The herbs are in it."

Aurelia was surprised at the pity and concern she felt for Richard. He had been so cruel to her, but nothing he had done warranted such a terrible fate.

Now he was just another helpless victim of the Blessed Mother. He was weak and scared and in pain. She could not hate him then. She just felt sorry for him.

Richard's eyes focused on Aurelia. The way he looked at her told her that he was trying to thank her and to apologize for what he had done before.

"You'll be all right. Just drink this."

Weakly, he nodded, never taking his eyes off

Aurelia's. He drank, and his moist hand slipped out from under the covers and reached towards her. She held it and smiled.

"Rest now." She stroked his forehead. He closed his eyes, trying to blank out the horrible memory and the pain. Aurelia's soothing voice helped him keep both away. He listened intently and drifted back into unconsciousness.

"How could she do this?" Aurelia asked as she got up.

"She is capable of much worse." Thomas was leaning his wide frame against the doorway. As she approached, he stepped back.

"At least he's out again." Aurelia sat down in the big chair in front of the fireplace. She was exhausted. She stared at the flames and sighed, listening to the thunder boom above the house and the rain increase.

All Aurelia could think of now was Joey. She blamed herself for not being able to stop the Blessed Mother from taking him. She was beginning to doubt she could ever do anything to stop the Blessed Mother.

Thomas Borg knew how much the boy meant to her. He wished he could tell her Joey would be fine, but all he could say was that they had to stand together against the Blessed Mother, and only in that way could they save him.

Aurelia was sick of hearing that.

The Blessed Mother had taken Joey, and they couldn't stop her. It was that simple, that obvious. All their plans, their grand theories, their hopes, were a farce. Aurelia had no power, no way to destroy the old woman. She had proved that this afternoon.

Aurelia straightened her legs out so her feet were close to the fire. She decided to go over it all one more time. No matter how hard she tried, none of it made sense anymore. There were no answers. No hope.

Aurelia turned in the chair and looked up at Thomas Borg.

"I can't stop her," she said. "Everything you have told me is wrong. You want to lead the people in my name. But I can do nothing."

"Together we can."

Aurelia looked back at the fire, tapping one finger on the arm of the chair. His optimism seemed ridiculously out of place.

"But the power—if I have it, why couldn't I use it to save Joey? I don't feel any power. I just feel scared and helpless and tired."

"Thee will have it. The children told thee. They picked thee. Tonight, do not worry. They have chosen thee for a great purpose." Thomas ran his hands through his hair.

And if she is right and I am wrong? he thought. Then I will be driven insane by the Blessed Mother. He shrugged. He was past being scared.

But what of this brave, kind girl? She would be trapped in a horror she never deserved. Trapped by a vengeance and a history she was never a part of.

It did not seem right or fair to Thomas, but it was irreversible.

Nothing could stop it now.

With unlit torches, the people gathered: husbands and wives, clutching together in fearful apprehension, men who had lost their wives, women who had lost their husbands or a child to the Holy Sacrifice. The memories of their dead loved ones gave them courage to go on, to face a foe who, for as long as they could remember, had manipulated every aspect of their lives with fear and self-loathing.

She was the Holy One. The One who could walk into the shadows of darkness, of Hell itself, and force it to do her bidding. She was their albatross, and yet she was their life's blood. Without the Blessed Mother, would a drought destroy their crops again? Would the spirits of the night, the horrors that live in the dark recesses of the cave, pour out against them as a plague? Would the Fallen Angel's horde of ghouls be let loose upon their valley and their souls and the souls of their children?

The people clustered together outside the porch of Aurelia's house, full of questions. Thomas stood on the steps, trying to appear strong and calm and confident of their coming success, their approaching freedom. He watched the crowd grow, its many voices whispering words of doubt and of courage, and he wondered how Moses had felt as he gathered the Israelite slaves together to flee from Ramses' cruel despotism and his all-powerful army.

Aurelia sat with her father, sponging his face and chest. His breathing had become irregular. He no longer trembled in unconscious fits of agony, but his stillness, broken only by quick, hollow breaths, was even worse.

Outside, she could hear the Holy Children speaking in hushed voices. She could not decipher their words. Then Thomas began to speak, and the people were instantly quiet. His voice fought the biting wind and the distant echoes of thunder. The rain had ended hours ago, but now had begun again, in a sudden downpour, as if the sky itself were weeping. It bombarded the roof like hail.

Aurelia leaned down. "We will stop her," she whispered, wringing fresh water from the sponge onto her father's cracked lips. "Then I'll take you out of here. We'll go far away. And we'll be happy again."

Water dribbled out the sides of his mouth. Suddenly his chest heaved. A horrible choking noise gurgled up his throat. Blood oozed out of his mouth and nose. There was no slight chest movement, no sign of breathing at all.

Aurelia wiped off the blood, then felt his chest. There was no heartbeat.

"Daddy?" She lowered her ear to his open mouth, hoping she was wrong.

Slowly she sat up. For a long time, she just stared, not even blinking. The sponge fell out of her hand and splattered on the floor.

"We march," Thomas ordered. "Light thy torches. Our time is at hand. For thy loved ones. For thy brother, Elena. And for thy wife, David. For the love of God and the salvation of our souls."

The people cried out the names of those in their families who had died in the Holy Sacrifice of the Cave. Their chaotic screams shook the house.

In slow motion, Aurelia's head turned towards the door. Then she gazed back at her father. She ached inside as she had never ached before. She wanted to die, wanted to crawl under the covers with her father and hold him and wait for death to come for her as well. For only in death would she be freed from the agony that drenched her very soul.

Again the Holy Children cried out the names of their dead.

Aurelia rose slowly from the bed and walked to the porch door. She looked at the mob. The torches lit their faces in reddish gargoyle-like masks. They peered up at the girl.

Thomas glanced over his shoulder.

"He's dead," she whispered.

Thomas closed his eyes and swallowed. Aurelia walked up to him and clutched his arm.

"I will walk by your side, Thomas," she announced

solemnly. "To avenge my parents. Nothing else matters now. Nothing."

Thomas lifted her chin and looked into her eyes. There was something overpowering in them then. He knew there was nothing more to say. He handed her a torch.

She descended the stairs into the rain. The mass of people opened up like the Red Sea as she walked silently through them towards the orphanage.

Joey heard the children's voices spread through the orphanage like a brush fire. He was locked in a tiny, third-story storage room with a small window overlooking the front grounds. He peered out through the rain to see what the commotion was about. The children's voices echoed hysterically through the halls.

Lightning cracked through the sky like a huge white branch falling from the heavens. In its glare, Joey saw the torch-lit mob crawling like one massive, hundred-eyed beast across the fields. He tried to jam the dirty window open, but it was nailed closed.

The Blessed Mother sat knitting by the fire. She was making a tiny sweater for one of her dolls.

The mute paced back and forth in the small parlor room on the fourth floor.

"Are they coming?" she asked calmly.

The mute stomped to the rain-drenched glass and peered out. Torches bounced and flickered toward the orphanage. They were almost at the barn. Thunder rolled over the valley. He clutched tightly at the window frame, turned and looked at the old woman. Her veiled eyes closely scrutinized him. His left eye twitched nervously. She had not seen that in fifteen years.

"Thee fears them." She put down the tiny black

sweater and hobbled over next to him. He gazed back out at the stormy night. She put her cold, gloved hand on his arm. His massive bicep quivered and flexed. "Do not fear them, Matthew. It was written that they would come again. The girl must prove she can lead them, that they will put their faith in her, even for the wrong reason. It will show the Children that she is worthy of their gift."

The mute grunted, marched to the fireplace, then to the door. He pounded his forearm against the wall. He did not like what must be done. The mob was led by his granddaughter. He feared them because of that, for even if he were commanded to do so, he could not harm the girl, blood of his blood.

"They will follow me still. They are scared of thee, Matthew, as they are of the Devil and the cave. But they fear me the most. In the end, that fear shall lead them again, as it has led them all their lives. I am their conscience and their judge. I am their salvation and their purgatory." She ambled over to the door and took his hand in hers. "Come. We shall meet them at the door."

The mute shook his head. The old woman smiled through her veil and squeezed his fingers.

"Do not doubt me, Matthew. The power is mine. Only when I give it to the girl, will she be able to lead them in the ways of the Holy Cave. It has been written in blood. Our blood. The Children await!"

Thomas lifted his torch by the steps to the huge oak doors of the orphanage. The mob crowded behind him. The storm heaved and rumbled across the sky. The cold night wind swept over the grounds, chilling the people's hearts and their courage.

The big doors swung open, and in the light of the foyer the black figures of the Blessed Mother and the mute were outlined. She stepped out onto the stairs and cast her gaze over the mob. Their torches flickered in the rain, spitting sparks up into the black, howling night.

Thomas looked down at Aurelia, then walked to the foot of the stairs. She started to go with him, but he pushed her back. This was for him to do. He had known that since he had quaked with fear again when he had faced the old woman that afternoon. He had to do this alone. For his Beth. And for a pride he had lost years ago, but finally found again in the eyes of a half-grown girl.

"Thy reign of terror and hate is over," he yelled over the storm. "We come for thee as thee had come for many of our loved ones. We shall stand thy sacrifices no longer. It is time thee met the fate thee has always relegated to others. A fate thee escaped from once in exchange for the souls of thy brethren."

The people cried out behind him, raising their torches.

The Blessed Mother descended halfway down the stairs and stopped to look into Thomas's face.

Aurelia felt the crowd, after pushing up against her, give way and slowly back up. She closed her eyes and tried to concentrate. She was trying to call back the haunting visions, the horrifying voices, even the terrible, cramping pain, to know the children were with her now. She could feel the fear scattering through the mob, drawing them closer together, away from her and from Thomas.

Her body tensed rigidly as she opened her mind to the dark memories of the cave. They must speak to me now, she thought. They must. The people are beginning to cower.

But nothing came. No faces. No words. No visions.

The Blessed Mother gazed over Thomas's head at the girl.

And suddenly Aurelia felt it. Like a small electrical shock, it coursed through her veins. She opened her eyes to see the veiled woman, staring.

Lightning lit the grounds and Aurelia could see the taunting smile behind the veil. It was not the children who had made her blood run hot. It was the old woman. She had the power still. She had just struck her with it.

Thomas! Aurelia cried, inside. Oh Thomas, we have been betrayed. The children lied to me. They are not with me now. It was all a lie. A lie, Thomas. A lie.

The Blessed Mother held up her skeleton hands. The crowd instantly hushed.

Thomas felt his body being drained of strength. His legs trembled as if they had no bones left in them. He lifted his face to the cold, sharp rain, squeezing his torch until his fingers screamed in pain. His skin felt as if it were on fire. His mind burned. He could hardly think.

"Thee has turned my people from me," the Blessed Mother cried, one hand slowly lowering until it pointed at Thomas. "Thee has filled their hearts with the Devil's blood, making them sin against God Almighty."

"No!" Thomas yelled. "I give them their freedom. With the girl's help and the help of the innocent souls thee condemned to Hell, I call their wrath down upon thee. Thy power is dead."

"Fool!" she barked. The old woman glanced back at the mute. The huge man stomped down the stairs. The crowd backed farther from Thomas. Only Aurelia stood her ground.

"Thee shall learn thy blasphemy is the most vile of all evils."

The mute's massive fingers reached out and clutched Thomas' throat, nearly lifting him off the ground. Everything started to spin. His throat was slowly being crushed.

Thomas felt his life flickering like the stub of a dying

candle. He lowered his torch hand. He was close to blacking out. There was no choice left. He shoved the torch forward. Its flame ignited the mute's coat. The huge man was instantly consumed in fire. The crowd gasped as the mute flailed wildly at his burning clothes. His screams shook the mob.

Thomas gasped painfully. He grabbed his torch with both hands and lifted it above his head. The mute dropped to his knees, grunting and slapping at the flames. As if chopping wood with an axe, Thomas began to club the burning mass of flesh. The mute's hair burst into flames. The skin on his face began to crack. Blood poured out under his eyes in small rivers.

The mob stared, opening its tight ranks to circle the horror. Aurelia turned her head and covered her eyes with both hands.

"Murderer!" The Blessed Mother screamed. "The blood of Cain runs through thee!" The mute slumped down in a pile of charred flesh. The rain quickly put out the last of the flames. "Thy life, thy soul has been condemned, Thomas Borg. Thee are no longer a Holy Child."

White saliva drooled out of her veil and down her black dress. She pointed at Thomas and thunder exploded.

The old man dropped his torch and clutched at his chest.

"No!" he whimpered. "Thee has no . . ."

Suddenly he twisted and flipped onto the ground as if hit by some incredible force. His body flopped and heaved like a fish thrown from the water. His face contorted into a tortured but silent plea. His arms flew out from his chest, his fingers pulsating as if each were a separate, quivering entity. Suddenly he sat up and screamed.

Aurelia ran to him. The Blessed Mother cried out to

stop her. Two men from the mob grabbed her by the arms and pulled her away.

Thomas's fingers, like the sharp talons of a hawk, slowly curled in towards his face. His eyes, huge and horrified, watched helplessly as they inched ever closer, reaching, snapping at his flesh.

"Look," the old woman cried. "Look to thy leader. See what happens to those who shun the cave, our Holy temple. To defy the sacred children is to destroy thy faith, thy soul, and the torment of Hell shall be upon thee."

Joey pressed his face tight against the glass. He couldn't take his eyes off the horror below.

He watched the Blessed Mother raise her arms and the crowd open up. Slowly, she hobbled between them. The two men holding Aurelia's arms yanked her roughly behind the old woman.

The girl did not resist. She moved with them, her head hung low, sometimes slipping and being dragged by the two men until she was able to regain her footing.

"Aurelia," Joey cried. He peered frantically around the small storage room. There was a half-full gallon of paint under the small broken end table in one corner.

Protecting his face with one arm, Joey smashed it through the glass. He took the bottom of the can and ran it along the frame, cracking off the jagged pieces still embedded in the wood.

He crawled out the small window onto the overhang, then stood up and started to side-step along the wet slippery ledge. He inched his way to the spiral corner. Holding his breath, he kicked at the curved window. He began to sway from the impact. He quickly hunched down and grabbed the frame inside the window. The glass cut his palms and wrists. Straining, his weight pulling him back, he dove, head first, into the room.

Two little girls huddled, frightened, in the corner of the room. He didn't even see them. He ran to the door and down the stairs.

When he dashed out of the orphanage, the smell of burnt flesh overcame him. He coughed and, holding his breath, hurried to Thomas' aid.

The old man was curled in the mud, his head tucked into his chest.

"Mr. Borg?" Joey bent down and shook his shoulders. "Mr. Borg, please, speak to me. They took Aurelia." Thomas did not budge. Joey had no time then to be sympathetic. He shook harder and yelled, "Mr. Borg, we must help her. Now!"

The old man slowly uncurled himself and rolled over. His bloody face, its flesh torn by his own hands, turned towards the boy. Joey jumped back and gasped.

"Mr. Borg?"

The old man's eyes peered at Joey. The boy gathered his courage and knelt next to him. He gently lifted his bloody head.

"I was wrong," the old man muttered. He clutched his chest and began to cough.

"Mr. Borg. Please, listen." Joey reached under the old man's arms and lifted him to his feet. Thomas swayed, but was able to stand. Joey kept a hold on him. "They took Aurelia. What can we do? We have to stop them."

"I killed her. She believed in me and I killed her." Thomas stared at the boy through the blood streaming down his forehead. There was no life left in his swollen eyes.

Joey backed away. "Mr. Borg. Can thee understand me?"

The old man lowered his gaze and said nothing.

He was waiting for his Beth.

CHAPTER XVI

THE HUGE, high-ceilinged cave danced with the flickering of the torches, the mob's massive shadow pulsating like some monstrous black creature come alive upon the cave walls.

The Blessed Mother climbed the boulder and stood, a haunting black apparition above them. The mob encircled Aurelia below her stone pulpit.

Aurelia's cheeks and shoulders were bruised, her blouse torn. Blood trickled from one nostril. The mob had taunted her, shoving her, scratching at her on the way to the cave, calling her a witch, the Devil's child, for turning them against the Blessed Mother.

Aurelia backed up until she was flat against the boulder, only inches from the wild, writhing mob. A gust of wind hurled through the cave. The torches fed upon it and grew huge, illuminating the frenzied, red-shadowed faces, reflecting the horrible mindlessness that filled the cavern like some thick, putrid stench.

Aurelia couldn't believe the change. She had been a part of these people earlier; their hope, their salvation. She and Thomas had led them. But now they were crazed with fear. All tried to out-shout each other, singing praises to the Blessed Mother, hoping she would recognize their voices so they would be held in her favor once again.

"Blessed are the children," the black apparition chanted, her skeleton fingers twisting and pulling above the mob like some insane puppeteer, the invisible strings tied to her fingers, controlling the bodies and limbs of the mass of humanity below.

Aurelia watched the torch-lit faces. She felt their insane frenzy swirl about her, pinning her against the rock. She had been abandoned by those she had sought to help. It had happened so quickly her mind was still whirling in confusion. There was no longer one among them she could turn to as a friend.

"Blessed is the cave, for it is the life of the Valley," the old woman chanted. "Bless this girl for the trial soon to come."

The crowd huddled closer together, suddenly quiet, all eyes upon the Blessed Mother.

As one, they sang out, "Amen," as she raised her hands.

Lightning cracked white outside, flashing brightly into the cave, its thunder bellowing behind it, crashing loudly into the cavern. The Blessed Mother held her hands high and threw her head back. Her body began to quiver, her torso heaving. Then she fell. Torches rose above the mob's heads. The people whispered, pointing.

The old woman shook, face-down, upon the rock, her limbs flailing about like the legs of a crushed black insect in its final death throes.

Silence again swept over the mob.

The Blessed Mother arose, wiping the white drool from her chest.

"This girl has been chosen by the children." She pointed down at Aurelia. All faces turned. Aurelia scratched her fingers into the cold stone she was leaning against. She could not meet their angry stares and averted her eyes. There was no pity now in their faces.

Slowly she peeked into the right corner of the mob. She saw Gertrude Throm staring back at her, tears streaming down her face. Aurelia's eyes fixed upon Mrs. Throm's. The woman's sadness and her concern gave Aurelia strength to hold herself up and not fall, trembling, before this monstrous human mass of cowardice and fear.

The crowd murmured, "Amen."

"She must be sacrificed for our salvation. She turned thy hearts against me, against God Almighty. But thee has seen the light and brought her to her judgment. Blessed is the cave, for within its walls, we are all forgiven. Atone for thy indiscretions. Atone, Holy Children. The cave awaits. Into its divine hands, we commend her spirit."

The crowd repeated her words. The Blessed Mother descended from her rocky pulpit and, taking Aurelia's arm, led her to the big tunnel. The mob, torches raised, followed behind.

They marched down into the bowels of the earth, the mob calling out to the darkness to cleanse them of their wicked sin. Turning into another, smaller tunnel, the Blessed Mother extended her hands, halting the people.

"Pray," she commanded. "Pray for thy salvation. Pray for thy tarnished souls. Pray that this child shall be chosen among all those who have gone before and never returned, for their hearts were tarnished with doubt."

The mob knelt before her. Aurelia listened to their buzzing, near-frantic prayers as the Blessed Mother led her down into the catacombs below.

They walked along the fast-rising stream and stepped down past the small waterfall to the bank of the underground lake. The Blessed Mother shoved her torch between two rocks.

"Thee has shown great power, Aurelia." The Blessed Mother raised her veil. "But thy destiny was not to save the people from the cave and the children's vengeance. It was to follow me and rule as I have ruled, forever bound by the souls of the lost children. That is thy fate. That is thy hope and glory."

Singing began to echo across the still, black water.

"Does thee hear them? They sing for thee, Aurelia. For thy soul. Soon it shall be theirs. It is thy blood that commands thee. Listen to it and be freed. Thee has no family, now, but the children."

The singing grew louder. The voices clanged against the huge cavern's walls like cathedral bells within their tower. Aurelia stepped back away from the old woman.

The singing suddenly turned into screeching howls. They filled the cavern, vibrating over the water. The Blessed Mother's head darted about, startled by the screaming, hysterical sounds.

Aurelia felt the pain then. It doubled her over, stabbing like a blunt sword, into her belly. She fell to her knees, gasping.

The howling stopped.

The cavern was as silent as a mausoleum.

Then the voices came back to her. Their words whispered in her mind like a fluttering cloud of bats. Aurelia stood up. She had no fear any more. She understood them now. Her glassy eyes peered ominously at the old woman.

"I have brought her to thee," the Blessed Mother cried. "My blood's blood. I sacrifice my grandchild to show thee my faith."

The terrible howls began again. The Blessed Mother held her ears, shaking her head. Aurelia walked towards her and yanked her hands away.

The echoing screams died as quickly as they had

come. The cavern was silent, except for the lapping of the waves against the rocks.

Then a crying, distant and mournful, filled the huge cavern.

"The children weep," Aurelia said, pointing across the lake. "They weep for the one who left them to die. The one who escaped their horrid fate. The one who sacrificed their souls for her life. But her soul is tainted, black as the Horned One who rules the Darkness."

The Blessed Mother rubbed her skinny hands together. Her eyes widened, trying to see into the shadows of the rocks near the lake. She glanced at Aurelia. The girl's cold, glaring eyes struck her skull like needles. Cautiously, the Blessed Mother inched back towards the edge of the lake.

"The children come for you," Aurelia said, smiling as she moved closer to the old woman. "Do you hear them?"

The Blessed Mother raised her hands and shouted, "I am thy life. Have I not always avenged thy fate? Did I not make the people who did thee harm suffer? Have I not—"

Aurelia yanked the Blessed Mother's arms down. The old woman jerked away from the girl, closer to the lake. Aurelia stepped nearer. The Blessed Mother backed onto the sharp, wet rocks of the bank.

"Thy lives are sacred because of me," the old woman cried, her frantic voice quivering. "I am thy—"

Aurelia waved her hands. The howling drowned out the Blessed Mother's words.

The old woman froze in midsentence; her mouth opened, formed into a word that caught in her throat. Only her eyes moved, darting like a small bird's suddenly caught in the shadow of a falcon.

Aurelia circled back, lifted the torch from between

the rocks and held it above her. It twinkled yellow in a line across the lake.

The howling stopped.

"For your life, you have caused their suffering," Aurelia said, pointing the torch at the Blessed Mother. "In your death, you shall know their pain. It shall be eternal. The children have spoken."

"Do not lie to me," the old woman moaned. "It is a sacrilege." She felt something slimy clutch her ankle. Then another and another. Like tenacles, they tugged at her. "All I have done, I have done for thee," she cried, losing her balance on the mossy rocks.

She twisted and stumbled backwards into the lake. Her garbled cries were muffled as the water churned about her. She clutched desperately at the slippery rocks. Her fingers found a crevice. She pulled herself up out of the water and crawled back onto the bank. Exhausted, she lay at Aurelia's feet.

The girl watched, never moving, only listening to the voices that now filled her mind.

The howling began again. The old woman contorted in agony, screaming as the horrible tremors of pain rippled through her body.

Then she lay still.

Aurelia gazed down at the black-clad body.

Many voices, some deep, others childlike, spewed in unison from the shadows. "Our fate is sealed. Now thine, old one, has been sealed as well. We have another who will bring the people's souls to our Master."

Aurelia silently unbottoned her blouse. Her eyes glowed, red and huge.

The torch, flickering behind her, suddenly burst into a massive flame and went out.

Rumbling laughter echoed through the cavern.

The people still knelt, silent, unmoving, too frightened

to whisper their apprehensions, their wonderment, as they waited, heads bowed in mock prayer, for the Blessed Mother's return. Their torches trembled in the darkness, reflecting the fake piety many felt in their hearts as they slowly realized just what they had done in their cowardly frenzy. The last glimmer of light in their lives of darkness, the last hope of salvation from their terrible oppression, had just been snuffed out by their own volition.

In the back of the column, Gertrude Throm wept silently for the death of an innocent girl.

Then they heard the footsteps, cold horrible sucking noises in the mud of the black tunnel below. Slowly they raised their heads as the shadowy vision shuffled towards them.

"Hallowed be the children," their chant began. The apparition grew in the torch light. "Glory to the Blessed Mother."

Suddenly a quick, choking gasp swept back over the kneeling column. Heads turned towards their neighbors in disbelief.

Could it truly be . . .

The girl, Aurelia?

But the Blessed Mother? Their faces questioned each other desperately.

Was she . . .

Almost too frightened to think it, the people began to rise, whispering among themselves. Quick nervous half-smiles flickered in the scattered light as a sudden, frantic hope filled their hearts. Aurelia had returned . . . alone. Were the words of Thomas Borg true? Have they finally, actually been saved?

Aurelia raised her black-gloved hand. Their voices quickly dimmed. The ominous silence they knew so well overcame them once more.

"I am the Choosen One," Aurelia announced. "As

my grandmother was, so then am I. See that I wear her vestments of authority, and take heed.'' Her words echoed sharply through the tunnel, like the burning sting of the leather whips the people had used to scourge themselves.

Almost in unison, the people knelt and bowed their heads once more. All hope, all joy, quickly emptied from their souls.

''Oh thee of little faith,'' Aurelia cried. ''For one brief instant, thee looked upon me for thy salvation. But no! Thee turned against me, as thy fathers and thy father's fathers turned against the sacred children. Again thee have sealed thy own fate in treachery and deceit. Punishment is thy only reward. Blessed be the children. For only through thy sacrifice and thy obedience to me will ye yet obtain salvation through them. It is as it was, and as it always shall be. The children have spoken.''

Like mere shadows, obedient and mindless, the people silently followed Aurelia as she led them back to their timeless and terrible fate.

A black-veiled figure emerged out of the cave as Joey watched from behind the trees. The others trailed behind. Not a word was uttered.

The storm still raged, but it had no fury compared to the storm inside Joey's heart. Aurelia was gone. The Blessed Mother had returned alone.

It was over.

All was lost.

The dark malevolent apparition commanded the people to disperse. Joey gazed numbly through the trees as they scurried out into the night like beaten dogs.

Then as she came closer, he saw.

Joey gripped the branch in front of him and stared. No longer did the Blessed Mother hobble like a brittle old woman. There was a sureness now, a surging, youthful energy to her gait.

"Aurelia?" Joey whispered, almost unable to let himself believe it.

The black figure stopped and turned in the cold wet-black night.

She was waiting.

Joey sensed it. She was waiting for him.

It was Aurelia.

Strengthened with a new hope, a new perception of life, as if being reborn from that dark oblivion to which he had succumbed, Joey dashed towards the lone figure.

As he neared, lightning flared above them and he saw the smooth, supple curves outlined against the damp black dress. And her face, Aurelia's beautiful face, carved within the translucent veil.

"Aurelia!" he cried, running to her. "It is thee. Please—the veil. Let me see thy face. Aurelia!"

But she made no move to reveal herself.

Joey clutched her shoulders. "Thee has beaten her. Thee has won!"

"How dare thee lay hands upon me," Aurelia growled.

Slowly Joey's fingers slipped from her arms. He smiled awkwardly, hoping it was a game, some sort of joke.

"Why does thee speak so?" he asked timidly.

"It is not thy place to question the Blessed Mother," she snapped.

"But . . . but thee has destroyed her. Thee has won. We are free."

"Blasphemy!" she screamed. "The power in me is the power of the Sacred Cave. In myself, I am nothing. Get thee back to the orphanage. The children have spoken."

Joey reached out to her again. "But . . ."

"Enough! If thee does not obey, thee will be punished. Now go!"

"Please," Joey pleaded, his heart tearing apart once more. "Aurelia, do not joke." His arms fell limply to his sides. "Aurelia, please?"

"Never call me that again," she hissed, pointing her black-gloved hand at his face. "Never."

Joey inched back away from the horror before him.

"No," he whimpered, slowly shaking his head. "No. No."

He couldn't stand it. Not this. He'd rather she had died, than this.

He turned and dashed, stumbling, into the woods. The cold wind blew through his drenched clothes.

The shock and the terrifying loneliness suddenly overwhelmed him, becoming an intensely physical pain. There was nothing left for him now. No one to turn to. Nowhere to go.

Mr. Borg, he thought suddenly. Maybe he is better now. He will know what to do.

Joey ran, slipping in the mud, falling, running again until he arrived at Thomas Borg's house.

He collapsed on the steps to the porch and waited until his breath returned.

"Thomas?" he called, standing up to open the front door. The house was dark and silent. Then he heard the barn door slamming. He spun around. It banged against the outside wall after each quick gust of wind.

Joey found a lantern on the porch and lit it. The rain beat his face as he stumbled towards the barn. Thomas was his last hope.

If he is coherent, Joey thought, we will escape together. It is all the hope that is left us.

Joey lifted the lantern in the doorway to light the darkness within. Cautiously, he entered.

"Thomas?" he whispered.

The door banged against the wall. Joey spun around, almost falling. He closed his eyes and took a deep breath.

He needed both hands to hold the lantern steady as he walked farther into the barn. A gust of wind hurled itself into the barn. Something squealed and flew out into the night. Joey squeezed the handle on the lantern.

Suddenly there was a loud creaking above him. Joey listened, paralyzed. Slowly, desperately, he lifted the light upwards and looked.

Thomas Borg's body hung above him from a wooden beam. His bloody head twisted as his body swayed, his eyes bulging grotesquely as the rope cut deeper into his broken neck.

EPILOGUE

"I FEEL sorry for the boy," the woman said. She was sitting on the porch with her husband, in the glow of the setting sun. The turquoise sky darkened on the horizon. She watched the boy herd the cows into the barn before the storm. "He never once has gone to town. It ain't right for a boy his age to always be stayin' by himself like that."

Her husband nodded, sucking on his pipe. "He hid again this week when the Hartfields came out. He's been gettin' worse. Don't talk no more. Couldn't find him until hours after they left."

"He's such a nice-lookin' boy, too. Talks funny, but works hard."

"Gotta give'm that. He's worth his wages and more."

Joey watched the storm creep across the purple sky. He had been living at the farm for a year now. They fed him well and he had his own room upstairs. He had made $1,100 so far and saved it all.

He had fled the Valley after the night they took Aurelia. He had run for days, stealing food when he could. Then he had come to Huntsville. Finding a job there had been easy. He knew farming and it was an agricultural community. The Bellstroms had been good to him. They left him alone and asked no questions about his family or where he was from.'

All he wanted was to be left alone.

But now he felt it again. It had been getting worse. All winter, he had felt safe at the Bellstrom's, but now, in the spring, all that had changed.

They were watching him. He didn't know how they could have found him, but he felt them, waiting, in the shadows of the woods.

The evening storm hit quickly. Rain pelted the barn. Joey stood in the doorway carefully observing the forest beyond the pea field. The couple on the porch went in for the night.

It was pitch-black now. Joey closed the barn doors and walked over to the pile of hay bales. The barn had felt safe to him before. Now it was huge and unprotecting, full of dark and dangerous places. It reminded him of that night of terror, one year ago today. He could almost hear the horrible creaking of Thomas Borg's body above his head.

Joey slapped the last cow into the stall.

"It is impossible to escape," he told the cow. Holding his breath, he looked into the shadows. Something foreign had moved in the barn.

Joey slumped down onto a bale of hay.

They have come, he thought. They have found me.

The Holy Children gathered around the boulder in the mouth of the cave. The Blessed Mother stood on its high crest and began to preach to the people, telling them again of their sins.

Next to her, Richard, dressed in black, held the white-haired baby in his arms. Her wide, pink eyes stared down at the torch-lit crowd. She gurgled, kicking her tiny feet.

The Blessed Mother cried out to her people. "The wicked shall perish in the name of the Lord. The children shall be His sword."

The people repeated the words, as most had all their lives, and as they now knew, they would for all time to come. As the chant grew frenzied, causing the very ground itself to tremble, they felt the immense power of the Blessed Mother surge through their bodies, binding them together, filling them with a strange, unnatural heat, as if the fires of Hell itself were flowing through their veins.

Suddenly Aurelia twisted, clutching at her throat, and fell. Richard held her down as her limbs stabbed the air. The baby clung to his shirt. It began to cry. Its small, bawling voice echoed in the cavern. The crowd murmured.

The Blessed Mother arose. The people instantly were silent. Her black-gloved hand drifted over them. Heads bowed. Eyes averted their neighbors, each too terrified to look up from the dust of the earth. It stopped in the middle, pointing down at Ruth.

"I never meant to hurt thee. Please forgive me," Ruth cried. "For a year I have obeyed thy every whim. Please Aurelia, forgive me."

Richard handed the baby to the Blessed Mother and climbed down the boulder.

"Richard. Thee . . thee was my . . ."

He grabbed her arm and yanked. Pain shot up her shoulder. The people shouted out to this poor sinner to repent, for her time was at hand. The salvation of the valley, once again, would be written in blood.

Richard began to drag her towards the black, dripping tunnel. The people chanted their praises to the

Holy Cave as they followed the Blessed Mother back down into their own eternal damnation.

A bolt of lightning exploded above the field. Joey stared out of the slit-like barn window at the woods.

"Thee will not take me," he whispered. "I would die first."

Joey knelt and fingered the blade of the long knife on his lap. He clutched the handle and lifted it in front of his face, mesmerized by its gleaming, reflecting steel.

Then he heard a loud scratching on the walls.

A voice, riding upon the wind, swirled in through the cracks in the barn.

Tears began to stream down his face. The knife quivered close to his eyes.

"Go away," he whispered softly. He gazed into the black corners of the barn.

Lightning flared ouside the door. Thunder exploded. Joey leaped up off his knees.

A terrible howling surrounded him. He spun in a circle, holding out the knife.

Suddenly it was silent.

Joey slumped down on the ground and closed his eyes.

"Oh, God," he whimpered, turning the point of the blade towards his belly. "Help me."

He stared down at the bright metal.

No, he thought, looking at his distorted face in the knife.

It is a mortal sin.

I cannot.

Joey threw the knife away and ran to the barn doors.

"Thee shall never make me," he screamed out at the night. "Never!"

In the shadows behind him, he heard the sound of children laughing.